"*Legendarium* does not disappoint ...
the very definition of a BLOCKBUSTER."
Phil Earle

"Sharp, fast-paced and full of heart."
Elle McNicoll

"A wonder of an adventure."
Jasbinder Bilan

"More immersive than any video game!"
Ellie Irving

"A thrilling, exciting, jam-packed adventure."
Mel Taylor-Bessent

"Fantastically imaginative."
Stephanie Burgis

"Clever, fast-paced, action-packed ...
grab your time-key and jump right in!"
Sinéad O'Hart

LEGENDARI⬦M

JENNIFER BELL

WALKER
BOOKS

First published 2022 by Walker Books Ltd
87 Vauxhall Walk, London SE11 5HJ

2 4 6 8 10 9 7 5 3 1

Text © 2022 Jennifer Bell

Cover illustrations © 2022 Paddy Donnelly

The right of Jennifer Bell to be identified as author of this
work has been asserted in accordance with the
Copyright, Designs and Patents Act 1988

This book has been typeset in Utopia and Futura

Printed and bound by CPI Group (UK) Ltd, Croydon CR0 4YY

British Library Cataloguing in Publication Data:
a catalogue record for this book is available from the British Library

ISBN 978-1-4063-9173-2

www.walker.co.uk

MIX
Paper from
responsible sources
FSC® C171272

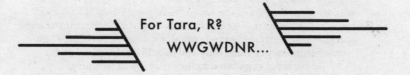

For Tara, R?

WWGWDNR...

The hotdog-eating contest was going badly.

"It's not funny," Arthur whinged, clutching his bloated tummy. "It feels like my stomach's about to explode."

His friend Ren laughed and slid another hotdog across the picnic table on a plate. "Ready to forfeit?"

She was much smaller than him, but dressed in her ripped black jeans, hooded tank top and massive combat boots, she looked ready for battle. Her silky black hair was fixed in a high ponytail with a thick fringe covering half her face. Arthur doubted that his baggy shorts and *The Mandalorian* T-shirt were as intimidating, so he adopted his most threatening game face as he pulled the plate towards him. "No chance."

They'd wagered that if Ren ate the most hotdogs that afternoon, Arthur would be her spotter every time she went rock-climbing during the rest of the summer holidays; but if Arthur ate the most, Ren would give him her copy of the latest *Spider-Man* game on Xbox – something he'd need five weeks of paper-round money to be able to afford otherwise.

"Can one of you *please* puke already? This is getting ridiculous," their friend Cecily complained beside them. If Ren had dressed for battle, then Cecily had styled herself for a photo shoot with a fashion magazine. Her amethyst-purple braids had been twisted into an impossibly intricate up-do, and she was modelling a vintage denim jacket and floaty maxi-dress. Sat in her lap was a scruffy white terrier, who yapped excitedly as Cecily unfastened the lead from around his red collar, and then scampered off to the pond at the bottom of Ren's garden. "See – even Cloud's had enough."

"It'll all be over when Arthur admits defeat," Ren promised, lifting her hotdog to her lips.

But as she opened her mouth to take a bite, a splash sounded at the end of the garden. Arthur glanced at Ren's pond and spotted the tip of a stubby white tail disappearing below the strangely misty surface...

"Cloud?" Cecily sprang to her feet. "Cloud, be careful! You might not be able to swim!" With the dog's lead flapping in her hand, she raced towards the bottom of the garden.

Arthur felt way too full to run anywhere, but Cecily was right to be concerned. Although Cloud looked like a typical West Highland terrier – with a fluffy white coat, round face and pointed ears – he was, in fact, a very advanced robot, or *mimic*, from four hundred years in the future. He'd been entrusted to their care by a twenty-fifth-century inventor named Milo Hertz, and there was still so much they had to learn about him ... including whether or not he could swim.

With a glance at the back door to check all their parents were still inside, Arthur pushed himself up and hurried after Ren and Cecily. When they all got to the pond, the mist had dissolved and the water was still. A dragonfly darted over the surface, but there was no sign of Cloud anywhere.

"I don't understand," Cecily said. "I saw him fall in."

Arthur knelt down and thrust his arm in up to the elbow. Wiggling it around, he could only feel slimy weeds. "Maybe he jumped out and we missed it?"

"Couldn't have," Ren said, nudging the pebbles at the water's edge with her boot. "These are all dry."

Cecily surveyed the rest of the garden. "So, then, where *is* he? Cloud!" she called. "Here, boy!"

Arthur waited for an excited ball of fluff to come bounding out of the bushes, but it didn't appear. His gaze drew nervously to the abandoned cottage behind Ren's garden, where, last year, the three of them had accidentally followed Cloud through a portal to the year 2473. After getting trapped in an in-reality adventure game, or I-RAG, called the *Wonderscape*, they'd barely escaped with their lives.

With a growing sense of unease, he searched the pond again. Buried in the silt at the bottom, he saw something glinting and reached towards it...

"Arthur, look out!" Ren yanked on the back of his T-shirt, just in time, as a jet of mist shot out of the pond with a loud hiss, narrowly missing Arthur's head.

"What's happening?!" Cecily cried.

Arthur's pulse quickened as he scrambled to his feet and saw that the mist had swirled around them, caging them in a spinning vortex that obscured Ren's garden. He grabbed his friends' arms and pulled them closer. "Stay together!"

There was a thunderous *boom* and the vortex rippled. Arthur felt a stab of brain freeze followed by the stomach-lurching sensation of ascending in a fast-moving lift. "Werrrr—!" As he spread his arms and legs for balance, the taste of fried onions burst at the back of his throat and before he could do anything to stop himself, he leaned forward and vomited. He briefly hoped the vortex wouldn't function like some kind of puke-nado and hurl the contents of his guts right back at him. "Ren?" he croaked, watching the mist curl around his toes. "Cecily?"

He flinched as something brushed his arm.

There was a high-pitched bark and Cecily yelled, "Cloud!"

Staring at his trainers, Arthur tried to steady his breathing. The vortex seemed to be moving slower and the mist was thinning. He could almost see the ground. He wiped his mouth clean on his T-shirt sleeve, lifted his head ...

… and let out a small yelp.

Ren's garden had vanished. They were all now stood on the floor of a vast concrete warehouse, filled with industrial-sized shelving units. Dim spotlights dangled from the ceiling, illuminating hundreds of coloured metal crates, organized in rows of blue, green and red. Several nearby crates had toppled over and a trail of sooty footprints led away from them, into the shadows. As the residual mist faded around Arthur's feet, he rubbed the sides of his face, convinced he was hallucinating. This couldn't be real.

"What happened?!" Cecily spluttered, pressing Cloud tightly to her chest. Strands of pondweed clung to the dog's damp fur, but his tail was wagging. "Where are we?"

Arthur shook his head, lost for words. He scanned the perimeter of the building, checking for whoever had made the footprints. At one side of the warehouse, stairs climbed up to a balcony with doors leading off into other rooms, but there was no sign of movement anywhere. Goosebumps prickled along his forearms as his skin adjusted to the cold. The place had to be a storage depot, although there were no clues on the walls or crates to indicate who it belonged to.

Shaking, Cecily fastened Cloud's lead to his collar and lifted him to the ground. "Hello?" she called. "Is anybody here?" Her voice echoed several times, but there was no reply.

"Never mind *where* we are," Ren muttered, rubbing her mouth on the shoulder of her tank-top. (Arthur guessed she'd suffered her own post-hotdog-eating misfortune.) "I'm more concerned about *when* we are. I got brain freeze. Did either of you?"

Arthur went rigid. The dull headache you sometimes get after eating ice cream too quickly was also a side effect of time travel. "For a split second," he admitted. "But there's no way we've time-travelled."

"No," Cecily said. "I mean – yeah, I felt brain freeze, too – but we *can't* have time-travelled."

They all looked at each other uncertainly.

"Maybe we should check our phones," Arthur suggested. "When we time-travelled before, they stopped working." He slipped his Samsung out of his pocket and his blood went cold. The screen was blank.

Cecily frantically pressed the power button on her dead iPhone. "But this makes no sense! We haven't walked through a Wonderway."

It was an excellent point. The portal they'd time-travelled through last year, a Wonderway, was opened using a small obsidian prism called a time-key; and Arthur hadn't seen either device in Ren's garden. He replayed the details of everything that had just happened, searching for an explanation. "When Cloud fell into the pond, there was mist on the water," he remembered. "It might have been the same fog spinning around us. Maybe when we thought we saw him sinking under the water, what we *actually* saw was him disappearing through the same portal we have?"

"So, it wasn't a Wonderway," Ren said. "It was a portal made of ... gas?"

"You can only get into the Wonderscape through a Wonderway," Cecily reasoned, starting to pace, "which means if we've travelled here through this ... this *mist-portal* ... we must be somewhere else in the future."

Arthur cast a nervy glance around the warehouse, knowing they could be anywhere – a different planet, a different solar system, a different galaxy... His chest tightened as the true horror of their situation hit him.

They were lost. In space *and* time.

"Great, and now we're facing the prospect of being turned into slime again," Ren grumbled, jamming her phone back into her pocket.

With a jolt, Arthur realized what Ren meant. When they'd time-travelled before, they'd upset the balance of the universe, triggering a sort of astrophysical autocorrect mechanism. As a result, if they hadn't returned home soon enough, their bodies would have broken down into a gloopy substance called protoplasm. "Oh no..." He fumbled to set the stopwatch on his Casio. "We don't know when it will happen."

Cecily stopped pacing. "What do you mean we don't know? We had fifty-seven hours to get home last time."

"Yes, but some of our variables will have changed, so it'll be different now." Arthur wished he'd paid more attention to the formula Sir Isaac Newton had used to make the calculation. The famous scientist had been one of many real-life heroes they'd met in the Wonderscape. "All we can measure is how much time has elapsed since we arrived – that's why I've set a stopwatch."

"So then ... it could happen at any moment," Cecily realized. "One minute we'll be standing here, and the next we'll be *you-know-what*."

Arthur tried to think of something positive to say, but there was no silver lining to this nightmare. He didn't know where they were, how they'd got there or how long they had to get home. The truth was, there was only one thing he knew for certain:

... a countdown had begun.

2

Thorny memories surfaced in Arthur's mind – of killer robots, ghostly mazes, evil villains and earth-trembling avalanches – everything they'd escaped in the future last time. He wasn't sure he had the strength to survive them all again.

"We need to focus," he heard Cecily saying, but his head was all over the place.

If they didn't make it home in time, he'd never see his dad again. His mum had passed away when he was young, leaving the two of them alone. Arthur's heart wrenched as he pictured his dad in Ren's back garden, earlier. Dressed in a short-sleeved summer shirt and a pair of flamingo sunglasses, he'd been trying to make everyone laugh by cracking awful dad jokes.

"Arthur?" Cecily squeezed his shoulder.

"Sorry, it's just—"

"I know." There was a haunted look in her big green eyes that made him wonder if the same memories had returned to her. "But we don't have time to freak out, OK? If we want to get home, we need a plan."

"And quickly," Ren added with a scowl. "I argued with my mum before the barbecue and I don't want that to be the last time we ever speak. It can't be."

Arthur felt a swell of gratitude that at least he had his friends with him. He tried to organize his thoughts. They had no control over when they might turn into protoplasm, so they should probably concentrate on something they could change. "We need to learn more about the mist-portal that brought us here," he said. "If we can find out how it was generated, we might be able to create a new one to return us to the twenty-first century."

Ren's ponytail swung as she crouched down. "Maybe these scorch marks are a clue?"

Arthur examined the concrete. A powdery black starburst covered the entire area where the three of them were standing. The footprints had probably been made by someone walking through it. He noticed a small, black object by his trainer and picked it up. It was the same shape as a hockey puck, but smooth and shiny, like glass.

"What's that?" Cecily asked.

Rubbing the object clean on his shorts, Arthur discovered it had a bevelled edge with tiny notches on it, like the dial on a kitchen timer. As he twisted it clockwise, he heard a satisfying clicking noise ...

... and a hole *vaporized* in its centre.

"Whoa!" He staggered back, almost dropping it. Solid matter didn't behave that way, at least not by the rules of physics he knew.

"We're definitely in the future," Ren muttered bitterly. "Do you think that doughnut is connected to the mist-portal?"

"Possibly." Hoping to learn more, Arthur rotated the dial anti-clockwise. This time, the centre of the object *reappeared*. He briefly considered experimenting with it – twisting the dial in different directions to see if it produced any mist – but without knowing where it might whisk them off to, it was too dangerous.

"Look – a way out!" Cecily said, over Arthur's shoulder.

He turned to find a set of large metal doors in the wall behind. They stood at least three metres high and were secured by a complex system of bolts.

Ren ran over and shook one of the bars fixed across the doors. "They're locked. Whoever owns this place obviously doesn't want anyone getting in – these are the kind of doors you'd have on a bank vault."

Arthur eyed the gloomy warehouse warily. Now he thought about it, the concrete walls did give off an end-of-the-world-bunker type vibe and the cold air probably indicated that no one spent much time in there. "But these footprints prove that someone else has been here recently," he said, studying them closer. They looked like they'd been made by someone wearing heavy boots like Ren's. He and Ren followed them a few paces until they abruptly stopped.

"I don't get it," she said, craning her neck to look above them. "Where do they go? It's like whoever made them disappeared into thin air."

Arthur considered the toppled crates and the scorch marks, trying to piece everything together. Had the owner of the footprints summoned them there? And if so, for what purpose? There were only a handful of people in the future that knew them...

"Hey, I've found something!" Cecily called, excitedly. "Look on the crate lids!"

Arthur stretched up on tiptoes to examine the top of the nearest red crate and spied a tiny gold arrow inlaid on the lid. As he reached for it, he heard a soft *hiss* and a cloud of glittering grey particles burst out. They promptly massed together and transformed into a paper-thin glass screen with images projected onto the surface.

He blinked. *Nanotechnology.* They'd come across it before in the Wonderscape. He swiped his finger across the screen, scrolling through a photographic inventory of items stored in the crate. The text was written in a language he didn't understand. And yet...

And yet as he skimmed the pages, the letters and words *became* English. His mind boggled trying to understand how it all worked. It seemed more like magic than technology.

He shuddered as his gaze moved through the list:

Shrieking Shuriken

Rock Blaster

Rex-Claw

Gamma Grenade.

The shrieking shurikens were razor-sharp throwing stars; the rock blasters looked like scope-mounted grey stalactites; the rex-claws were daggers with dinosaur-claw handles; and the photo of the gamma grenade showed a small glass bauble filled with writhing blue flames. He quickly checked the inventory of the next crate along, and swallowed. "Bad news. I think the red crates all contain *weapons*," he told the others.

Ren poked her head around the corner of a shelf. "The green ones are full of different gadgets – strange goggles, armoured jackets, expanding shields – there's even a pair of boots with hover-engines in the soles." She flipped around the glass screen. "And then there's these *evaders*, but I don't understand what they do."

Arthur squinted at the image on screen. The evaders looked like large silver pebbles, as reflective as mirrors. *Weapons, armour, shields* – he could only think of one type of organization that used those. "Perhaps this is some sort of military building? The mist-portal could be top-secret military technology."

"I'm not so sure," Cecily said, over by some blue crates. "There are bars of precious metals in these, as well as jewels and minerals. Why would soldiers need those? Oh, and this is interesting." She patted one of the toppled crates nearest to where they'd been standing when they'd first arrived. "This one has a hole burned in it."

Curious, Arthur and Ren went over to investigate.

"I can't see anything inside," Cecily told them, peering through the fist-sized opening, "and the nano-screen isn't working." She demonstrated by swiping her hand over the arrow on the lid, but nothing happened.

Arthur ran a finger around the melted edge of the hole and it came back streaked with charcoal. Testing a suspicion, he held the hockey-puck-doughnut up against it.

They were a perfect match.

"It must have contained *this*," he realized, with a buzz of excitement. "If we can get the nano-screen working, we might be able to figure out what it is and how to use it."

Right at that moment, Cloud made a strange whirring noise and went rigid. He looked like one of those stuffed-toy puppies that do back-flips in toy shops.

"No, not now!" Cecily pleaded, tugging on his lead. "He's been freezing like this for the last few weeks. I don't understand what's causing it."

Cloud's right ear snapped up and a beam of light shot out of it, coalescing into a 3-D hologram. The hologram showed a burly, scruffy-haired man in a white lab coat. He was sat hunched over a desk strewn with multiple whirring, bubbling and hovering pieces of apparatus. As he leaned forwards, a pendant fell from a chain around his neck; it matched the red colour of Cloud's collar exactly. "Arthur?" the man cried, almost falling off his stool. "Cecily! Ren!"

Arthur jerked his head back. *"Milo Hertz?"* The inventor had a lot more wrinkles than when Arthur had last seen him, but Milo's kind grey eyes and gorilla-like size were instantly recognizable. Arthur felt some of the tension of the last few minutes dissipate. Wherever they were, and whatever had happened to them, Milo would help sort it out. The man had designed Cloud and the Wonderscape. He was a genius.

"What in Newton's name are you doing *here*?" Milo hissed, checking over his shoulder in case anyone was listening. "You should all be in the twenty-first century!"

Cecily started. "Don't you know? Isn't that why you're speaking to us?"

Milo frowned and lifted his pendant closer. Arthur saw tiny specks of light whizzing under its surface. "Cloud is linked to this device I'm wearing. I programmed him to open a direct transmission to me if he ever moved through time again. *That's* why I'm speaking to you – Cloud contacted me."

Arthur glanced at Cloud, still frozen in position. "Then, you *don't* know why we're here?" His insides tightened as all his anxiety rushed back.

"You need to tell me *exactly* what's happened," Milo said, grabbing a pencil and notepad off the desk beside him.

As Cecily sped through the events of the last half hour, Milo jotted down various details. "If you really are in a high-security military building, it might make it more difficult to get a fix on your location," he warned, tapping several commands on a holographic keyboard next to him, "but I'll try my best. In the meantime, show me this mysterious device you've found."

Arthur reached into his pocket and pulled out the hockey-puck-doughnut he'd collected off the floor. Milo snatched a pair of black sunglasses off his desk and pulled them on. "Let me take a peek inside," he murmured, adjusting a dial on one side of the frames. The lenses went from being matt black to transparent green with blinking red dots. Arthur could only imagine what they allowed him to see.

After only a few seconds of scrutiny, Milo's jaw went slack.

"What is it?" Ren asked.

"I don't understand..." Milo's voice faltered. "What you're holding is a *time-key*."

"What?" A thousand questions spun through Arthur's mind, making him feel dizzy. He steadied himself against the nearest crate, resting the device on top. "But it doesn't look anything like a time-key! And anyway, we thought they'd all been destroyed."

"They *were* destroyed," Milo told them worryingly. "And not just the devices themselves, but all the designs, notes and recordings I created when I invented them. As you three know better than most, time travel is too dangerous a power for anyone to possess. That's why I went to great lengths to erase every possible trace of the time-keys' existence." He pushed up his sunglasses with a shaky hand. "The device you've found is an exact copy of a time-key, with a few added updates. That's why it looks and works differently to the time-keys you've used before."

That explains the mist-portal, Arthur thought.

Cecily rubbed her temples. "So, it's like a time-key 2.0?"

"Exactly," Milo said, his brow fraught with worry. "The question is: who engineered it? It's inconceivable to think that someone could have built this *without* using my old designs, because they include an incredibly unique time-compressing coil, which I developed in secret. The problem is I can't fathom how anyone would've got hold of them. Nobody else knows about the time-keys or about you three being time-travellers."

"Maybe your brother had something to do with it?" Ren grumbled, folding her arms. "He could have boasted to one of his prison mates about the time-keys."

Arthur remembered Milo's stone-hearted brother, Tiburon, with a shiver. Not only had he repeatedly tried to kill them, he'd also stolen one of Milo's time-keys in order to travel back through history and make digital copies of the consciousnesses of famous heroes. Later, he'd rebuilt them as mimics and cruelly enslaved them to play roles in the Wonderscape.

"I don't think so," Milo said. "It isn't in Tiburon's interest to say anything. He's still serving a prison sentence for kidnapping me and if he ever divulged the truth of his *real* crimes, his jail term would be extended. No, this has to be my doing. I must have slipped up somehow when I was destroying the time-key designs..." He took a regretful sigh. "I'm so sorry you've been caught up in all this again. Just sit tight. Once I pinpoint your location, I'll come to you and configure this new time-key to send you back to the twenty-first century."

Arthur gave the others a forced smile. Sure, they might have found a way to get home, but it was difficult to feel relaxed when anyone in the Known Universe could soon have the power to reshape the path of history. "Are you going to look for this new time-key engineer?" he asked anxiously. "You don't know how many devices they've built or who they could have given them to."

"That's what troubles me," Milo admitted. "I need to find out how they know about my design. Whatever's happened, it's my responsibility to set things right. Inventing the time-key was my mistake."

Cecily started pacing again. "Maybe the engineer is someone who works for you in the Wonderscape? You could interview all your staff—"

"The Wonderscape is closed," Milo interrupted. "It's 2493 now, twenty years since you were last here."

2493! It was no surprise Milo had more wrinkles.

"What's making that noise?" Ren asked, as a creak reverberated around the warehouse.

Cecily spun around. "I think it came from the doors…"

The creak sounded again, followed by a long groan, like a heavy object being dragged across concrete.

"Stand aside so I can take a look," Milo suggested, pulling down his sunglasses.

He immediately tensed. "No, it can't be." He tapped his pendant and his hologram began to dissolve. "It's *raiders*," he told them, his voice thick with fear. "They'll kill you if they see you. Hide!"

3

A column of light raced across the floor as the warehouse doors started to open. Multiple figures stood silhouetted in the widening gap.

"This way!" Ren hissed, tugging on Arthur's T-shirt. She pulled him behind a row of red crates where Cecily was already crouched, holding a wriggling Cloud.

Arthur's heart raced as he shuffled into position between two containers and peeked through a slit in the middle. Outside the warehouse, torchlight flickered over a rough, sandy wall where a golden sun-shaped statue stood in an alcove. It seemed odd that blazing torches were being used outside when the building interior had electrical lighting.

"Arthur, your toes!" Cecily whispered, nudging Arthur's leg. With a jolt, he realized his foot was exposed and slid it into the shadows just in time.

There was a shuddering *boom* as the warehouse doors ground to a halt; then heavy footsteps reverberated around the walls. Arthur watched three figures dressed in grubby brown trench coats and tall leather boots trudge into the clearing. As their faces passed under a spotlight, he saw they could have only been a couple of years older than him. At the head of the group strode a stout boy with cold, dark eyes and a shaved head. He was followed by a red-haired girl carrying a clunky backpack, and a tall youth with a small barrel-shaped contraption attached to his right shoulder.

Raiders, Milo had called them. Arthur distrusted them instantly, and it wasn't just because of their shady name. As their coats flapped open, he saw they were wearing harnesses equipped with rock blasters, shrieking shurikens and gamma grenades.

"How'd that job go last night, Vorru?" the red-haired girl asked, grinning. She had an unusual, lilting accent that Arthur couldn't place. "I heard you faced a bit of *resistance*."

The tall youth tapped the contraption on his shoulder, which Arthur was beginning to suspect was another weapon. "Nothing I couldn't handle. And it was worth it. Twelve rex-claws and two vats of firebrew – they'll fetch Deadlock a decent price on the Dark Market." As the boy scratched his neck, Arthur spotted a tattoo poking above the edge of his collar. It looked a bit like a skull and crossbones, except the bones were actually a pair of rusty spanners. He noticed the same motif on the girl's wrist and wondered if it was a gang symbol, the mark of a raider.

"With any luck, Deadlock will give you another mod,"

the girl said, slapping Vorru's empty shoulder. "Perhaps a second shoulder-cannon, or even a new leg?"

Vorru's face paled. "But ... I like my leg. I don't want a new one!" He turned to the dark-eyed boy, walking ahead. "Rultan, did you hear that? Tide thinks Deadlock's going to take my leg!"

Tide burst into laughter, making Vorru flush. As they both drew closer to where Arthur and the others were hiding, Arthur realized what Tide had meant by "mod". The base of Vorru's shoulder-cannon was joined to a lumpy mound of flesh that poked through a hole in his coat – the weapon was *fused* to his body. The mods had to be some form of cybernetic modifications.

And it wasn't just Vorru who had one. As Tide turned her shoulder, Arthur saw her rucksack was, in fact, a smoke-stained jetpack bonded to her spine.

"Don't be a baby, Vorru," Rultan growled, scuffing the toe of his boot through the sooty footprints on the floor. He narrowed his gaze on the damaged blue crate that had once contained the time-key. "And be careful what you touch, both of you. It looks like something volatile was being stored here, and one of the others set it off and did a runner. We must have only just missed them."

Tide's eyes sparkled as she saw the hole. "Oh, Deadlock is *not* going to like this. I bet it was that annoying brat in the other crew – the one with the skull-launcher mod. She's always knocking stuff over."

Ren nudged Arthur's knee and murmured, "So we're here by accident?"

Arthur shrugged, although he understood what she was getting at: if the time-key had been triggered by a clumsy raider, then maybe it was just bad luck that the three of them had been sucked through the mist-portal. Still, there had to be a reason why the portal had opened at their specific time and location – that couldn't be a coincidence. It left Arthur with the unsettling feeling that someone, somewhere, knew all about them and had programmed the time-key to seek them out.

Rultan peered through the hole in the damaged crate. "You two had better search the area. Whatever was inside here is missing."

"What are we looking for?" Tide asked.

Arthur held his breath as her gaze passed over where they were hiding. Milo had said the raiders would kill them if they saw them...

"Not sure yet." Rultan swiped his hand above the arrow on the crate lid. When no nano-screen materialized, he rolled back his sleeve to reveal something *embedded* in his forearm.

Arthur tried not to retch. What looked like an over-sized penknife was sardined into the cavity between Rultan's radius and ulna. With practised ease, Rultan slid free a cylindrical silver attachment and pointed it at the arrow. A puff of glittering dust escaped, and a glass screen solidified in mid-air. Rultan read the inventory with interest.

"Well, well." He whistled through his front teeth. "This must be something Deadlock's been working on in secret, 'cause I've never heard of it before. Says here it's one of a kind, too. Pity we can't take a peek at what it looks like – there's no photo."

So, the time-key is one of a kind? Arthur felt a momentary wave of relief, knowing Milo would only have to destroy the one they had. He slipped his hand into his pocket, reaching for the smooth feel of the device...

But it wasn't there.

Heat rushed to his cheeks as he patted his other pocket. Also empty.

No! How could he have been so careless? He'd left the time-key resting on top of that crate!

Cecily poked him in the arm and he gingerly showed her his empty pockets.

WHAT? she mouthed.

Ren must have been following their silent exchange because she started gesturing wildly.

Arthur lifted his hands. *I know, I know!* Unless they wanted to end their days as puddles of gloop on the warehouse floor, they needed to retrieve that time-key. It was their only ticket home.

With the raiders nearing, they didn't have much time to formulate a plan. Arthur peeked through the gap and spotted the time-key sitting on a green crate in the next row. It was the one containing those weird silver pebbles – evaders. "Think you can snatch it?" he whispered to Ren, who was closest.

Rultan's footsteps came to an abrupt halt. "What was that? I thought I heard a voice."

Arthur went rigid.

"Probably just Vorru humming," Tide muttered, checking down another aisle, further along. "I can't see any important-looking gadgets around here. Think this thing was stolen?"

Rultan scoffed. "Steal from *Deadlock*? Even Vorru's not that stupid." He skimmed the crates with a scowl. "Let's just get what we came for and clear out of here. We're already running late and I don't want this blamed on us." He tinkered with his arm-mod and a small panel of light projected out of it. There was text written on the surface, but Arthur was too far away to read what it said. "Our job is to deliver an evader to one of the isports champions competing in the Irontide Tournament. Search the green containers – there's bound to be a stash of them somewhere."

Vorru's shoulder-cannon rattled as he plodded towards the nearest row of green crates. "What does an evader look like again?"

"Small, shiny, intelligent," Tide snapped. "Opposite of you, you big lump."

As the two of them began studying nano-screens, panic

seized Arthur's chest. The time-key was only three crates away from them!

"We've got to do something," Cecily hissed. She rotated Cloud's collar so the silver tag that dangled from it was at the top. It was etched with the words *Cloud. West Highland Terrier. Male.*

But not always.

Cloud had a secret ability. Two beads – one on either side of his tag – could be twisted to transform him into one of eleven other animals from the Chinese zodiac. It was a trick that had helped them escape several dangerous situations in the Wonderscape.

Cecily fiddled with the right-hand bead, changing the text on the tag:

Cloud. Corn Snake. Male.

Cloud. Breton Horse. Male.

Cloud. Capuchin Monkey. Female.

Arthur signalled to the tag. A monkey would be useful. Cloud could swing between the shelving units to the other side of the warehouse and knock something over, diverting the raiders' attention long enough for Arthur to dash out and retrieve the time-key.

But before Cecily could activate Cloud's transformation, Ren squeezed Arthur's knee and pointed through the gap. Vorru had reached the crate of evaders. Arthur felt a spike of dread as the raider reached for the time-key with his meaty fingers...

"Small, shiny, intelligent," Vorru mumbled, turning the device over in his hands. He scanned the crate's nano-screen and gave a goofy smile. "Rultan, I've found an evader!"

Arthur gave a silent cry of frustration. There was no point monkey-Cloud creating a distraction now. Vorru had the time-key in his clutches, and he wasn't going to put it back while he thought it was an evader.

"Good work!" Rultan called over from another row. "Let's get out of here and see it delivered. We'll have to travel there directly or we'll be late."

Arthur wasn't sure what Rultan meant until the warehouse doors started to slide closed. As the raiders drew back together, Rultan entered a few commands into his Swiss-arm-mod and a three-metre-tall column of red light rose out of the floor near the warehouse door.

Tide tapped her boot against the concrete. "Red *again*. Why is traffic always this bad getting into Atlantis?" She waited until the light changed to green and then, with a satisfied grin, stepped forward ...

... and *evaporated*.

Cecily stifled a gasp.

"It must be another kind of portal," Ren whispered, shifting her weight. "If we lose track of that time-key, we're done for. We're going to have to follow them."

Arthur didn't know what would happen if they went into that light. It was entirely possible that their twenty-first-century bodies might not survive. But as he watched Vorru and the time-key disintegrate into the green haze, he knew they had no choice. There was no other way to leave the warehouse, and if they remained there, they'd be slime before they ever found the time-key again.

As Rultan followed his colleagues into the portal, Cecily stuffed Cloud under her armpit like he was a rugby ball. "Come on, it's now or never!"

She sprang to her feet and ran out from their hiding place. Arthur and Ren were hot on her heels.

"Hurry!" Ren yelled, her boots pounding the concrete. "It's closing!"

As the pillar of light started to fade, Arthur willed his legs to go faster. Cecily and Cloud reached the portal first, vanishing as soon as they touched it.

Arthur was next. As he drew closer, he hesitated.

"Go!" Ren said, shoving him from behind. "You'll be OK. Just try not to die."

4

Light blinded Arthur. For the briefest of moments, he felt weightless, like he was floating. He wiggled his fingers and toes and found he could move them with only the slightest effort.

Ren's words returned to him. *Just try not to die...*

Wait. Maybe he *had* died?

"Ren!" he cried, panicking. "Cecily!"

A blast of wind socked Arthur in the face and, with a jolt, mass returned to his body. As his vision cleared, a wave of nausea rolled over him and he lurched forwards, swallowing breaths of salty air. There was gravel under his trainers now and noise roared all around him – voices shouting and laughing, the splash of water, the crackle of footsteps – wherever they were, they were surrounded by people.

A hand gripped his arm and he turned to see Ren bent over beside him. "Next time we move through a portal, remind me *not* to eat four hotdogs beforehand."

"Me, too," Arthur agreed, relieved to see her. As he straightened up, he lost his breath.

They'd materialized in the middle of an enormous square, teeming with people. Colourful buildings shaped like giant nautilus shells, barnacled treasure chests or ancient shipwrecks loomed at the edge, with moving holographic signs flashing for attention on every wall:

THE MERMAID'S COVE
100% Official Merchandise!

Stay where the action is at
BLACKBEARD'S BED & BREAKFAST!

SUNKEN WONDER SOUVENIRS
for clothing, armour, weapons and more!

Arthur blinked stars from his eyes, gawping. "This place is incredible!"

Despite the bright sunshine, everything was made to look as if it was underwater – from the knobbly coral lamp posts and driftwood street signs, to the holographic fronds of seaweed that swayed up from the ground, giving the impression they were all stood on the seabed. People wandered around sipping foamy rainbow-coloured drinks, or jostled in and out of shops, chatting. Arthur didn't notice anyone with a cybernetic mod, although lots of people were dressed in loose-fitting clothing made from strange materials that appeared to glow or change pattern of their own accord.

"There's so many people here," Ren said, scouring the crowds. "Can you see the raiders?"

Arthur tried to pick out Tide, Vorru or Rultan among the masses, but it was like looking for three needles in a haystack. "No, I think we've lost them."

Clutching Cloud's lead, Cecily rubbed the spot between her eyebrows. "Ugh, talk about a head rush." She steadied herself against the arm of a nearby bench, then recoiled when she saw it was sculpted into an enormous eel. "Oh no. Where are we?"

Cloud sniffed the air, his ears alert.

"One of the raiders called it Atlantis," Arthur remembered. Given the underwater theming, he wondered if its design was inspired by the lost island of Atlantis. He and his dad had watched a documentary about it once. According to legend, Atlantis was an ancient Greek island that sank beneath the Atlantic Ocean.

"It's ... amazing," Cecily realized, staring. "But we've got to find out where the raiders have gone with the time-key."

"They were told to deliver an evader to one of the *isports champions competing in the Irontide Tournament*." Ren phrased the sentence carefully, like she'd been repeating it in her head ever since she'd heard it.

Arthur was keen to unpack what they'd discovered in the warehouse – about this creepy *Deadlock* person, and everything Milo had told them – but their immediate priority was to retrieve the time-key. "Isports champion." He thought carefully. "We have *e*sports in our century – the sport of competitive video games. Maybe *i*sports is similar, but for I-RAGs?"

"Which means the Irontide Tournament could be an I-RAG event," Cecily reasoned. She shifted her gaze warily. "Do you think we're in an I-RAG right now?"

It was difficult to tell. Arthur spied a few people trudging around wearing rugged combat gear and heavy packs that had tools and ropes dangling from them – they could be I-RAG players – but everyone else strolled around like they were on holiday. Atlantis didn't seem like the kind of place where danger would be lurking around every corner. "I don't know, but we need to find out. Fast."

Ren scanned the area. "There's a bookshop over there. If we are in an I-RAG, it might tell us more. The bookshops in the Wonderscape did."

The bookshop had a dark-green front with a striped awning, and a shimmering holographic sign at the top that read: *Legend Has It.* "Good idea, but let's try to keep a low profile while we move around," Cecily said, pulling up her jacket collar. "We need to keep our existence a secret – we don't want anyone asking questions about who we are or what we're doing here. No one can know time-travel is actually possible."

Arthur wished he had a jacket to help him cover up; the Baby Yoda on his chest could well be a dead giveaway that he was from a different time. His nerves jangled as they crossed the square. Fashions appeared to have changed in the twenty years since they were last inside an I-RAG. A lot of people were now wearing holographic jewellery and neon stripes of make-up around their eyes and forehead. Hairstyles were short and slick, with a few kids sporting glossy, wet-look dos that made them look like they'd just gone for a swim. Arthur caught fragments of conversations in multiple different languages, most of which he'd never heard before.

"Is it just me, or are a few adults giving us strange looks?" Ren said out of the corner of her mouth.

Arthur thought he saw a flicker of recognition in one man's face, but he told himself it was just his anxiety talking. "It's probably nothing. Just keep moving."

Fortunately, there was no one milling around outside the bookshop when they got there. Behind the window, a collection of books bobbed up and down in mid-air like ducks at a fairground shooting range. One was titled *Ghost Ships of the Orion Nebula* and had a picture of the scorched metal carcass of a spacecraft on the front cover; another, *Legends from the Planet Hoodal*, featured a photo of a hairy brown animal with long whiskers and a flat tail, not unlike a giant beaver. Below each book was a price in DIRT – Dynamic Intergalactic Real Tender – the same currency that was used in the Wonderscape.

Hovering in the middle of the display was a crinkled old map drawn on tea-stained parchment. It depicted hundreds of small islands floating on a body of dark water. The central island, labelled *Atlantis*, was joined by dotted lines to each of the others. Written in large gold letters at the top of the map was the word *LEGENDARIUM*.

"Well, that confirms it," Cecily said. "We're in an I-RAG, all right. That has to be a map of the game. *Legendarium* – the name makes it sound like it's themed around legends."

Ren pushed her face up against the glass. "Those other islands all have names, too – the Land of the Hunt, the Land of Wishes, the Land of Moving Shadows – nothing that mentions the Irontide Tournament, though."

"According to the key, those other islands are called *quest-lands*," Arthur said, studying the list in the top right-hand corner of the map. "It says the dotted lines are portal routes."

"Maybe the quest-lands are the different levels of *Legendarium* and players travel to them from Atlantis?" Ren speculated with a shrug. "There are always safe zones in games where you can upgrade your character armour, heal wounds or buy supplies. Atlantis could be similar to that."

Scanning the other book titles, Arthur noticed *How to Be a Successful Quester* and *Top Ten Things Every Quester Should Know*. "I think players are called *questers*. Maybe we should go inside and search under 'I' for Irontide?"

As Cloud pressed his nose against the window, Cecily crouched down to rub the wet mark off with her sleeve.

"Milo would be able to help us with this. Why hasn't he got back in touch?" She turned Cloud around to face her. "Can you contact him again, boy? Please?"

Cloud cocked his head and blinked.

Cecily groaned. "I'll take that as a no."

Arthur checked his watch. They'd been in the future just over an hour; who knew how long they had left before they turned to protoplasm. "Milo will find us; I know he will. We've got to concentrate on tracking down the time-key."

Just then, a bell rang as the front door of the bookshop opened. Arthur pretended to be interested in *Ghost Ships of the Orion Nebula,* as a teenage boy walked out, dressed in a camo T-shirt and faded jeans. "Thanks for the help, Tar!" he called, waving to the assistant inside.

"No problem," a warm voice called back. "Good luck in the Land of Half-Truths, and enjoy the tournament!"

Arthur's ears pricked up. He gestured to Ren and Cecily as the boy proceeded into the square. "Did you hear that? The bookseller said *tournament.*"

"Come on, let's follow him," Ren said. "If we can find where the Irontide Tournament's being held, we'll find the competitors. The raiders have probably delivered the time-key by now, so we'll need to steal it back from whichever isports champion they gave it to."

With their sights fixed on camo-boy, Arthur and the others snaked their way across the square and onto an adjoining street. Atlantis bustled with activity at every level. Seagulls swooped and cried overhead; musicians played sea shanties from balconies; and carts shaped like giant crabs scuttled along the roads, ferrying goods around. Arthur spotted a clock on one building that read 11.10 a.m. and noted that Atlantis was four hours behind twenty-first-century time.

Noise built as people crammed the pavements. Cecily pointed up. "Look!" Floating between the rooftops was a holographic banner written in large Greek-style letters with the words *IRONTIDE TOURNAMENT 2493*. Projected beneath the text was a looping video montage of several people fighting shadowy monsters, racing across crumbling stone walkways, dodging fireballs and paragliding off cliffs.

"That's it!" Arthur felt a slither of hope. Finally, they were getting somewhere. "It must be an annual isports event, like the World Cup for professional questers."

As they got to the end of the street, people dressed in yellow, black, red, blue or white outfits joined the throng until it became impossible to pick out the boy they'd been tailing. Arthur listened carefully to the voices of passers-by, trying to glean more information about where they were headed. It was tricky, as only a few people spoke English.

"Stay close to me," an elderly lady said, squeezing the hands of two small children. "I don't want you getting lost in the Kraken."

Two teenagers ran through the pack shouting, "Griffon Ramsay!" at the top of their lungs.

Someone called after them, "It's Yesenia Colt's tournament this season. That girl is *ice*!"

"We should have gone to the Stadio del Mistero," one man muttered irritably. "It's always less crowded than the Kraken."

Arthur guessed the Kraken was one of the stadiums where you watched the tournament. On Earth, it was also the name of a legendary sea monster… "Keep your eyes and ears open for any information about the competitors," he told Ren and Cecily.

They heard the Kraken before they saw it. A rumble filled the air, making all the buildings along the street tremble. The din grew louder until they turned a corner and Arthur's breath caught.

The Kraken looked like its namesake – a mammoth oily-blue sea monster with a swollen head and glowing amber eyes. It was so enormous that Arthur had to tip his head back just to see the top of it. Towering banks of seating rose under the arches of its tentacles and spectators swarmed inside through large silver security gates.

"No way," Ren said, gaping up at it. "Why can't stadiums look like that in our century?"

Surrounding the Kraken was an expanse of pavement dotted with merchandise stalls and carts selling cones of fried seaweed. A few of the flagstones were inlaid with golden five-armed starfish and whenever someone walked over one, a holographic statue rose out of the ground on a rotating podium.

"This reminds me of the Hollywood Walk of Fame," Cecily commented, tapping her foot against the nearest starfish. The hologram of an athletic young man with long brown braids projected into the air beside her, his expression hidden by dark sunglasses. His muscular torso was strapped with lightweight body armour, and in one hand he wielded a baton that crackled with sparks of blue energy. A ring of text scrolled around the bottom of his podium:

Griffon Ramsay – Irontide champion – 2491.

Arthur shrank back just looking at him.

Suddenly, a siren pierced the air, making them all jump. A ring of huge holographic screens dropped down around the Kraken, all displaying the same flashing message:

KRAKEN GOING LIVE IN 10 … 9 … 8…

As the crowds continued pouring into the stadium, Arthur noticed a number of floating, bare-chested security guards shepherding everyone through the gates.

"Are those –" Ren squinted – "*mermen*?"

They were obviously mimics because they had forked fish tails for legs. Arthur wasn't sure how they stayed afloat – they appeared to be swimming through the air.

… 3 … 2 … 1.

The countdown vanished from the big screens and was replaced by a live view inside the Kraken. Rather than a grassy pitch, the ground was a rippling lake of liquid silver. Supporters crammed the dizzyingly high stands, cheering and waving coloured flags. Arthur had visited high-capacity football stadiums before, but the scale of the Kraken was on another level. He could only imagine what it might feel like to be inside, surrounded by all that noise and heat.

There was a loud, reverberating *bong* and the crowds hushed. Arthur watched in amazement as the lake undulated and a name rose out of the surface:

LAZARUS SLOANE.

The liquid silver heaved with waves. One moulded itself into a slim, smartly dressed man with scaly green skin and wide yellow eyes. Arthur recoiled, even though he'd seen a lizard-headed man before in the Wonderscape.

"Good afternoon, fellow isports fanatics!" the lizard-headed man announced. Arthur tried to concentrate on what he was saying and not be distracted by the thin black tongue flicking between his lips. *"My name is Lazarus Sloane and it is my pleasure to welcome you to the greatest isports show on holovision:* The Lazarus Show. *Beginning today we will be presenting live uninterrupted coverage of the Irontide Tournament 2493!"*

The crowd roared as a countdown clock appeared in the top right of the screen. Outside, Arthur felt the ground tremble.

"We're just forty-five minutes away from the opening ceremony and the atmosphere in the Kraken is electric," Lazarus continued. *"The rules are a little different this*

season. Questers can now compete as individuals, or in teams of up to four. So far, we have five entrants."

As he spoke, the lake divided itself into five different coloured squares – red, black, white, yellow and blue. There were three teams and two individuals, all posed in combat-ready stances, so they looked more like video-game characters than real people. Most had snarling faces or smug grins.

"Well, they seem like a friendly bunch," Cecily remarked unhappily. "And we've got to steal the time-key back from one of them…"

Stood in the black square, Arthur recognized Griffon Ramsay. His braids were slung up in a band on one side of his head and he was wearing the same black body armour as his holographic statue. The other solo quester, in the yellow square, was a hawkish young woman with white-blonde hair. Her neon-yellow catsuit was plastered with various company logos and she was posed holding a strange bubble-shaped gun with the words *Magmaflo-3000* written along one side. Her name was Yesenia Colt. A spear-wielding trio of men in sleek scarlet outfits made up the red team. They had blazing flame motifs stencilled on their hair and their team's name, *Savage Strike,* printed on their chests. The blue team, *Transonic,* consisted of two heavily armed older teenagers in tailored navy suits; and the white team, *The Ghost League,* comprised four ragtag adult questers dressed in matching white puffer jackets.

Lazarus cleared his scaly throat. *"Long ago,* Legendarium's *designer, Pierre Irontide, created a suit of gaming armour with extraordinary powers. The armour consisted of five grouped components – a helmet, a pair of boots, a pair of gauntlets, a tunic and a shield. Copies of each of these components have now been hidden in five quest-lands of* Legendarium. *Tournament competitors must complete a unique challenge in each quest-land in order to win one component of armour. The champions will be the fastest questers to collect the full set, which can then be exchanged for our three* billion *DIRT grand prize!"* He raised a clawed finger. *"Remember: you can watch all-day live coverage, exclusive interviews and analysis on* The Lazarus Show. *For now, please enjoy a message from my sponsors."*

Lazarus disappeared as the lake reshaped itself into a giant drinks can with the word *NOVAFUEL* written on the side. Fireworks burst over the Kraken as the ring pull snapped and a fizzy orange liquid bubbled out.

"Over here," Cecily said, viewing another of the holovision screens. "I think it's a news channel."

Arthur read a few of the headlines scrolling around the screen's edge:

CONTINUED UNREST ON THE PLANET YIM...

RAIDERS ATTACK SUPPLY CARRIERS IN THE ROZT SYSTEM...

GALACTIC HIGHWAY 24 CLOSED IN TRADING DISPUTE...

He wondered if the raiders' attack had anything to do with Tide, Vorru or Rultan. In the centre of the screen a smartly dressed presenter appeared outside a grand building, where some of the Irontide Tournament contestants could be seen entering a set of revolving doors. A brass plaque on the wall was etched with the words: *HOTEL LOCH NESS.*

"... *As per tradition, each of the questers has been given a room at the same hotel and checked in two days ago to start preparations,*" the presenter was saying. "*It's impossible to know who will be the tournament victor this year, but current favourites are the only former champions taking part: Griffon Ramsay and Yesenia Colt.*"

"The raiders were delivering the time-key to an isports *champion,*" Ren remembered, "So if Griffon Ramsay and Yesenia Colt are the only champions competing, then one of them must have it. We just need to figure out which one."

Cecily looked thoughtful. "I've got an idea, but it's risky."

"Go on..." Arthur said.

"Well, we *could* try to enter the Irontide Tournament ourselves. As contestants, we'll get unhindered access to that hotel and we'll have a better chance of getting closer to Griffon and Yesenia to work out which one of them has the time-key."

Ren blinked at her. "Actually, that might work. If they're keeping the time-key in their room, it'll also make it easier to break in and steal it back."

The thought of being in competition with someone like Griffon Ramsay made Arthur's stomach shrivel to the size of a walnut. He knew entering the tournament was an extremely dangerous plan, but it also seemed like the fastest way to locate the time-key. And given that they could turn into protoplasm at any moment, speed was of the essence. "All right," he said, with a deep breath. "Let's do it."

"We need to find out how you enter," Ren decided, surveying the area around the Kraken. "Cecily, why don't you ask one of those mermen? They look official."

Cecily pointed to her chest. "Why do *I* have to ask them?"

"Because out of the three of us, you're the most persuasive," Ren replied. "It certainly isn't me. I couldn't even convince you to enter our hotdog-eating contest."

"That's because the contest was moronic," Cecily said flatly. "And wasteful."

Arthur rubbed the back of his neck, feeling embarrassed. "Ren's right – it needs to be you. Plus, you have purple hair. A mer-mimic might relate to that."

"*All right*, fine." Cecily straightened her jacket and marched up to the nearest merman, whose seaweed-green hair was styled into a scallop-edged mohawk. "Excuse me, I was wondering if you could tell me how to enter the Irontide Tournament?"

The merman peered down at her. "And you are?" His booming voice was like waves crashing against rocks.

Cecily shrank back. For a moment, Arthur thought she'd lost her nerve, but then she cleared her throat and said, "My friends and I are new here. We haven't visited Legendarium before."

"So, you're a nobody," the merman clarified. "I doubt Lazarus Sloane will let you enter the tournament if you don't have any fans. Fans mean views and views mean advertising. But before Lazarus, you'd need an isports licence from the UGP."

"The UGP?" Cecily echoed.

The merman folded his sizeable arms. "You mean you've never heard of the Universal Gaming Police? Where are you from, the outer rings of Navagool? The UGP oversee every isports tournament in the Known Universe. Anywhere there are professional players, you'll find UGP officers. They prevent the use of illegal equipment and stop people cheating."

"I see." Cecily bit her lip, thinking. "And do you know where the Hotel Loch Ness is?"

The merman pointed his tail in the direction of the Kraken's head. "Two blocks that way, on the corner." His fins bristled as a shout went up by the security gates. "You'll have to excuse me." And, with a flick of his tail, he swam off.

"Well, that was gross," Cecily complained, when she arrived back. "He had really bad BO – smelled like tuna."

Arthur wrinkled his nose. That was a fact he didn't need to know.

"You heard him, I suppose," she continued. "We need an isports licence from the Universal Gaming Police. If you can find UGP officers wherever there are professional players, there must be one stationed at the Hotel Loch Ness."

Arthur turned in the direction of the Kraken's head. "Good thinking."

As they set off, Ren walked over one of the five-armed starfish in the pavement and another hologram ascended from the ground. "What the—?!" she exclaimed, almost falling over.

Three people were rotating in mid-air in front of them. Arthur didn't need to read the scrolling text to identify who they were because it was like looking in a mirror.

It was a statue of them.

5

Gazing up at their holographic likenesses, Arthur cringed. It was as if they'd all frozen in the middle of an argument. Cecily was shouting, Ren was pointing at her and Arthur had his hands held high in the air like he was begging them both to stop. At their feet, Cloud had hidden his face under his paw, like he was embarrassed. It couldn't be more different to Griffon Ramsay's statue.

"This must have been taken when we first arrived in the Wonderscape," Ren said, blushing. "*Before* we became friends."

Cecily absent-mindedly ran her fingers down the nape of her neck – back then, her braids had hung loose over her shoulders. "But how does this exist? Milo said that nobody in this century knows about us."

"He said nobody knows about us being *time-travellers*," Arthur corrected. He wondered now whether those strange looks they'd received in the square had been because people had actually recognized them. "I suppose lots of people must have known about us as players – our success in the Wonderscape was front-page news." He examined the caption below their hologram:

The Mysterious Pipsqueaks – The Wonderscape – 2473.

Due to a frustrating name-calling incident, they'd been forced to use "Pipsqueaks" as their team moniker. Arthur had never lived it down. "When we returned home, it must have seemed like we'd just vanished from the twenty-fifth century. Maybe that's why they've added *mysterious* to our name?"

"You know what this means, don't you?" Cecily said. "We're *famous*. We might even have fans. Lazarus Sloane is bound to want us in the tournament!"

"Don't you think he'll find it suspicious that we haven't aged in twenty years?" Ren said, pointing to the date on the podium. She made a quick calculation on her fingers. "We'll have to pretend to be the Pipsqueaks' children. At least nobody will be able to deny the resemblance."

"You want us to pose as our own children?" Arthur's brain went fuzzy just thinking about it, but he supposed if it made Lazarus Sloane more inclined to give them a place in the tournament, it was worth it. "Come on, let's get to the hotel. The clock's ticking."

Following the merman's directions, they made their way through the remaining crowds around the Kraken, before turning onto a quieter street lined with what Arthur suspected might be ice-cream parlours. Strange flavours like

Marine Honey and Sweet Atlantean Kelp were displayed in revolving silver bowls, topped with fruit wedges and multi-coloured sprinkles. Smartly dressed servers scooped the ice cream into silvery wafer cones shaped like oyster shells. If Arthur hadn't been racing against time, he would have liked to try some.

"There it is," Ren said, pointing to an elegant building on the far corner of the road. "The Hotel Loch Ness."

Compared to some of its gaudier neighbours, the hotel looked rather plain. It stood five storeys high, fenced by black iron railings and decorated with neat window boxes brimming with heather. A rabble of dark-clothed men and women jostled for position outside. Arthur noticed a few of them holding devices with large lenses and decided they were probably paparazzi.

"I thought there might be a sea serpent swimming up the wall," said Cecily, surveying the building as they approached. "That's the legend, isn't it? That there's a monster living in the loch?"

"Yeah, but I saw a photo of it once and it looked more like a cardboard cut-out," Ren told her disappointedly. She nodded towards two hotel porters dressed in blue kilts, waiting at either side of the revolving front doors. "Any idea how we're going to get past them?"

Cecily smirked. "Oh, leave that to me."

They gave the paparazzi a wide berth before proceeding through a gate in the iron railings. As Cecily marched up to the revolving doors, one of the porters stepped into her path. "Sorry, Miss, no fans allowed."

"A *fan*?!" Cecily staggered back like the word had wounded her. "I'm not a fan, you moron."

The porter's expression faltered. "Uh…"

"I'm a guest," she snapped. "Although *guest* is putting it nicely. Your general manager assured me that this hotel is used to catering for celebrities, but my friends and I have had nothing but hassle from your staff since we checked in!" She threw a glance over her shoulder at the waiting paparazzi. "Now let us pass, before one of them realizes who I am."

"So sorry, Miss," the porter said, blushing. "Of course." And he hastily moved aside, allowing the four of them to enter.

"That was brilliant," Arthur whispered, bundling through the revolving doors behind Cecily. Cloud trotted beside them with his chin held high.

Cecily gave a shy smile. "I've stayed in fancy hotels like this before with my parents. There are lots of rude guests, unfortunately."

The lobby of the Hotel Loch Ness was dominated by a dazzling chandelier, floating just under the ceiling. An auburn-haired receptionist in a smart tartan suit moved behind a desk to one side, and a shiny grand piano sat on a stage, opposite. There were fluffy sheepskin rugs spread over the floor; pine-green cushions on all the armchairs and sofas, and the air smelled of woodsmoke and whisky. Guests lounged around chatting while *The Lazarus Show* played on a huge holovision screen above a fireplace.

Arthur noticed a slender shadow sliding over the floor, up the wall and then across the ceiling. As he looked around, trying to see what was causing it, he realized it was shaped like a long hump-backed creature with fins and a tail. "There's your loch monster," he told Cecily, wondering how the guests didn't find the effect off-putting. "I can't see any of the Irontide competitors, or any UGP officers, but then I don't really know what the UGP look like."

"Maybe we should ask at reception?" Ren suggested.

Arthur was about to agree when he spotted a door in the far wall decorated with a large silver lantern. It looked like an official symbol, so on a hunch he led the others over. They all stopped outside when they heard voices behind the door.

"... only they didn't realize it *was* illegal," someone was pleading.

"That doesn't matter," replied a husky speaker. "They broke the rules. You were right to bring it to my attention."

"Yes, but—"

"Listen to me, Ribbon. You're only sixteen; there's still a lot you need to learn about our line of work. Your talent is unquestionable, but if you want to complete your apprenticeship and become the youngest UGP officer in history, you need to prove that you're capable of rooting out the cheats."

It went quiet. Arthur wanted to continue listening, but someone in the lobby was bound to notice the four of them earwigging outside. With a deep breath, he rapped his knuckles against the door.

"Come in," said the husky voice.

Cecily bundled Cloud into her arms and they piled into a small office. The walls were decorated with posters depicting scenes you might see in an action movie: a man running across a collapsing bridge; a figure escaping from a rampaging dinosaur; a woman leaping across rooftops. Somewhere in each poster – whether hanging from a tree, jammed between two rocks or nestled in some long grass – was a silver lantern like the one on the office door. A slogan at the bottom of each poster read: *Universal Gaming Police: the Light of Justice.*

A bespectacled woman with a steel-grey bob sat behind a desk, monitoring several holographic screens. A polished brass sign on her desk read: *Chief Inspector Doveton.* Over her shoulder stood a rosy-cheeked girl with a quiff of black hair. Both of them wore a similar uniform: a snug-fitting navy jumpsuit with a silver lantern emblazoned on the chest, and a matching cross-body satchel. The only difference was a coloured braid stitched over their shoulders. The chief inspector's was gold, whereas the girl's was white.

"If you have a violation to report, you should use the hotline," the chief inspector muttered. She pointed to a poster that read: *Have you noticed any illegal in-game activity? Report anonymously to the UGP on 880-909-4*4.*

"Actually, we're here to get an isports licence so we can enter the Irontide Tournament," Arthur said. "Can you help?"

The chief inspector regarded him languidly over her spectacles. "Am I supposed to know who you are? Lazarus didn't notify me of any last-minute entrants."

"That's because Lazarus doesn't know about us yet," Cecily said delicately. "But we're sure he'll want us to take part. Our parents were famous I-RAG players – the Pipsqueaks."

The apprentice at the back of the room stifled a gasp.

"The *Pipsqueaks*?" the chief inspector said, lifting her eyebrows. "You're the children of those *Wonderscape* players who disappeared in the seventies?"

"That's right, the *2470s*," Cecily said, like she was trying to remind herself. She pointed Cloud in the chief inspector's direction. "We have our parents' mimic, too. They gave him to us for luck."

Cloud yapped happily, but the chief inspector made a shushing motion with her hands. "Very well. I'll let Lazarus know." She tapped at one of the screens in front of her. "In the meantime, please stand still." Opening a drawer in her desk, she lifted out a small silver lantern, just like those in the posters. She tampered with something on top and a bright light flashed in Arthur's eyes, making him flinch. When he looked down, a pale line was skimming his body.

The chief inspector seemed to notice his surprise. "You've never been bio-scanned before?"

"No, err..." Bio-scanning hadn't been used in the Wonderscape. Arthur remembered something the merman had mentioned to Cecily and ventured, "We're from the outer rings of Navagool."

"Ah, that explains it," the chief inspector remarked, studying the top of the lantern. "This bio-scan takes a copy of your vitals and tells me whether you've got any previous offences on your gaming record. Actually ... you've no previous *anything* on your record. Have you never played an I-RAG before either?"

Arthur smiled gingerly.

"Isports competitions are dangerous," the chief inspector warned. "*Legendarium*'s safety features are switched off during the Irontide Tournament. That means you can be seriously hurt – or *worse* – while you're playing. Do your parents *really* approve of you being here?"

"Actually, this was their idea," Cecily explained. "Look, we really want to take part. We've been training for months."

At the back of the room, the young apprentice cleared her throat. "If I may, ma'am? I know they're inexperienced, but so were their parents. The Pipsqueaks had no history of ever having played an I-RAG before, and they proved to be formidable competitors in the Wonderscape."

She smiled encouragingly at Arthur and he remembered what they'd overheard outside, about her aiming to become the youngest UGP officer in history. She probably understood what it felt like to be an underdog.

"Hmmm." As the chief inspector rubbed her chin, something flashed on one of her screens. "Well, it seems you were right about Lazarus – he *does* want you in the tournament. He's decided that your team colour can be green." She considered them thoughtfully. "Very well. I'll issue you each with an isports licence, but remember my warning: your lives will be at risk in the quest-lands."

Cecily beamed at Arthur and Ren. "What happens now?" she asked. "Should we check into the hotel?"

The chief inspector signalled over her shoulder. "My apprentice here will guide you through orienteering, but it'll have to be brief. The tournament opens in twenty minutes. You're lucky you turned up now and not half an hour later."

As the girl guided them out of the office, Arthur felt a weight lift off his chest. Step one, complete. Now all they needed to do was figure out whether Griffon Ramsay or Yesenia Colt had the time-key, and steal it back. "Do all the Irontide competitors stay in the same part of the hotel?" he asked the apprentice, fishing for more information.

"That's right. Competitors are on the second floor; coaches are on the first." She turned to him. "Do you have a coach? If so, they're entitled to a room, too."

Arthur presumed Milo could pose as their coach when he found them. "Yeah, he might be arriving later."

He shrugged at the others as they all walked into a mirrored lift. Seeing his reflection, heat rushed to Arthur's cheeks. His T-shirt was stained with ketchup and there were charcoal smudges up his legs. Ren and Cecily didn't look much better. The bottom of Cecily's dress was torn and there was pondweed sticking out of Ren's ponytail. Still, considering they'd travelled over four hundred years through time, Arthur supposed it could have been worse.

The UGP apprentice removed three silver bangles from her satchel. Arthur noticed she was already wearing one around her wrist. "Put these fazes on," she said, handing one to each of them. "I don't suppose you use them on the outer rings of Navagool, but they're invaluable in Legendarium. I've loaded them with your isports licences and portal permits, as well as a copy of the tournament guidelines." She ran a finger over her faze in a clockwise direction and a semi-transparent panel of light opened at chest-height in front of her. Arthur guessed the panel was some sort of futuristic notepad as the girl started tracing her finger over it. "Fazes have several other applications – an automatic translator, a navigator, a holovision viewer, an information directory and space to store your DIRT. Plus, you can use them to contact the UGP if you have any questions or concerns regarding security. Not all the apps work in the quest-lands, of course, only in Atlantis."

As the lift juddered into action, Arthur pushed the faze over his wrist and stroked his finger across it, like the apprentice had. A golden rectangle of light appeared hovering in front of him. As he lifted his head, the rectangle floated up, anchored to his line of sight.

Experimenting, he swiped across the display and a document appeared with the UGP logo at the top. It was entitled: *THE YOUNG PIPSQUEAKS – Guide to the Irontide Tournament.*

"Our team name is the Young Pipsqueaks…" he realized gloomily. He hadn't thought there could be anything worse than the Pipsqueaks, but adding the word *young* in front of it, made them sound even more cutesy.

The apprentice chuckled. "Nothing I can do about that, I'm afraid. Lazarus Sloane has chosen it. But that guide has some useful sections to read."

The lift came to a smooth stop and the doors opened to reveal a long, beautifully decorated corridor. The tail of the loch monster's shadow was just slipping over the pine-green carpet at the far end.

"Check out page four for rules on sponsorship, and page sixteen for a catalogue of illegal items," the apprentice suggested, leading them past several numbered doors.

Turning to page sixteen, Arthur found a long list of objects that he recognized from Deadlock's warehouse, including rock blasters, shrieking shurikens and evaders. "Do you suspect any of the other competitors are using these?" he asked, hoping the apprentice might offer some insight into whether Griffon or Yesenia was more likely to have the time-key. One of them obviously intended to use an evader to cheat.

"That's for me to worry about," she insisted. "But I can assure you, everyone taking part in the tournament has a clean isports licence."

Flicking through the guide on her faze display, Ren frowned. "The weapons we saw the other contestants holding aren't in here. Yesenia Colt had a Magmaflo-3000."

"Not all weapons are illegal, only those traded on the Dark Market," the apprentice explained. "They're unregistered, which means mimics don't always have the right skills to heal the wounds they can inflict. All isports fatalities in the last six years have been caused by the use of illegal weapons."

Arthur shuddered, horrified that these weapons were being used in a game. What a gruesome business this Deadlock was in.

The apprentice stopped outside a door with a glowing red seal. The number 235 flashed over the doorknob. "This is your suite. You'll need to tap your fazes against the handle to gain entry."

Arthur took note. That meant they'd need to pinch Griffon's or Yesenia's faze in order to break into their room. Ren held her wrist near the handle. The seal glowed green; there was a click and the door swung inwards.

As Arthur ventured inside, part of him wished they really were staying there on holiday. It was easily the fanciest hotel room he'd stepped foot in. The welcome area featured a plush velvet sofa and armchairs nestled around a carved stone fireplace. A holovision screen shimmered on the wall above the mantelpiece, and a basket of strange jelly-like fruits sat atop a polished wooden dining table.

Ren took a peek into one of the adjoining rooms. "No way! Four-poster beds!"

"If you need me, you can contact the UGP on your fazes, or knock on my room door," the apprentice informed them. "I'm in the coaches' corridor, Number 167."

"Thanks for all your help," Arthur said.

The apprentice nodded. As she turned for the door, she hesitated. "I wasn't even born when your parents made a name for themselves, but my dad told me what happened to them." Her voice faltered. "He ... passed away a few years ago, but it was one of my favourite stories that he used to tell."

Arthur felt a pang of sympathy. "I'm sorry for your loss," he said sincerely. "It's nice to meet you. I'm Arthur, by the way, and this is Ren and Cecily." He tensed as soon as he'd finished speaking, wondering if the apprentice knew the names of the original Pipsqueaks.

But she couldn't have, because she only smiled and said, "My name's Ribbon Rex, but just call me Ribbon. Everyone does."

"Ribbon. All right, well we'd better start preparing for the first quest in the tournament..." Arthur didn't want to be rude, but they needed to get on with finding the time-key.

"Yes, of course," Ribbon replied. "You don't want to be the first out at midnight."

"First *out*?" Arthur said. "What do you mean?"

Ribbon blinked. "You do know about the eliminations, right? You must begin your first quest at some point in the next twelve hours. As soon as you start, a timer begins that only stops when you complete the quest and win your first component of Irontide armour. At the end of the twelve hour-period – midnight tonight – the slowest team is then eliminated from the tournament live on *The Lazarus Show*. The process repeats every twelve hours until only one champion remains."

"Do we have to start our first quest right away?" Cecily flapped.

"Depends on your strategy," Ribbon said. "Every competitor is given a different quest, so your progress is timed separately. If you choose to start yours after your opponents have finished theirs, you'll have a better idea of the times you need to beat, but you'll also have less time to finish. Questers traditionally start the first quest as early as possible. I expect the others will already be at the Great Library of Alexandria, ready to begin."

"At the Great Library...?" Arthur's head swirled with questions.

"Well, good luck!"

As Ribbon closed the door behind her, he stared at the others. "What are we going to do? If we get eliminated, we'll be thrown out of the hotel before we've even had a chance to look for the time-key."

"We're going to have to complete the first quest," Cecily decided, opening her faze display. "And we need to do it faster than another team. Didn't Ribbon say our fazes had a navigator app? We've got to find a way to the Great Library of Alexandria."

6

Another flashing triangle appeared on the pavement ahead of Arthur, pointing left. "This way," he said, jogging around a corner.

The navigator on their fazes had plotted a route to the Great Library and then projected a series of arrows on the ground to direct them there. It felt a bit like being inside a digital map, which was a little creepy, but as long as they reached their destination, Arthur didn't mind.

"The Great Library of Alexandria sounds familiar," Ren said, hurrying beside him. "Have you ever heard of it?"

"Yeah, it was in my old Wonders of the Ancient World Top Trumps set." Arthur tried to remember the information on the card. "There's a legend about the library. It was said to contain every book ever written, but I think it burned down in a fire and everything was lost."

Speeding past them, Cecily forked right. "This way!"

Cloud was racing along at her side, his pink tongue lolling out of his mouth in an expression of pure doggy joy.

At least one of us is enjoying this, Arthur thought.

Veering onto the next street, he almost tripped over as the Great Library appeared in the distance. The Top Trumps illustration had depicted the library as one large building, but here it was a sprawling mass of different structures. Sloping terracotta rooftops, colonnaded walkways and domed towers peeked above the parapet of an imposing stone wall. The entrance was marked by a limestone portico flanked by twin Ionic columns the size of giant sequoias.

"No way," Ren said, staggering to a stop outside. "You probably *could* keep every book ever written in there."

A steady stream of questers dressed in practical hiking gear tramped in and out through the portico, talking and sharing information on their faze displays.

Rushing inside, Arthur and the others entered a bright and airy room, with a high, arched ceiling and bare stone walls that were open at the top to allow light in. Questers marched to and fro across the gleaming mosaic floor carrying various books and scrolls in their arms. Arthur assumed news of their entry in the tournament hadn't yet been announced, as no one paid them any attention. "Where are the other Irontide competitors?" he asked.

"Let's ask someone." Cecily nodded to a man sitting on a nearby bench, sipping from a mug with the slogan *Nice as π* written on the side of it. He was balding with a curly white beard and heavy, wrinkled brow. Unlike the questers, he was dressed in a comfortable knitted jumper, loose brown cords and battered loafers. "What about him? He doesn't look like a quester; maybe he's a librarian?"

They approached him hastily. "Sorry to bother you," Arthur said. "Are you a librarian?"

"Yes, but I'm on a coffee break," the man replied, sounding irritated. As he lifted his head, whatever he was about to say got caught in his throat. "I... My goodness," he spluttered. "Arthur Gillespie? Ren Williams? Cecily Madaki?"

Arthur froze. "How do you know our names?"

"Because you three are my saviours," the librarian replied, smiling broadly. He rested his coffee mug on the bench and pushed himself to his feet. "We've never met but I've heard everything about you from the others. Wangari even showed me photos."

Wangari? It took Arthur a moment to figure out what the man must mean. Wangari Maathai was a hero they'd met in the Wonderscape, a Nobel prize-winning environmentalist. "Wait ... you're a hero from the Wonderscape?"

"Archimedes of Syracuse," the man said, extending his hand. "It's a pleasure to meet you all."

Arthur shook Archimedes' hand in a daze, unable to believe who he was talking to. He'd done a history project on Archimedes during the spring term. He was a famous inventor, engineer and mathematician who had lived more than two thousand years ago.

Ren's jaw dropped. "You're Archimedes? Like, *the* Archimedes? You invented the catapult and the hydraulic screw, and – you were the first person to say *eureka*!"

Clearly, Ren had done the same project.

The tips of Archimedes' ears went pink as he shook hands with Ren and Cecily, too. "Yes, that's true. But enough of me – what are you three doing here? Shouldn't you be in the twenty-first century?"

Arthur glanced warily around the hall, checking that none of the other questers had heard. "Archimedes, we're in trouble," he whispered. "We've lost contact with Milo Hertz and in order to get home, we have to steal a time-key from one of the competitors in the Irontide Tournament."

"We're competitors, too," Ren added glumly. "And unless we complete the first quest fast enough, we're going to be eliminated at midnight."

The scholar's bushy white brows jumped. "Oh dear. You'd better follow me."

He steered them out of the hall and along a narrow corridor filled with desks where questers were sat studying more books and scrolls, some holographic. Gazing at Archimedes' back, Arthur started thinking. Like all Wonderscape heroes, Archimedes had a mimic's body implanted with the consciousness of the *real* Archimedes of Syracuse. Milo Hertz had promised to give all the heroes the option to live a "second" life as a mimic in the twenty-fifth century, if they so wished. Archimedes would have been able to do whatever he wanted in the Known Universe... So why had he chosen to spend his time in Legendarium?

They made their way into a circular gallery where bookcases lined the walls, right up to the ceiling. The air smelled of dust and old leather. Inhaling deeply, Archimedes smiled. "I used to frequent the *real* library in Alexandria," he told them. "Since leaving the Wonderscape, working here is the closest I've felt to home."

Arthur stared at the shelves, crammed with all sorts of manuscripts and scrolls. Some were so ancient that their bindings were crumbling away. The marble statues of nine elegant women stood in recesses around the room. In their hands they each held a different musical instrument, theatre mask, celestial sphere or scroll. They reminded Arthur of the golden sun statue he'd glimpsed outside Deadlock's warehouse.

"Those are the nine Muses of Greek mythology," Archimedes explained. "The Great Library was dedicated to them. Everything you see here is a faithful recreation of the Great Library as I remember it. There are a few differences, of course – the coffee machines on the second level are a new addition." He sighed. "It's a real pity we didn't have coffee in ancient Greece; my friend Eratosthenes would have loved it."

Arthur was sure the ancient Greeks hadn't been reading *holographic* scrolls, either, but the library was now part of an in-reality adventure game and he supposed it had to function as such.

"I spend a lot of time helping questers with their research," Archimedes continued brightly. "That's what most of these texts are – stories of legends from across the Known Universe. I've been curating the library's collection. Can you believe that there are over one million written languages of intelligent life out there?"

Arthur wondered if Archimedes still did mathematics and engineering in his spare time. There were so many questions he wanted to ask the scholar about his new life, and the lives of the other heroes, but there just wasn't time. "We're here by accident, we think," he said, launching into a speedy account of what had happened to them in the last few hours.

Archimedes rubbed his beard, looking curious and troubled in equal parts. "Hmmm. I'm not in direct contact with Milo Hertz, but I know heroes who are. I'll ask them to send him a message. In the meantime, you've got to win your first component of Irontide armour. I haven't been paying close attention to this season's contestants, but I've heard the names Yesenia Colt and Griffon Ramsay before. They both have fierce reputations. You need to be careful." He pushed open a heavy door and ushered them into a long, empty passageway.

"I assume you've worked out the essentials of how *Legendarium* works," Archimedes continued. "But how much do you know about *legends*? The word *legend* actually has several different meanings. In the tournament, your knowledge could be the difference between life and death."

Arthur gulped, remembering Chief Inspector Doveton's warning that *Legendarium*'s safety features would be switched off for the tournament. "Legends are stories," he said, thinking of that Atlantis documentary he'd watched with his dad. "Mysterious ones. No one really knows if they're true or not."

"Like the Loch Ness monster," Ren voiced. "Some people claim to have seen it, but no one can be sure whether it's really down there."

Archimedes nodded. "Exactly. Legend has it, this library and all its treasures were destroyed by a terrible fire. In fact, there was a small fire once, but it didn't cause much damage." He shook his head before continuing. "The point is: although there is a seed of truth in most legends, their stories have been embellished over time. Legendarium is where those stories come to life. In the quest-lands you will meet legendary people and beasts, and explore legendary places. Everything's mixed together so my advice would be to expect the unexpected."

Arthur fiddled with a thread on his shorts, wondering what kind of challenges they might face. "Are the mimics in Legendarium as real as you?"

Archimedes winked and tapped his scalp. "They don't have the consciousness of a real person inside their heads, like me and the other heroes, if that's what you mean. But most people don't know that. The mimics in Legendarium are upgrades from those you met in the Wonderscape, who can think and act for themselves. They have been programmed with the same personalities, skills and memories as the legends they represent." He added with a tone of caution, "Which means they're not always *good*, unlike the heroes in the Wonderscape."

As Archimedes led them through another door, Arthur shared a wary glance with Ren and Cecily. The heroes of the Wonderscape had been their allies. Clearly, they wouldn't be able to rely on such help in Legendarium.

They entered a brightly lit hall, bustling with people. In the centre of the marble floor, a triangular-based pillar of light soared thirty metres up to the ceiling. Questers moved in and out of it from all sides, closely monitored by a number of UGP officers, who stood at intervals around the room holding their lanterns. A balcony overlooking the floor was crammed with dark-clothed paparazzi and several camera operators wearing T-shirts with a yellow reptilian eye printed on the front.

"That, believe it or not, is the Bermuda Triangle," Archimedes said, with more than a hint of irony. "It's a portal that allows questers to move between Atlantis and any of the quest-lands."

Arthur was fairly sure that the *real* Bermuda Triangle was a legendary region in the Atlantic Ocean where ships and planes would mysteriously disappear...

"When you're close enough to the Bermuda Triangle, a quest-map will appear," Archimedes explained. "Study it carefully. It will show you which quest-land you will be travelling to, and give you a clue about how to win your first component of Irontide armour. Every competitor will have their own quest to complete and their own set of armour to collect within the same quest-land. It will be closed to other questers, so the only people you'll see will be your opponents or characters in the game. You'll be timed from the moment you enter the Bermuda Triangle, until the moment your quest succeeds or fails, at which point you will automatically return here."

Arthur repeated everything slowly in his head, trying to commit all the advice to memory. Glancing at the media balcony, he wondered if the yellow reptilian eye was the logo of *The Lazarus Show*. "Will *The Lazarus Show* be following everything we do?"

Archimedes grumbled disapprovingly. "Their cameras will be filming you the entire time, but to avoid revealing your tactics to other competitors and their coaches, they don't record sound. That means you can speak freely. Just don't let your actions betray who you really are."

"Right." Arthur swallowed. "Thanks for the help, Archimedes."

The scholar nodded. "Good luck, my friends."

As they crossed the floor towards the Bermuda Triangle, Arthur noticed how much fun the other questers seemed to be having. Most were laughing and joking with each other, examining one another's equipment, or sharing stories.

But they weren't at risk of death. He doubted the other Irontide competitors were looking so jolly. "If our opponents are anything like esports players, they'll have been training for months for this," he told Ren and Cecily, miserably. "I can't see how we'll be faster than any of them."

"We've got to stay positive," Cecily insisted. "We were successful in the Wonderscape, and you do as much gaming as any of this lot, just in a different century."

Arthur tried to take confidence, but it was difficult to believe they wouldn't get eliminated. All they could really do was try, and hope that luck was on their side.

They were a few metres from the Bermuda Triangle when a sheet of brightly coloured fabric materialized in mid-air and flopped to the ground at Arthur's feet. As he reached down to collect it, he noticed a haze of fading particles and knew it must have been nano-generated.

"It's a tapestry," Ren realized, as Arthur spread it between them.

Arthur had only ever seen huge tapestries hanging on the walls of medieval castles. They normally portrayed knights on horseback or scenes from everyday life in the Middle Ages.

This tapestry, however, was a map. It depicted a wide oak forest with a road running through it. A castle stood to the north and embroidered inside the castle walls was a pair of armoured gold boots. Sewn around the edge of the map were the words:

LEGENDARI◈M

– *THE LAND OF OUTLAWS* –

Choose wisely who to follow
if you want to see tomorrow.

"Outlaws?" Cecily read worriedly. "Does that mean it's going to be filled with bandits and criminals? Why couldn't it be the Land of Kittens?"

Arthur tried to put the outlaws to the back of his mind. "The Irontide boots must be in the castle. That's obviously where we need to go when we arrive." He still didn't know how much time remained before they all turned into slime, but to have any chance of going home, they needed to win those boots as fast as possible. "Come on. Let's do this."

Stuffing the quest-map in his pocket, he summoned some courage and stepped into the light.

7

Travelling through the Bermuda Triangle felt similar to moving through the raiders' light-portal, only even faster. One moment, Arthur was surrounded by blinding white light, his weightless body bobbing like a cork on water …

… the next, he was stood on a patch of damp soil in the middle of a bare, twiggy wood.

He reached for a trunk to steady himself as his senses adjusted to their new scenery. Gnarly oak trees with thick, moss-covered trunks were rooted all around and the scent of fresh-turned earth hung in the cool air. A pale sun was just dawning, meaning the Land of Outlaws had to be in a different time zone to Atlantis, possibly even on a new planet entirely.

"Everyone all right?" Cecily asked, unfastening Cloud's lead. The little dog wiggled his bottom as he prepared to spring into a pile of leaves.

"Fine, if you don't count being cold," Ren replied, rubbing the backs of her arms.

Arthur was feeling the chill, too. His shorts and T-shirt had been perfect barbecue attire, but now the climate had changed, he was desperate for a hoody and jeans.

He scoured the trees for landmarks. Ahead of them, a wide, muddy road cut through the undergrowth. "We must be somewhere in the forest on the quest-map," he said, fetching it from his pocket. "We need to get our bearings to work out which direction the castle is in. The sun rises in the east, but that might not be true if we're on another planet."

As he examined the map, the hairs on the back of his neck bristled and he sensed the air shift over his shoulder. He turned around to find a small mirrored drone floating a few metres away. It had a large camera lens on one side with a yellow reptilian eye printed below. It hovered for a moment, and then its mirrored surface rippled and it turned invisible.

"I think this means the show's started," he warned the others, ominously. "Don't forget: we're being watched."

Ren tramped over to a tree at the edge of the road and hung off a branch to test its strength. "We'll get a better view of the area if we climb one of these." She pressed her toes against a knot in the trunk, reached for an overhead branch and heaved herself up.

"I'll just wait down here..." Cecily said, hugging her elbows.

Arthur gave her a thin smile. She suffered from vertigo whenever she was up high. "Can you take another look at this?" he asked, passing her the quest-map. "Archimedes told us to study it carefully and there might be something we've missed."

As he started climbing, he remembered the first time he'd scaled a tree in the local park. He could still hear his dad now, calling up instructions: *Look for sturdy footholds! Swing your legs! Grip the trunk with both hands!* He felt a twinge of pain, thinking that if they failed this quest, he might never hear his dad's voice again.

"I think I'm high enough," Ren yelled down. She performed a careful about-turn so her back was against the trunk, and settled herself on a branch. "Arthur, can you see this?"

Arthur manoeuvred himself into position and peered out at the view. The wood continued for a couple of kilometres and then opened onto a wide heath. In one direction, an imposing stone castle rose beyond the edge of the trees, surrounded by a dark moat. Red flags with gold crowns fluttered from the turrets, and guards in steel armour marched up and down the battlements. The central keep was square, with four white towers. There was something familiar about its design, but Arthur couldn't understand why.

He spied four white figures scrambling across the heath, being chased by a terrifying beast with a leopard's body and a snake's head.

"I think I can see the Ghost League," he told Ren, grateful

that the leopard-snake was far away, "but none of our other opponents so far."

"Something's coming this way!" Ren blurted. "Cecily, hide!"

Arthur and Ren scrambled down the trunk as a clatter of horseshoes sounded along the road. Dropping to the ground, they spotted Cloud and Cecily cowering behind a bush and ducked behind a large shrub of their own.

Arthur's heart thudded, wondering what was coming. At first, an old-fashioned stagecoach rattled past, pulled by four brown mares. The vehicle had four wooden wheels and was painted with glossy scarlet and black lacquer. Sat atop was a driver dressed in smart red-and-gold uniform, and another uniformed man pointing a large shotgun behind them. Both were sweaty-faced and trembling, and it wasn't long before Arthur realized why.

The trees rustled and the ground shook as a monstrous black dog, the size of a tank, came charging after the stagecoach. Putrid yellow breath fogged around the dog's mouth and nostrils as it snarled. Arthur caught a whiff of something foul and covered his nose. He'd never heard stories of a giant black dog before, but perhaps it was a legend from another planet. He froze as the beast passed by, desperately hoping it wouldn't notice them. Eventually, the clop of horseshoes faded and the smell disappeared. Everyone waited until the creature was out of sight before rising to their feet.

"What *was* that?" Ren asked, walking out into the road.

Arthur glanced unnervingly at the trees, thinking of all the other legendary beasts that could very well be lurking around them right now. "I don't know. Let's just win these Irontide boots and get out of here as soon as possible."

Cecily brushed dirt off her dress. "Did you see the castle from up there?"

"Hang on..." Ren said, examining the trees on the other side of the road. "You two should take a look at these."

Frowning, Arthur and Cecily followed Ren over to where several sheets of parchment had been nailed to the trees. They all had the words *WANTED: DEAD OR ALIVE* written at the top in thick black letters, and a charcoal sketch of a person's face underneath.

Outlaws, Arthur realized. The first poster showed the face of a man named John "Swift Nick" Nevison. He had wild, dark hair, a torn shirt and cold, beady eyes that watched Arthur disconcertingly. In small text at the bottom was a paragraph describing Nevison's crimes:

10,000 DIRT for the capture of John "Swift Nick" Nevison, notorious rogue and highwayman, charged with the robbery of twelve stagecoaches travelling on the Great North Road between York and London.

"No wonder that coachman was carrying a gun," Arthur remarked. "They have to protect themselves from monsters *and* thieves." He examined the next poster along. It featured a scruffy-looking man in a ragged suit.

A bounty of 15,000 DIRT will be paid to anyone who can surrender, dead or alive, one Claude Duval, illustrious thief and rabble-rouser, to His Majesty's Guard.

Ren pointed to a group of posters further along. "They're from all over the world – Mexico, India, Cuba, Australia. There's a whole bunch of Wild West gunslingers from North America, too."

Arthur thought about what Archimedes had told them – that Legendarium was home to a mixture of different legends. "Maybe the Land of Outlaws is home to every single outlaw who's ever had a story told about them?" He scanned some of the other posters. None of the outlaws' names were familiar, but he got the sense from their varying styles of clothing and headwear that they had lived at different times in history. Women were in the minority, so they all stood out; especially Katherine "the Wicked Lady" Ferrers, who wore a striking black scarf covering her mouth. Their crimes ranged from petty theft and train robbery to cold-blooded murder.

"I hope we don't come across any of these people on our way to the castle," Cecily said, turning her nose up at the nearest poster. "Maybe we should stay off the road? Highwaymen probably got their name because they robbed coaches on the highway."

"Good idea," Arthur said, taking the quest-map back off her. "Through the trees it is. We'll just have to be careful not to encounter any unfriendly legendary beasts."

Ren was stood staring at another poster. "Actually, I'm not sure the outlaws or the beasts are our biggest problem…"

As Arthur drew closer to the poster Ren was looking at, he got a horrible sinking feeling. It didn't have just one face on the front.

It had three.

"Not again," Cecily moaned.

Just like the statue outside the Kraken, the poster depicted the three of them. Ren and Arthur were both snarling and Cecily had her head thrown back, laughing maniacally.

"A special reward will be granted to the captor of the Young Pipsqueaks," Cecily read, *"known crooks, brigands and vagrants."* She folded her arms. "Well, that's just rude."

"This must be part of the game," Ren said, tapping another *Wanted* poster depicting the three flame-haired men from the Savage Strike team. "Maybe this quest-land is like an RPG?"

"RPG?" Cecily repeated.

"Role-playing game," Arthur clarified. He pictured the stack of video-game cases in his bedroom at home. At least half of them were RPGs, where you play the role of a character in a story… Except now, *they* were the characters. "Normally in an RPG, you interact with other characters and are given several choices. If you make the right decisions, you end up fulfilling your objective."

Cecily regarded their poster thoughtfully. "These rewards are all paid by His Majesty's Guard. If we're playing the role of outlaws, they'll arrest us if they find us."

"That's going to make getting inside the castle difficult," Ren said. "I'm pretty sure it was flying a flag with a crown on it – for His Majesty."

Arthur thought of the guards he'd seen patrolling the battlements; there would be more inside. "We'll have to formulate a plan on the way. Let's just get to the castle without being captured, eaten or robbed first. Then we can think about how to get inside and find the Irontide boots."

With their senses on high alert, they ventured back into the forest and set off in the direction of the castle. Cloud foraged ahead with his nose pressed firmly to the ground, sniffing for danger. Arthur supposed the invisible drone with the lizard eye was following behind. The thought made him feel uneasy.

"Who do you think's more likely to have the time-key?" Ren asked as they trekked, "Yesenia Colt or Griffon Ramsay?"

Cecily opened her faze and tapped at the screen. "I'm not sure, but that info directory that Ribbon told us about seems to be working. I'll see what I can dig up on them both."

Arthur pictured the two isports champions – effortlessly cool Griffon and laser-eyed Yesenia. He almost had to pinch himself to make sure he was really in competition with them. "You'd have to be pretty desperate to make a bargain with someone like Deadlock and both of them seem too successful for that. Why would they risk it?"

"Perhaps they're under pressure to maintain their success?" Cecily said. "It says here that Yesenia's won thirteen isports tournaments in her career, while Griffon's won eight and been runner-up in six. When you're at the top, it's a long way down." She grimaced, reading on. "During Yesenia's last competition, she sabotaged one of her opponents by pushing them into a pit of snakes. And Griffon seems just as ruthless. His fans call him the "Lone Wolf" because he likes to hunt down his opponents. Sounds like they'll both do anything to win."

They'd been hiking a few minutes longer in the direction of the castle when Cloud took an abrupt left turn, following a scent. Arthur noticed tracks in the mud. Given their size, he presumed a vehicle had passed through, although the grooves were too smooth to have been made by tyres. "Careful," he whispered, lowering his head. "There could be someone else here."

They crept to the edge of a wide, leafy clearing. A brightly painted wagon was parked in the centre and a dappled grey pony stood chewing on a clump of grass beside it.

"Do they belong to His Majesty's Guard or to outlaws?" Cecily whispered.

Arthur scoured the area but couldn't see anyone. The castle's four white towers peeked above the treetops. "I don't know, but this is the direction we have to go. Stay vigilant."

They ventured out into the open. Arthur pivoted his head in all directions, checking for threats. As they snuck past the wagon, he noticed the ground around it was covered in footprints.

"What-ho, questers!" called a cheerful voice, suddenly.

Arthur nearly jumped out of his skin as a cloud of glittering particles burst from under the wagon. The dust converged into a portly man with unruly dark eyebrows and a friendly smile. He was dressed in a long velvet robe, knee-high leather boots and a maroon cup.

"By my troth, I've got some bargains today!" the man promised, excitedly. He pulled a canvas sheet off his wagon to reveal several baskets of bread, fruit and veg; a stack of home-made country pies, and a large barrel. Rising in the middle of them was a holographic menu of other items with prices listed beside them. "Food and drink, weapons, armour, power-ups, info packs – you name it, I've got it!"

"You're a trader," Arthur realized, crumpling with relief. The guy wasn't there to kill them, only to sell them stuff. Here was something that video games and I-RAGs had in common: there was always a shop.

"Maybe he's got something that can help us sneak into the castle?" Cecily said hopefully. But before she had a chance to browse what was on offer, a shadow streaked past the tip of her ear. Staggering back, she swatted her hands either side of her head. "What was that?!"

Cloud's fur bristled. He gave a warning bark as several dark objects whizzed through the air around them.

"Get down!" Ren yelled.

Arthur ducked just as a voice at his back shouted, "NOW!"

In a blur of colour, three strangers sprang from the trees and started sprinting towards Arthur and the others. Their faces were covered by ornate Venetian masks and they all wore tricorne hats, polished leather boots and thigh-length jackets with upturned collars. One had a bow slung across their back; the other two brandished old-fashioned pistols that Arthur recognized as blunderbusses (one of his favourite *Super Smash Bros.* characters used one).

He knew at once that they were outlaws. And that meant one thing.

"It's an ambush!" he cried. "Run!"

8

Arthur flinched as a loud *BANG* reverberated around the clearing. The trader's pony gave a startled bray and galloped off.

"They're firing at us!" Cecily shrieked, bundling Cloud into her arms.

Ren darted behind the trader's wagon. "Over here!"

Pulse racing, Arthur scrambled around the wagon and dropped into a crouch beside the trader, who had already taken shelter. Cecily and Cloud were close behind. "How are we going to escape?" Cecily asked, breathlessly. "If we run, they'll fire at us!"

Arthur peeked around the side of the wagon. The outlaws were stalking closer. The tallest of the trio, who wore an ostrich feather in his tricorne, pointed his blunderbuss in Arthur's direction. "Let us take what we want and no one will get hurt!" he called in a smooth, French accent.

Without warning, the trader grabbed a baton of crusty bread from the wagon and jumped out into the open.

"Stay back, foes!" he cried, waving the loaf madly. "These supplies are for the questers. You can't have them!"

In a flash of sparks and smoke, the outlaw with the ostrich feather fired his blunderbuss and a patch of ground exploded near the trader's feet. The trader yelped, threw the bread in the air, and dissolved into a cloud of nano-particles that vanished under the wagon.

"Fat lot of good he was," Ren muttered. "Now what?"

Cecily fiddled with the disc on Cloud's collar. "We'll have to use Cloud." As she twisted the right-hand bead, the outlaws fired another shot. Cecily's hand slipped …

… and suddenly, Cloud was transforming. It happened so fast that Arthur only caught glimpses. Cloud's stubby snout elongated; his body mushroomed; hooves sprouted from his shaggy paws and his coarse white fur turned dark and shiny. In seconds, a sturdy chestnut-brown horse with a flaxen mane was stood between them all, flicking its tail.

"Oh." Cecily stared. "I was aiming for *Siberian Tiger*."

A volley of arrows sailed over the wagon and hammered into the grass around them. Arthur, Ren and Cecily scrabbled back out of the way, but Cloud was too big to take cover. Neighing loudly, he reared on his hind legs and bolted to safety in the trees.

"Cloud, wait!" Cecily called.

Clenching her jaw, Ren grabbed a beefsteak tomato from a basket behind them. "There's nothing else for it; we'll have to throw food – come on!" Springing to her feet, she hurled the tomato at one of the outlaws, who gave an irritated yell as it hit its target. Following Ren's lead, Arthur and Cecily snatched a couple of speckled green squashes and flung them at the outlaws.

Arthur's squash collided with the Frenchman's thigh and burst into a shower of stringy seeds; Cecily's splatted against the shoulder of the outlaw with the bow.

"*Mon ami*, stop! Stop!" the Frenchman shouted, brushing squash remains off his trousers. "If you keep throwing produce, there'll be nothing left for us to steal!"

The outlaws all lowered their weapons.

"I propose a truce," the archer said, resting the end of her bow in the grass. "Leave the food where it is; come out slowly with your hands up, and we'll let you go free."

Cecily looked across at Ren and Arthur. "They're outlaws," she whispered. "They're probably trying to trick us. Archimedes said some of the legends in this game are bad, remember?"

"Yeah, but Robin Hood was an outlaw, and he was a *good* guy," Ren pointed out.

Arthur wasn't sure what to do, but he got the feeling this was their first important choice in the game. The correct decision would set them on the path to the Irontide boots. "How do you expect us to trust you, when you're wearing disguises?" he yelled.

"A fair point," the Frenchman agreed, slipping off his mask to reveal a well-groomed moustachioed face with sparkling blue eyes. "How about some introductions, no? My name is Claude Duval, and these are my friends, Katherine Ferrers and John Nevison."

The other two took off their masks and bowed their heads. Arthur recognized them instantly from their *Wanted* posters, although they looked much cleaner and better dressed in real life. The archer, Katherine, had dark curls, a sharp chin and a small, bow-like mouth. John was slim with salt-and-pepper hair and delicate features. Arthur tried to remember the crimes they were accused of. "You're thieves, robbers and criminals," he said.

"Thieves, yes," Duval admitted, removing a sack from his belt. "But once we've taken these supplies, they'll refresh in an hour, anyway."

That was probably true. If *Legendarium* was anything like the video games Arthur played, everything was designed so that players made repeat visits to spend more money. "Do you give what you steal to the needy, like Robin Hood?" he asked.

Nevison laughed jovially. "No, but we only steal from those who can afford it. I'd wager half the legends about Robin Hood aren't true. Stories are fickle things. They change depending on who's telling them. His Majesty's Guard, for instance, recount one version of our legend. But our friends and families have a different story to tell. Come out from behind there and you'll be safe. We promise."

"I still don't trust them," Ren hissed, "but I think we

should risk it. The clock's ticking and the other competitors might be further ahead than us."

Cecily gave a resigned sigh. "You're right. We need those boots as fast as possible."

Slowly, they crept out from behind the wagon with their hands in the air. Arthur's stomach twisted with nerves, hoping they'd made the right decision. If they'd judged this wrong, they might never retrieve the time-key and get home.

Once they were a few paces from the wagon, Ferrers squinted at them. "I've seen your faces before," she said with a tone of surprise. "You're outlaws, too!"

Arthur tensed as Duval lifted his blunderbuss. "West of the main road is *our* territory," he growled. "What are you doing here? Come to spy on us?"

"No!" Arthur exclaimed, lifting his hands higher.

"We're just trying to get to the castle," Cecily spluttered. "We're not spies!"

Ferrers frowned. "The castle? Why would you want to go there? It's crawling with His Majesty's Guard."

Staring down the barrel of Duval's blunderbuss, Arthur tried to quash his panic and think. "There's something inside that we need," he replied carefully. "Treasure. We're planning to sneak in and steal it."

"Treasure, you say?" Duval's blue eyes gleamed. "In that case, we'd be more than happy to assist you with your raid."

Ferrers gave a sharp nod. "Agreed. A fifty-fifty partnership seems fair. You can share your plans with us back at camp."

"Err…" Arthur hadn't intended to invite the outlaws along, although he got the impression he had no choice in the matter. They were the ones holding weapons.

Nevison swung his blunderbuss over his shoulder and signalled to the trees. "Our camp is in that direction. We'll collect your horse on the way."

As they all set off across the clearing, Ren shuffled closer to Arthur. *"Choose wisely who to follow if you want to see tomorrow,"* she mumbled, reciting the line from the quest-map. "I hope we've done the right thing, or we'll never get those boots."

They found Cloud trotting happily through the undergrowth, poking his long nose into all the high places he couldn't reach as a dog. Ren grabbed hold of his collar and led him along. The outlaws' camp was a fifteen-minute trek through the forest, in the opposite direction to the castle. The entrance was marked by several green-and-white-striped ribbons, tied around the branches of a large oak tree. In the clearing beyond, a modest fire was surrounded by log benches, canvas tents and a few horse-drawn wagons. Several other outlaws dressed in tricornes, knee-high boots and velvet jackets were sat whittling arrows, sharpening swords or cleaning their blunderbusses. Most of them scowled at Arthur, Ren and Cecily as they entered.

"Have a seat," Nevison said, kicking off his boots before relaxing on a log bench beside Duval. "And don't mind the others. They're wary of new faces, is all."

Ferrers poked at the fire. A steaming kettle and a tray of rectangular scones were heating on top. "When there's a bounty on your head, you have to be suspicious of everyone," she muttered. "It's a matter of survival."

Exactly, Arthur thought, perching on a bench beside Cecily and Ren. He was sure one of the outlaws would notice how much his legs were twitching. Part of him wanted to make a run for it – to get as far away from all these dangerous criminals as possible – but he knew if they were going to win the Irontide boots, he had to keep his cool.

Using a long stick, Duval drew a square in the dirt between them, which he marked with crosses at three different points. "So, how are you planning to sneak inside the castle?"

"Well, uh…" Cecily's cheeks flushed as she studied the drawing in the dirt. "Legendary outlaws like yourselves can probably guess the answer to that already."

Arthur wasn't sure the outlaws would take the bait, but Nevison gave a crooked smile and pointed his toe at one of the crosses Duval had drawn. "The drawbridge here is lowered every three hours to let supplies in. I'd position us further up the road, hijack one of the incoming coaches and slip in disguised as traders."

"That could work." Duval stroked his moustache. "Or

you might want to hide in the woods until the guards change on the east tower. When the coast is clear, someone can climb the barbican wall and lower the drawbridge from the inside." He peered across the fire at Arthur, Ren and Cecily. "Which option is it?"

Another choice. Arthur threw a sidelong glance at Ren and Cecily, who both shrugged. "Umm, the second one?" he said. He didn't much fancy hijacking a coach.

The outlaws all nodded.

"Once inside, you can lead us to the treasure," Ferrers decided, offering them each a mug of tea and a rectangular scone slathered in melted butter. "Let's eat. We'll leave in ten minutes."

Arthur was too nervous to eat, but he reached for a scone anyway, his mind whirring. In an RPG, it didn't matter if you made a mistake – you could always return to your last save point and start the level again. But here, every choice was final. Whatever path they'd just set themselves on, there was no going back...

Half an hour later, Arthur, Ren and Cecily found themselves hiding on the edge of the forest, waiting for a signal from Claude Duval.

The castle loomed in front of them, as heavily guarded as when Arthur had last seen it. Soldiers wielding sharp pikes patrolled the battlements and archers stood poised between the crenels, ready to shoot. The wind had dropped, so the red-and-gold flags hung limply from their poles. The surface of the moat was still and the guards at the east tower had just left their post. Everything was set.

Crouched behind a bush, Arthur and Cecily took shallow breaths. A few metres behind them, Ren was mounted on horse-Cloud, her face taut with concentration. Arthur didn't know she could ride, but he wasn't surprised when she'd volunteered. Nevison and Ferrers, also on horseback, were positioned further along. If all went according to plan, the three riders would race to the east tower and use grappling ropes to climb the walls and get inside the castle. Everyone else would dash to the drawbridge and wait for it to be lowered.

Arthur glanced expectantly at Claude Duval, nestled between some shrubs with his blunderbuss gripped tightly in his right hand.

Any ... moment ... now...

Trying to settle his nerves, Arthur ran through the plan one last time. Once inside the castle, they'd split up to search for the Irontide boots. It was too difficult to predict what further challenges they might face, so they'd have to think on their feet.

Suddenly, a shout went up from Nevison, and Duval looked around, startled. Arthur caught a flash of red-and-gold uniform in the trees and tensed. Something had gone wrong.

"It's His Majesty's Guard!" Ferrers yelled, redirecting her horse. "Scatter!"

Arthur and Cecily shot to their feet as soldiers sprang from the undergrowth all around them. Some were armed with swords and bows; others carried trumpets and banners.

"This way!" Cecily cried, spotting a gap.

Ren tugged on Cloud's collar, turning him around. "Go! I'll follow you!"

Hurdling roots and brambles, Arthur and Cecily raced into the forest. Birds erupted from the trees as gunfire echoed and the smell of smoke filled the air. Arthur's pulse pounded as he bobbed and weaved, trying to avoid soldiers running at him from all directions.

Cecily screamed as a guard darted out from behind a tree and seized her. Before Arthur could do anything to help, strong arms wrapped around his shoulders and lifted him in the air. "Get off me!" he roared, struggling to break free.

Another soldier swung down from a tree and snatched Ren from Cloud's back. Cloud whinnied and kicked his front legs as more of His Majesty's Guard swarmed around them, but Arthur could see it was no use. They were surrounded.

One of the soldiers shouted instructions to take Cloud to the castle stables, and the horse snorted ruefully as he was led away.

"No!" Cecily whimpered, reaching for him. But the soldier holding her pushed her hands down and bound her wrists together with a length of coarse brown rope. Arthur felt the same itchy cord tightening over his hands as they were fastened in front of him.

An armoured white horse cantered out of the trees. Sat in the saddle was a knight in gleaming silver armour with a long red-and-gold cape draped over their shoulders. With a clank, they pushed up their visor, revealing a chiselled olive-skinned face with deep brown eyes. "The Young Pipsqueaks, I believe?" The knight had a rough, croaky voice, like he'd spent far too much time shouting orders.

"Yes?" Arthur croaked.

The knight smiled. "You're under arrest."

9

The knight's armour creaked as he crossed his arms behind his head, leaning back in his chair. "I have a proposition for you," he said easily. "Tell me the location of the outlaws' camp and I will ensure that you each receive a full pardon for your crimes."

Arthur glanced uncertainly at Ren and Cecily, sitting beside him. They'd been escorted to a small, windowless room inside the castle, furnished with a wooden table and a few chairs. Footsteps echoed in the passageway outside, and the air reeked of paraffin and gunpowder.

"You can do that?" Cecily asked.

The knight studied the text on a sheet of parchment. "Theft, deception, vagrancy – I see nothing here that isn't forgivable."

There was something decidedly *off* about this knight. Arthur thought knights were meant to abide by a chivalric code of honour, but this one seemed happy to sweep all their supposed crimes under the carpet. For a price. It reminded him of something John Nevison had said earlier – that stories can change depending on who is telling them. In legends, knights were always the heroes but perhaps that was because some of them were telling their own stories.

Ren hadn't moved since she'd sat down. Her bound fists rested on top of the table and she was scowling intensely at the knight like she was trying to win a staring contest. "We can't tell you what we don't know," she said firmly. "We've never been to the outlaws' camp."

Credit where credit was due, Ren was a good liar. Cecily remained still but Arthur nodded as earnestly as he could. It wasn't because he felt any loyalty to the outlaws, but at least their motives had been clear. The knight's intentions were more suspicious. Who was to say he wouldn't double-cross them as soon as they'd revealed the camp's location?

The knight ground his teeth. "You might think those thieves are your *friends*, but I'm telling you, they're out for themselves. I implore you to reconsider. You will not get another opportunity to redeem yourselves."

This had to be another decisive moment of gameplay. If they cooperated with the knight and he kept his word, then they'd go free, but the outlaws would be captured. On the other hand, if they refused to tell the knight what they knew, they'd probably be imprisoned themselves … or worse.

"Well?" the knight said.

"Can we, err, discuss this in private?" Cecily asked.

With a smirk, the knight leaned closer. "I don't think so. I want your answer now."

Arthur tried to garner the others' opinions. Biting her lip, Cecily looked torn, but Ren's jaw was set. He focused on their objective: finding the Irontide boots. If they walked free, they would probably be cast out of the castle, but the Irontide boots were somewhere *inside*... "Ren's right," he decided quickly. "We've got no idea where the outlaws' camp is, and even if we *did* know, we wouldn't tell you."

The knight's face reddened. "Fools!" He flew out of his seat and marched towards the door.

"Sir?" a guard asked, opening it from the other side.

"Lock them in the dungeons!" the knight barked. His cape billowed behind him as he thundered off into the castle.

Dungeons?! Arthur felt the blood drain from his face. Had he made the wrong decision?

Before he could move, four beefy soldiers armed with razor-sharp pikes filed in. "You three are coming with us," one grumbled.

Sandwiched between the four guards, Arthur, Ren and Cecily were escorted down a wide spiral staircase, deep into the bowels of the castle. Arthur shivered as they walked along a torchlit passageway, passing the barred doors of several dingy cells. A skeleton was manacled to the floor in one of them and the *drip, drip, drip* of water echoed around the cold stone walls. Arthur looked around frantically, searching for possible escape routes. Before he knew it, one of the soldiers heaved open a door and jabbed the wooden shaft of his pike hilt into Arthur's ribs. "In you go," he grunted. "Move!"

Arthur had no option but to shuffle into the cell with Ren and Cecily. The room had no windows, but torchlight filtered through the barred door casting flickering shadows up the walls.

"Wait!" Cecily said, as the door was locked behind them. "Where are you going? You can't leave us in here!"

But the guards didn't reply. As the sound of their footsteps faded, Arthur turned on the spot, inspecting their cell. The air was damp and smelled like a drain. Graffiti had been scratched all over the grey stone walls. Most of it was written in languages Arthur couldn't understand, but he could make out a few words in English:

Dead End

No Escape

Legend Losers.

"Well, this is just great," Ren said, kicking her foot against the floor. "There's no way we'll be faster than any of the other teams now."

Cecily shook her head. "*Choose who to follow if you want to see tomorrow...* We must have made a bad choice somewhere, or we wouldn't have ended up here."

Guilt tugged at Arthur's insides. Maybe if they'd told the knight what they knew, they'd be walking free right now. "It's my fault," he admitted, slumping against a wall. "I shouldn't have made such a quick decision."

"None of this is anyone's fault," Cecily said firmly. "We're not supposed to be in this century, let alone in this tournament." With a tearful sigh, she sank to the floor beside him. "I was going to tell you both at the barbecue – I'm meant to be packing for Nigeria right now. My parents had organized a surprise trip for me to meet some of my dad's family. Our flight was leaving tomorrow."

"Your *flight*?" Arthur couldn't hide his surprise. Since meeting Wangari Maathai in the Wonderscape, Cecily had been determined to lower her carbon footprint.

"Yeah, I know," she said flatly. "I wanted to sail there – you know, Greta Thunberg-style – but my parents refused."

"Still, I bet even Greta Thunberg would be impressed by all the changes you've made this year," Ren said, encouragingly. "You persuaded your parents to turn their business carbon-neutral, and even the Year Tens were using those make-up recycling bins you installed in the school toilets."

Cecily picked at a patch of moss growing between two slabs in the floor. "Yeah, maybe. Sometimes it's difficult to believe that all the little things I'm doing will really make a difference to the climate emergency." She glanced around the walls of the cell. "Not that it matters now, I guess. I won't be able to do anything when I'm slime."

Ren sat cross-legged in front of them. "Well, my summer

was shaping up to be duller than this dungeon. I was meant to be doing work experience at my mum's garage."

"I didn't know you wanted to be a mechanic," Arthur said.

Ren huffed. "I don't, but my mum believed it would be good for me. I think she wants me to follow in her footsteps, but I'm just not like her. We kept having the same row about it, over and over. That's what we were arguing about before you all came over…"

Arthur offered Ren a sympathetic smile. It must be tough knowing that possibly the last words they'd exchanged were sour ones.

"What about you, Arthur?" she asked. "Were you attending that video games workshop that was advertised in school?"

Despite everything, Arthur still felt a twinge of disappointment. He'd spotted the flyer on their school noticeboard – a dream two-week workshop where you learned about game design, 3-D modelling and animation. But he hadn't signed up. The other students were a lot older than him and he was worried he'd spend the whole time trying to keep up. "Nah, it wasn't really my thing."

Ren arched an eyebrow, but didn't press him.

"Hey…" Cecily said, frowning at the patch of moss she'd been picking at. A length of green-and-white-striped ribbon was now protruding from the muddy crack between the stones. "Isn't this the same ribbon that was tied around the branches of that oak tree outside the outlaws' camp?"

Arthur moved onto his knees and shuffled closer. "Yeah, I think you're right. Maybe it was left here by one of Duval's crew?" Carefully grasping the ribbon between his tied hands, he tugged and felt one of the floor stones come loose.

Cecily gasped. "Look – the ribbon's buried under the floor! Keep pulling."

Arthur heaved. Slowly, a large slab in the middle of the floor lifted up. With their hands still bound, Ren and Cecily managed to grip one side each and move it away. Revealed beneath was a dusty hole that opened into a tunnel lined with wooden planks.

"An escape route!" Ren cheered, swinging her legs over the edge. "Perhaps we *did* make the right choices after all? If we hadn't followed the outlaws to their camp, we never would have recognized that ribbon."

The tunnel was wide enough to crawl through one behind the other, although it was difficult with their hands still tied. After only a few minutes, light shone ahead and they clambered awkwardly up a ladder and out into a large, bustling courtyard. There were so many people around, nobody seemed to notice them emerge. Shouts reverberated around the walls as a company of archers performed target practice in one corner, while a team of engineers repaired a wooden catapult in the other. Servants dressed in medieval clothing were busy batting dirt from rugs or lugging sacks of grain. Arthur recognized the four white towers at the heart of the castle, looming over them.

As he got to his feet, he wondered again why the castle keep seemed so familiar. He didn't know any legendary castles, although he was sure they existed. He'd seen photos of creepy Gothic fortresses in Romania and grand châteaux in France, but he'd never visited any of them, and he got the distinct feeling he'd been *inside* this castle before...

"Where do you think the Irontide boots are?" Ren whispered, her eyes darting around warily.

"In a treasure room?" Cecily guessed. "We need to find a way inside before someone notices us."

They dashed around a corner into a smaller courtyard with a stable off to one side. Arthur had to pull his T-shirt up over his nose using his thumbs, to filter the stench of manure. Several horses poked their heads over their barn doors, chewing sleepily on mouthfuls of hay. He jolted as he recognized one with a glossy chestnut coat and flaxen mane. "Cloud?" he exclaimed.

Cloud's ears twitched, and he turned his head towards them.

A stable boy also looked over, frowning. "Can I help you?" he asked, taking a step closer.

"Err ... yes," Cecily answered, hastily hiding her bound wrists in the folds of her dress. Ren and Arthur copied her. "We're lost. We're ... pot-washers. We need to find our way back to the kitchen."

The boy narrowed his eyes. "You don't look like kitchen staff..."

Cloud snorted and stamped his feet, obviously trying to communicate. He aimed his muzzle at a couple of birds, strutting a short distance away. They had coal-coloured beaks and iridescent black plumage.

Ravens.

Arthur had a flash of recollection. A couple of years ago, he'd been on a school trip to London to visit some of the city's historical landmarks. One of the places they'd toured was a fortification on the banks of the River Thames, famously home to six ravens: *the Tower of London.*

That was why this castle seemed so familiar! It had to be a replica. He craned his neck to check the keep's turrets. They all had curved lead roofs that came to a sharp point and, notably, three of them were square and one was circular – exactly the same as those on the Tower of London. *"Psst,"* he hissed into Ren's ear. "I think I know what building this is: the Tower of London."

She blinked. "There's a legend about it. The ravens—"

"You're not pot-washers!" the stable boy called, closer now. "Guards? Guards! We have escaped prisoners!"

Arthur turned and was about to flee when he remembered something that the Tower of London tour guide had told his class: legend has it, should the ravens leave the Tower of London, the building and country would fall.

And in Legendarium, legends were real…

Footsteps sounded over his shoulder as a troop of archers came hurtling around the corner, drawing their bows.

"Hide!" Cecily yelled.

But Arthur grabbed her arm before she could run. "No – we need to scare away the ravens. Trust me!" It was risky, but if the ravens left the castle grounds, it might create a big enough distraction for the three of them to find a way inside without being caught.

An arrow suddenly skimmed Ren's shoulder and landed in a nearby pile of hay. Her face paled. "Whatever we're doing, we need to do it now!"

Arthur counted four ravens pecking around the courtyard and two perched on the battlements. All six were in sight. "Let's draw their fire towards the birds – come on!"

They split up, zigzagging in different directions across the courtyard. Arthur's feet hammered the cobbles as he charged towards the stables. Two arrows soared over his head and hit the ground close to one raven, who cawed in alarm and flew from the castle to the safety of nearby trees.

Hurdling a pile of manure, he snatched an apple from a bucket and lobbed it, hands together, at another raven on the battlements. The bird dodged the fruit at first, but Arthur grabbed another and threw again. This one made target, knocking the bird off its perch, out of sight on the other side of the castle walls.

Ren and Cecily made quick work of another three ravens, luring the archers' arrows close enough to frighten the birds away. "There's only one left!" Ren called, pointing to the final raven, who stood preening itself in the middle of the courtyard.

Just then, a booming *thud* resounded around the walls and the door to Cloud's paddock went spinning across the cobbles, having been kicked off. Cloud galloped out with his head lowered, charging straight towards the raven. The bird took one look at him and leaped into the air, its dark shape quickly becoming a dot in the sky.

"The ravens have gone!" a servant yelled. "Take cover!"

The ground shook, making the stable doors rattle. Dust and rubble skittered down the castle walls as the servants dropped what they were holding and scattered. Several archers took shelter behind a hay bale, covering their heads with their hands.

"It worked!" Arthur cried, as the others ran towards him. "Now let's get inside and find the treasure room."

But just then, a gong sounded. Arthur squinted as a bright light burst at the centre of the courtyard. As his eyes adjusted, he saw a pair of armoured gold boots materialize out of thin air, rotating like a trophy. "Are those—?"

"The Irontide boots!" Ren yelled. Dodging another arrow, she side-stepped the nearest servant and sprinted as fast as she could towards them.

Arthur and Cecily gawped at each other, completely flabbergasted. Banishing the ravens must have been the key to completing the quest. He couldn't quite believe it, but they'd done it.

Ren's wrists were still bound as she reached up and gathered the boots against her chest. Instantly, their surroundings changed. The crumbling castle with its foul smells and clanging echoes melted away, and the brightly lit hall of the Bermuda Triangle came into view around them.

Cloud nickered as a couple of questers pointed at him, looking surprised. A shout went up from the media balcony and a dozen camera lenses angled towards them. Heat rose to the surface of Arthur's cheeks as he remembered that their progress was being broadcast live on holovision.

"Do you think we were fast enough?" Cecily asked, breathlessly. She stared as a mist of silver particles evaporated away from her hands, where the ropes had been.

Arthur checked his watch. "There are still two hours until midnight. We'll find out if we've been eliminated then." He scanned the hall for their competitors. The Transonic duo, looking muddy and tired, were being hassled by several members of *The Lazarus Show* crew. Lazarus Sloane himself was stalking towards one of the Savage Strike questers, who was sat slumped against a wall with a bandage around his head. Lazarus was taller and thinner than he'd looked on-screen, with glistening acid-green scales and bulbous black eyes. Arthur felt relieved the presenter hadn't spotted them.

As Cecily reached for the disc on Cloud's collar, a shadow fluttered at the end of Ren's nose. She almost dropped the

Irontide boots as she staggered back, scrunching up her face. "What was that?"

Arthur bent down and collected a sheet of grey tissue paper off the floor.

"Another map?" Cecily asked.

He held it up. It was completely blank except for six words, scribbled in charcoal at the top:

LEGENDARI◈M
- *THE LAND OF THE LOST* -

10

Hoping to avoid Lazarus Sloane and his crew, the team made a quick exit from the Great Library. Atlantis seemed even more "underwater" after dark. Bioluminescent coral had appeared on all the buildings, and holographic jellyfish swam through the streets, carrying neon advertisements in their tentacles. Above the rooftops, great clouds of twinkling plankton drifted by, looking like distant nebula.

As they approached the black railings of the Hotel Loch Ness, Arthur's mind drifted to home. They'd been missing for a full twelve hours now and his dad would be worried sick. Arthur's chest felt hollow, thinking just how far apart in space and time they both were. All he could do was hope that they found the time-key. With it, they could journey back to the exact moment they left and it would be as if they'd never gone missing at all.

The hotel lobby was almost empty. A lady with a bow tie played jazz on the grand piano while a receptionist studied his nails behind the desk. Sitting alone in one corner of the room, Griffon Ramsay stared angrily at them as they entered. His body armour was gone, replaced by a loose-fitting black tracksuit. Although he had no visible injuries, Arthur knew he must have already completed his first quest.

"Why's he looking at us like that?" Ren hissed. "Is he trying to psych us out?"

Arthur remembered what Cecily had read about Griffon – that he had a reputation for hunting down his opponents. "If he is, it's working," Arthur admitted, quickening his steps.

As they hurried towards the hotel lift, another guest leaped out of an armchair. "There you are!" Milo Hertz exclaimed.

Cloud barked jubilantly and scampered towards his inventor, dragging Cecily along with him.

"Nice to see you, too, boy," Milo said, patting Cloud's head. Milo had removed his lab coat and sunglasses and was now dressed in grey joggers, a brightly coloured Hawaiian shirt and a pair of battered flipflops.

Cecily put a hand to her chest. "You found us."

"A friend told me that Archimedes had met you in Atlantis," Milo explained, standing back up. "Then I saw the news that you'd entered the Irontide Tournament and I figured you must be here. I managed to convince the hotel staff that I'm your coach. I'm sorry I couldn't locate you sooner. When I saw those raiders..." He shifted his gaze warily. "Perhaps we should talk somewhere more private. Did they give you a room?"

"A suite," Arthur said. "And you can have one, too, I think."

Milo fetched a large rucksack, propped up against the armchair he'd been sitting in. The pockets were stuffed with tape, reels of wire and various tools. "Sounds good. Come on, we've got a lot to discuss."

After Milo had checked in, they took the lift up to Arthur, Ren and Cecily's suite. Everyone bundled onto the sofa near the fire, where *The Lazarus Show* was playing on mute above the mantelpiece. Lazarus Sloane had left the Great Library and was now interviewing fans outside the Kraken.

"Those raiders work for a nasty trader called Deadlock," Milo said, unpacking some of the things from his rucksack. It looked like he'd brought half his lab with him. "That warehouse must have belonged to Deadlock because something there was blocking my scanners – something illegal. That's why I couldn't get a fix on your location."

Distracted by something on the dining table, Cecily muttered, "That wasn't there before," and got up to collect a garish green envelope from beside the fruit bowl. As she opened it, she frowned. "OK..."

She handed a sheet of headed paper to Arthur. At the top was a reptilian eye logo with the words *The Lazarus Show* beneath. *"Dear Young Pipsqueaks,"* Arthur read. *"Following your entry in the Irontide Tournament, the production team and I are delighted to extend an invitation for you to take part in an interview tomorrow..."*

Cecily huffed as she reclaimed her seat beside Arthur. "They're only delighted because they think having us on will make them loads of DIRT. We can't waste our time with that."

Arthur read on. "Yeah, but Sloane will also be interviewing the two current leaders of the tournament – Griffon Ramsay and Yesenia Colt. If we accept the invitation, it might give us the opportunity to determine which one of them has the time-key."

Milo flinched. "Wait. Don't *you* have the time-key? We need it if I'm going to help send you back."

Heat rushed to Arthur's cheeks. He still couldn't believe he'd been careless enough to leave the time-key on top of that crate. Feeling mortified, he explained what had happened in Deadlock's warehouse after Milo's hologram had vanished. When he repeated the conversation they'd overheard between Tide, Rultan and Vorru, Milo's expression tightened.

"Did you know those particular raiders?" Arthur asked.

"Not those exact three," Milo growled, "but I've dealt with others like them. Twenty years ago, after what happened with you and Tiburon, the UGP temporarily shut down the Wonderscape in order to do a thorough investigation of my brother's former operations. I couldn't risk them learning about my time-keys, so I decided to break in to Tiburon's old headquarters and search the place." Milo sighed. "At the time, the UGP were guarding the building and I knew that

the only way to sneak past them would be to use an evader –
the same device those raiders were meant to deliver."

"We saw evaders in Deadlock's warehouse," Ren said.
"What do they do?"

Milo shook his head disapprovingly. "They turn you
invisible, but they can only be used once, for a short period
of time. After some panicked enquiries, I managed to
procure one from a mysterious Dark Market trader who
employed those raiders in their workforce."

"Deadlock," Arthur realized with a shudder.

Milo nodded, his eyes full of guilt. "I was desperate.
I thought I had no other choice. Using the evader, I slipped
inside Tiburon's old headquarters. It was fortunate I did,
because I discovered that Tiburon had made a secret copy
of one of my technical drawings of a time-key and I was
able to burn it to ash."

Arthur felt at once relieved and anxious. Sure, the
drawing no longer existed, but the fact that it had been
created in the first place left him uneasy.

Milo reached into one of the pockets of his rucksack and
pulled out a smooth silver stone, the size of Arthur's palm.
"This is the evader the raiders gave me. It's been sitting in
my scrap drawer for years. I was going to re-engineer it for
another project, but I never got round to it. After I received
that call from you, I gave it a thorough examination."

Arthur shuffled closer to get a better view. It was easy
to understand how Vorru had mistaken the time-key for

an evader. Both gadgets were the same size and shape; the only difference was their colour, and the fact that the time-key had a dial around the outer edge. "Is there something unusual about this evader?"

"Not that you can see with the naked eye, but take a peek at it through these X-focals." Milo retrieved three pairs of sunglasses from his pack – the same ones he'd been wearing during their call earlier – and handed them to Arthur, Ren and Cecily.

Eager to learn what they did, Arthur tugged his on.

"No way!" Ren said, turning her head to and fro. "This is incredible!"

Blinking through the lenses, Arthur viewed the room in a strange new level of detail. The colours were brighter; the textures were more defined; and when he focused on an object, he found he could see *through* it. Behind cupboard doors, under floorboards and inside bags – it was like the sunglasses had given him X-ray vision.

He turned his attention to the evader. He wasn't sure what it was made of, but a mass of tiny green lights moved in different directions under the surface. In one place, they formed a circle around a small, black hole. "Is that a camera?" he guessed.

"Well spotted," Milo remarked. "It's switched off now, but I suspect it was planted there in order to spy on me. Deadlock must have captured an image of that technical drawing before I destroyed it – it's the only way to explain how the new time-key uses my time-compressing coil in its design."

Cecily stiffened. "But if Deadlock has copies of that drawing, what's to stop them making more time-keys? And what will they do with them?"

Pulling off his X-focals, Arthur considered everything they'd learned about Deadlock and quickly decided that whoever they were, they could only have bad intentions for a time-key. "Tiburon caused enough pain and suffering with just *one* time-key. If Deadlock has the power to make more of these new versions, the consequences could be unthinkable."

"The lives of millions of people throughout time could be at risk," Milo agreed, seriously. "That's why I've got to stop them."

Ren squeezed her fists. "But how? Even if you destroy the time-key that brought us here, so long as Deadlock has a copy of that drawing, they'll be able to make a new one."

She was right. Trying to stop Deadlock would be like fighting a sea monster with infinite tentacles. Every time you chopped one off, another would regrow in its place.

"I have a plan," Milo said, rooting through his rucksack. "Deadlock will have kept that drawing closely guarded, for fear a rival would get hold of it. I doubt they would have shared it with anyone, except maybe one trusted engineer. The only copies are therefore probably being stored on

Deadlock's mainframe computer, located at their base of operations. If I destroy the mainframe, those copies will be lost for ever."

"But how are you going to locate Deadlock's base?" Arthur asked.

Milo motioned to the evader. "I'm going to trace where the data on that camera was sent. Deadlock probably has all kinds of firewalls in place, so it'll be difficult. And I'll have to work quickly, before Deadlock realizes what's happening. That means you three will have to try to recover the time-key on your own for a while."

Arthur nodded. It was his fault they didn't have it, anyway.

"Finally," Milo moaned, removing a large roll of paper from his pack. "Here, this is for you."

He handed the paper to Arthur, who unfurled it across his lap so Ren and Cecily could see. It showed the architectural blueprints for a sleek glass building surrounded by landscaped gardens and sparkling fountains. A huge sign on the roof read, *WONDERSC2PE*.

"What's this?" Ren asked. "Are you working on a new version of the Wonderscape?"

"Well, yes, but –" Milo stretched across to flip the blueprints over – "you're reading the wrong side."

Written in scruffy handwriting on the reverse was a long algebraic formula filled with Greek letters, numbers and symbols. The number "58" was circled at the bottom.

Arthur's skin tingled, realizing what he was looking at. "This is Newton's formula! Does this mean we have fifty-eight hours before we turn into protoplasm?"

"That's one more than last time," Cecily noted with a hint of optimism.

Milo flashed an awkward smile. "Actually, that's how long you had when you first arrived in the future. You need to deduct the length of time you've already been here."

Checking his stopwatch, Arthur made the calculation. "In that case, we've now got a little over forty-four hours left," he said jumpily, setting a timer.

"Forty-four hours?" Cecily exclaimed. "That's not even two days to find the time-key!"

Ren gestured to the holoscreen above the fireplace. "We've got one thing going for us at least."

The Lazarus Show had cut to outside the Hotel Loch Ness, where a camera crew was following Lazarus inside. The name of each team – and the time it had taken them to complete their first quest – was displayed at one side of the screen, listed from 1 to 6. There was also a golden boot symbol beside each name, which Arthur guessed indicated that every team had successfully won a pair of Irontide boots. Griffon and Yesenia occupied the top two places, followed by Savage Strike and the Ghost League. The Young Pipsqueaks were in position five. The team at the bottom, Transonic, was flashing red.

As Lazarus stalked into the hotel lobby, the two teenagers from Transonic were sat by a holoscreen with their heads in their hands.

"Transonic are the first team eliminated!" Arthur realized, feeling a pang of sympathy for the two questers as Lazarus started firing questions at them. "We made it through!"

With a triumphant yap, Cloud jumped into Ren's lap and rolled onto his back. "Mostly thanks to you, Fuzzball," Ren said, tickling his belly.

Cecily exhaled deeply. "That means we've got access to the hotel for the next twelve hours at least. Let's make them count."

Chewing on another mouthful of Zoorflakes (they looked like purple confetti, but tasted like puffed wheats), Arthur tapped his spoon against the invitation from Lazarus Sloane, lying in front of him. "We have to be careful not to reveal who we really are during this," he mumbled. He hadn't watched enough of *The Lazarus Show* to be able to predict what Lazarus would ask them, so they would be taking a risk. If the interview gave them the opportunity to learn more about Griffon and Yesenia, though, it would be worth it. "We've got to give the impression that we're taking the tournament seriously. That we're in it to win it."

"Lazarus might ask us for our predictions about the Land of the Lost," Cecily said, digging her fork into a bowl of colourful fruit salad. "There has to be a reason the quest-map is blank. Maybe we have to do something to activate it?"

"We could try submerging it in water or setting it on fire?" Ren suggested.

Cecily studied her worriedly. "It's made of paper, Ren. I don't think that's a good idea."

It was the following morning and the three of them were sat around the dining table in their hotel room, which, thanks to Milo, now smelled like freshly squeezed orange juice and hot tea. Before they'd all gone off to bed, he'd transferred some DIRT into their faze accounts, so they could now order room service and make purchases anywhere in Legendarium. Despite the urgency of the tournament, they'd decided it would be worthwhile to try to get some sleep. Who knew what challenges lay ahead, and they'd be better prepared if they had more energy.

Arthur's night had been restless. He'd drifted off to sleep a couple of times, but always woken from the same nightmare.

In it, he was running across a castle drawbridge when his fists turned into globules of acid-green goo, his legs melted and he fell to the floor with a loud *splat!*

That was when he'd woken up.

"Perhaps the design of the quest-map is connected to a legend in the Land of the Lost?" he speculated. Sliding a finger over his faze, he opened the screen and navigated to the information directory.

"I wouldn't bother," Cecily said. "I searched 'Land of the Lost' last night, and the device found references to thousands of different legends with that name. It's impossible for us to know which might be the right one."

Sighing, Arthur closed his faze and collected the Irontide boots off the floor beside him. "All right. Well, what about these? Lazarus Sloane said the Irontide armour has extraordinary powers. Maybe the boots can help us in the next quest?"

"What do you think they do?" Ren asked.

Arthur examined them more closely. They were knee-high, made of a combination of leather and golden metal, with thick greaves and pointed toes. "Not sure. Maybe they make you run faster? Or help you walk in the right direction?"

He was about to try them on when there was a knock at their door. Arthur frowned at the others before rising from his seat and walking over to open it.

Even though they'd arranged to meet later, Arthur half expected Milo Hertz to be stood outside, but he was, in fact, greeted by the hum of five small drones. They were black and saucer-shaped, and each carried an improbably large cardboard box.

"Delivery for the Young Pipsqueaks," a voice buzzed. *"From a concerned benefactor."*

"Oh. Err, thanks?" Arthur stepped aside as the drones floated in and deposited the boxes onto the carpet.

As they hovered away, Cecily left the table and got down on her knees to study one of the boxes. She ripped off a length of tape and peered inside. "Oh no." Her face dropped as she pulled out a baggy moss-green sweatshirt with a glittering stripe down both arms. Printed on the breast was a motif that reminded Arthur of the New York Yankees baseball team logo – a capital "P" with an upside-down "Y" written over the top. "YP – that must stand for the Young Pipsqueaks."

"It's on everything," Ren observed, rummaging through another box. "Hats, T-shirts, water bottles, bags – whoever our *concerned benefactor* is, they want us to be branded."

Cecily wrinkled her nose. "Do you think we have to wear it?"

"Probably not, but all the other teams have colour-coordinated clothes," Arthur said. "And we're trying to fit in."

Ren held a pair of khaki cargo trousers against her legs and shrugged. "At least these have pockets."

After searching through all the boxes, they reluctantly decided on an outfit each. Arthur opted for a forest-green T-shirt and matching tracksuit bottoms; Ren chose the same T-shirt (with the sleeves ripped off) and the cargo trousers; and Cecily eventually fixed on an emerald jumpsuit and belt with a YP buckle. With her denim jacket over the top, she somehow still managed to appear stylish.

Cecily looked Arthur and Ren up and down. "Maybe try to seem more relaxed in front of the cameras?" she suggested delicately.

Ren scowled and bent down to turn up the bottoms of her trousers. "I can't relax knowing millions of people will be judging us. What if they expect us to be like Yesenia Colt or Griffon Ramsay?"

"Tell me about it," Arthur admitted. The thought of being compared to the other contestants made him feel nauseous. "I hope Lazarus doesn't ask us anything personal."

Cecily flashed him a sympathetic smile. "Don't worry. I'll try to answer all the questions. You two, just remember to breathe."

After breakfast, they made their way down to the lobby. It was early and the hotel was quiet. A handful of staff were busy serving tea to guests, cleaning surfaces or tending to the fire. Arthur spotted the three Savage Strike guys talking heatedly with an older woman in a flame-red suit, whom Arthur guessed might be their coach. Judging by the team's immaculate scarlet outfits, Arthur thought they couldn't have completed their second quest yet. He wondered if they were discussing tactics; there was still plenty of time for them to journey to the Great Library to start.

He took a seat on a bench under one of the front windows, with Ren and Cecily beside him. He placed the Irontide boots by his feet, and Cloud flopped next to them with his snout in his paws. The invitation from Lazarus Sloane had told them to wait in the lobby until transport arrived to take them to the studios where the show was filmed.

A clamour sounded outside. Arthur peeled back a curtain to see the crowd of paparazzi had doubled since yesterday. There was also a growing number of fans on the street, waving banners and cheering. Mostly they shouted their approval for the other teams, although Arthur definitely caught someone yelling, "Young Pipsqueaks!"

"It'll be difficult to move around Atlantis without attracting attention now," he realized. "We're overnight celebrities."

Ren drummed her fingers against the edge of the sofa. "Hopefully, we won't be here much longer, anyway. Once we get the time-key, Milo will use it to send us home."

"Young Pipsqueaks!" Ribbon Rex hurried towards them from across the lobby, her black quiff bouncing. Her UGP uniform looked like it had been freshly pressed. "Congratulations on surviving the first elimination."

"Thanks," Arthur said, as Ribbon bent down to stroke Cloud. "We're just waiting to go for our interview with Lazarus Sloane."

Ribbon nodded. "Yes, an autoshell is due to pick you up outside. For security, I've arranged to have one follow you around Atlantis. That means it will always be waiting to transport you anywhere. With so many fans about, it's safer than going on foot."

A car horn sounded outside and Cecily drew back the curtains. "Looks like the autoshell is right on time," she whispered to Ren and Arthur. "I think they're hovercraft, but they look like cowry shells."

Arthur picked up the Irontide boots and the four of them rose to their feet and made for the front door. Arthur was just about to step inside the revolving compartment when a voice at his back snapped, "Out of my way, clowns."

He turned to see Yesenia Colt barging past Cecily. Her white-blonde hair was slicked back over her head and she was dressed in the same slinky yellow catsuit her avatar had been wearing in the Kraken. The flicks of black liner at the edges of her eyes gave her a distinctly feline air.

"Who are *you* calling clowns?" Ren retorted. "We're not the ones who have *NOVAFUEL* written across our butts."

Yesenia peered down her nose at Ren. "*I* am a professional. You are a joke. Children shouldn't be allowed to compete in the Irontide Tournament. It makes a mockery of us all." She gave Cecily a sniff of indignation and pushed past Arthur, through the front doors.

"Try not to listen to her," Ribbon said, stepping closer. "She just feels threatened because you're the youngest in the tournament and it'll make her look bad if you do well. Adults don't like being outshone by young people. My advice would be to prove them all wrong." She glanced surreptitiously at the white braid on her shoulder, and Arthur wondered if she was thinking about her own experiences training to be the youngest UGP officer in history.

He smiled in thanks. "We'll do our best to ignore her."

When they got outside, Yesenia was already gone. Arthur hesitated before approaching one of the waiting autoshells. The vehicle was the size of a small hatchback car, with blacked-out windows and a rubber skirt, from which air blustered out. Arthur guessed that a thin gap in the side of the craft might be the outline of a door, but there was no handle.

The paparazzi started shouting.

"Over here, Young Pipsqueaks!"

"Young Pipsqueaks, care to comment on the recent elimination?"

"How does it feel competing against previous champions like Griffon Ramsay and Yesenia Colt?"

"Where are your parents, Young Pipsqueaks?"

Arthur really wanted to get out of there. He pushed his hand against the door in different places, experimenting to see what might make it open.

"We need to hurry," Cecily said, casting wary glances at some of the cheering fans. "How does this thing *open*?"

Right then, there was a hiss and the door released, lifting vertically up.

"Voice activation," Arthur realized. "Thank goodness."

They bundled inside and the door closed automatically behind them. The autoshell had a luxurious interior with velvet seats and a tortoiseshell-patterned sideboard. Chilled bottles of Novafuel nestled in all the cupholders and Arthur was pretty sure the stainless-steel contraption fitted to the seat in front was an ice dispenser. The vehicle must have been soundproofed because he could no longer hear the paparazzi's shouts, or the roar of the craft's blowers.

"Destination?" asked a familiar voice. Arthur stiffened. It was Lazarus Sloane's.

But the lizard-headed presenter wasn't inside the autoshell. It had to be a recording.

"This must be a driverless vehicle," Ren said, excitedly. She cleared her throat. "Can you take us to *The Lazarus Show* studios?"

The autoshell vibrated and sped forward. "Estimated journey time: twelve minutes," responded Lazarus's voice.

"Do you think Yesenia has the time-key?" Cecily asked, rubbing the spot where Yesenia had pushed her.

"She's certainly mean enough to be a cheat," Arthur said, "and ruthless, given that she's sabotaged her opponents before. But cheating is risky. If Yesenia was caught, her career would be over. We need to listen carefully to what she says at the studios."

The autoshell arrived, on time, outside a knobbly coral tower covered in spiky black sea anemones, which Arthur speculated might be satellite dishes in disguise. A silver-haired gentleman dressed in black greeted them as they stepped onto the pavement. He was wearing a glowing earpiece and had his faze display open in front of him.

"Young Pipsqueaks? Excellent. You're right on schedule. I'm one of the producers of *The Lazarus Show*. Follow me, please." He escorted them inside the building, past a row of merman security guards, and into one of several lifts.

Arthur noticed the reptilian-eye logo of *The Lazarus Show* printed on the back of the producer's shirt.

"You'll be taken through hair and make-up before going onto the sound stage," the producer said, checking something on his faze display.

"Sound stage?" Ren queried.

"It's a soundproof room where we record the show. Lazarus only has a couple of questions, so you won't be on for more than a few minutes. Just be yourselves and everything will go smoothly."

As they ascended, Arthur glanced nervously at the others. The very last thing they could do was be themselves.

The lift opened into a narrow corridor decorated with blown-up photos of Lazarus Sloane. One showed him winking at the camera with his forked black tongue poking through his lips; in another he was grinning with his arms spread wide. Half of the hallway was taken up by large black crates with metal edges, all stamped with *The Lazarus Show* logo. Another member of staff was sticking labels to them.

"*The Lazarus Show* provides coverage and analysis of the most popular isports tournaments in the Known Universe," the producer explained as they edged past. "This equipment is being shipped out ahead of a contest in *Mythopoeia*."

Arthur assumed *Mythopoeia* was the name of another I-RAG, and although it spiked his interest, he knew it was safer not to ask questions. The producer stopped outside a green door labelled *MAKE-UP*. "In you go. I'll meet you on set in five."

They entered a small room with a brightly lit mirror hung on one wall and a long table below it. Arthur expected there to be an array of make-up palettes, brushes and cotton buds strewn across the surface, but all he saw were what looked like three VR headsets. The air smelled like hairspray and a tall member of staff with a twirly ginger moustache stood in one corner, examining his faze display. "You can each put one on," he said, pointing to the headsets.

Cecily took one tentatively. "Do we really have to wear make-up?"

"Lazarus likes you to look healthy," the man explained. "No one wants to see bruises on holovision."

Arthur placed the Irontide boots on the floor and collected a headset. "I thought you'd be OK with this," he told Cecily. She wore make-up all the time at the weekend. Arthur, on the other hand, had never worn it in his life. Well, not serious make-up. He'd had his face painted to look like Wolverine a few times.

"I like make-up, but it should be something you wear for *you*," Cecily said confidently. "Not because someone tells you to."

Grabbing a headset, Ren lowered her voice. "Anything that helps us fit in is a good thing."

She had a point. Arthur pushed his headset on. Lights

danced in his eyes as he felt a cool mist fall onto the surface of his skin.

"All done," the moustachioed man said. "You can take them off."

Arthur removed the headset and peered into the mirror. His skin looked dewy, like he'd just got out of the shower. Ren and Cecily were the same as before, just … shinier.

The man assessed them with a sigh. "That'll have to do. Follow me." He steered them back into the corridor and through a padded door with a sign on the front that read, *STUDIO 9*.

Arthur tensed as they walked into an echoless hall, full of people. The set of *The Lazarus Show* sat under glaring lights in the middle of the room, surrounded by more staff operating hovering cameras with numbered labels. The silver-haired producer was there, waiting for them. He held a finger against his lips and motioned for them to follow.

As they walked behind the cameras to the far side of the room, Arthur studied the set. Lazarus Sloane was sat cross-legged on a green suede chair to one side, with the show's logo floating behind him. He was dressed in a tailored crimson suit that made his glossy acid-green scales pop. Griffon Ramsay and Yesenia Colt were perched opposite him on a long, curved sofa. The backdrop looked like Atlantis at night, twinkling with sea life and bioluminescent coral.

Arthur tuned his ears into their conversation.

"... both your careers have seen their fair shares of controversy," Lazarus was saying. "Last season, Yesenia, you came under criticism for the so-called 'Snake-Pit Incident'. Although it's not against the rules to sabotage your opponents, it is seen as bad form. Do you regret your actions?"

"A win is a win," Yesenia said coolly. "I pride myself on my reputation. My fans know I will do whatever it takes to get the result I want. If that means removing someone who is in my way, then so be it."

"Is your desire to win what helped you survive without food or water for five days on Doom Island, last season?" Lazarus asked. "It was considered a major upset when you beat the favourite to the title."

Yesenia smirked. "It's amazing what you can withstand when you put your mind to it." Her ice-blue eyes glinted with assurance and Arthur shivered, hoping he and the others never had the misfortune to get in her way.

"Griffon, you finished as runner-up in your last tournament," Lazarus continued. "It was a contest marred by scandal. Do you think the allegations against you affected your performance?"

Griffon shuffled in his seat. "The allegations were lies. I paid them no attention." He had a gruff voice perfectly suited to his tough image.

"Of course, but it must have shaken your confidence being called a cheat," Lazarus said.

A cheat? Arthur whacked Ren on the arm, checking she and Cecily were listening.

"I am not a cheat!" Griffon declared, flaring his nostrils. "That equipment had been planted there to frame me."

Lazarus nodded. "Yes, we all know what you *said* happened, and the UGP cleared you of any wrongdoing, but in certain parts of the isports community, people have been asking questions—"

"I *don't* want to talk about this!" Griffon exclaimed, standing up.

The silver-haired producer signalled madly to Lazarus, who gave a wide grin. "In that case, why don't you take a seat while my next guests arrive?" he suggested smoothly.

The producer gathered Arthur, Ren and Cecily around him and pointed to a small light on one of the cameras. "Red means recording; amber means standby," he whispered. "Look at camera number four when you're on the sofa."

Arthur barely had time to register the information as he and the others were ushered on set in a blur of lights and faces.

"I'm delighted to welcome to *The Lazarus Show*, for the first time, the surprise last-minute contestants that everyone's been talking about – the Young Pipsqueaks!" Lazarus got to his feet, clapping his claws as recorded applause played around the sound stage.

The Irontide boots rattled in Arthur's trembling hands. Light fell on his shoulders, making him blink. *Focus,* he told himself. *Stay in character.* But it was all he could do not to trip up as he took a seat on the sofa, beside Griffon and Yesenia.

"It's so great to have you here," Lazarus said warmly, sitting back down. "And I see you've brought your mascot with you – your parents' mimic."

Lifting Cloud into her lap, Cecily searched for camera four. "That's right. He, uh, really enjoys being part of our team."

"I'm sure he does," Lazarus said. "In fact, I must ask you about your parents. Where are they? How are they doing? Were they supportive of you entering the Irontide Tournament, or did they advise against it?"

Arthur ran a clammy finger around the collar of his T-shirt. He started to imagine what he must look like, sitting next to Griffon and Yesenia. Like a loser, probably. Part of him wanted to shrivel up and fall down the back of the sofa. "Actually, this was all their idea," he answered, finding his voice.

"That's right," Cecily agreed, giving Arthur a concerned glance that said: *You look awful. I'll do the talking.* "But they'd like to remain out of the spotlight, so we can't tell you any more about them."

Lazarus's tail flicked. "I see. But I'm sure they have high expectations for the three of you. Have you always been interested in becoming isports players, or did you feel pressured to pursue the career after your parents' success?" He aimed his question at Ren, who looked like her body temperature had just risen ten degrees.

"Well, uh..." She fiddled with a loose thread on her new YP-branded combats. "We have lots in common with our parents, but we're our own people. I wouldn't say they pressured us, exactly..."

Arthur could tell by how awkward she sounded that she was answering the question for real. She must be thinking about her mum and their arguments over her doing work experience at the garage.

Lazarus flashed a crooked smile. "And where do you see your isports career going in the future?"

At this, Ren went bright red.

"We just want to make our parents proud," Cecily interjected. "And do our best." She glared at Lazarus, trying to draw his attention away from Ren. Arthur was beginning to think they'd underestimated Lazarus Sloane. He gave off the impression of being flashy and shallow, but there was something sinister and calculating about the way he probed for answers.

"That's admirable," Lazarus told Cecily. "But really, what chance do three amateurs and a second-hand mimic have in a tournament like this? Do you genuinely believe you can become champions and win the three billion DIRT prize?"

No! Arthur wanted to reply. They didn't have a hope in hell of winning the tournament. They were only taking part so they could retrieve the time-key and return home. Of course, he couldn't say that...

"We can win it," Cecily said, sounding far too hesitant to be convincing.

Lazarus stared at her while she blinked back at him. "Very well." There was a pause before he continued, this time addressing Griffon and Yesenia, too. "There's just over four hours until the next elimination and after this, I know you all have to rush off to your next quests. I was wondering if you could share with our viewers any predictions you have about the Land of the Lost?"

Griffon pressed his lips together and folded his arms, clearly unwilling to answer. Arthur gazed helplessly at Ren and Cecily, whose faces were blank.

"Oh, come *on*," Yesenia jibed. "You'd have to be an imbecile to not know what's next. The Land of the Lost is inspired by the Earth-legend of Biringan, an invisible city in the northern part of Samar, in the Philippines." She widened her eyes at camera four and put on a spooky voice. "Seafarers claim to have seen the city rising out of the sea on moonless nights, or tell tales of others being lured there by its supernatural inhabitants..."

The operator behind camera four started mouthing a countdown – ... *seven, six, five...*

Lazarus clapped his hands together. "And with that,

we're going to go to a break sponsored by our friends at Novafuel. When we come back, one lucky viewer will get a chance to win a holovision set and all these goodies."

As soon as the lights on all the cameras had turned amber, Griffon sprang from his chair and steamed out of the studio, ignoring the pleas of several producers. Lazarus was swarmed by staff, who glossed his scales and asked him to check things on their faze displays. Yesenia gave Arthur and the others a stiff look, before striding away.

Arthur was too dazed to move but Cecily tugged on his arm, pulling him up. "Come on, we've got to follow Griffon. You heard what Lazarus said – Griffon's been accused of cheating before."

Ren held on to Cloud as they wound their way off set and out of the sound stage. Arthur wanted to reassure her after the interview, but he could tell by the way she hid her face behind her fringe that she was embarrassed and wouldn't want to talk about it. None of Lazarus's staff seemed to care that they were leaving; they were all busy focusing on the next segment of the show.

Outside, a trio of autoshells hovered kerbside, the gust of their engines roaring loudly. Cloud flattened his ears as Griffon charged into the first, slamming the door behind him.

"Take me to the Great Library," Yesenia barked, climbing into the second.

Arthur and the others scrambled inside the third and Cecily told it to follow Griffon.

"Shouldn't we return to the hotel?" Arthur said. "If Griffon *is* the cheat, then he won't have the time-key on him now, not with all the cameras watching. It'll probably be back in his room."

"But if we want to break in there, we'll need to get hold of his faze," Cecily reminded him. "I was thinking … maybe we can trap him in the Land of the Lost?"

Arthur almost laughed. The chances of them outsmarting Griffon had to be nigh on impossible. Still, he pulled the quest-map out of his pocket. Other than the title, it was still blank.

"Yesenia mentioned a Filipino legend," Ren said. "An invisible city named Biringan. Maybe the map is invisible, too?"

Of course. Arthur wondered what they could use to read it. A pair of Milo's X-focal sunglasses might be handy. He certainly couldn't use his eyes. *Unless…*

He held the tissue paper squarely in front of him and blinked. A dark shape flashed on the insides of his eyelids.

"What is it?" Cecily asked.

Arthur blinked again, more slowly this time. He could see the dark shape in more detail. "Maybe the only way to see the invisible part of the map is … to not see anything at all."

He shut his eyes. On the insides of his eyelids, a gloomy map appeared. It depicted a floating city of soaring skyscrapers and gravity-defying bridges. The city buildings were arranged in a circle and in the very centre was a tall tower made of black stone. At the top of the tower was drawn an armoured gold helmet, the only feature in colour. Scribbled beneath the map's title, was now a clue:

LEGENDARIOM

- *THE LAND OF THE LOST* -

Tread with care up in the skies,
the shadows here have many eyes.

12

Footsteps echoed throughout the porticos of the Great Library of Alexandria as questers hurried back and forth between reading rooms, carrying books and scrolls. A frizzy-haired girl with purple glasses looked up from her faze display as Arthur, Ren and Cecily dashed past. "The Young Pipsqueaks!" she gasped

"Sorry!" Arthur called, over his shoulder. As he swerved around a corner, he adjusted the Irontide boots tucked under his arm. They were awkward to run with.

"Was that all the map said – *the shadows here have many eyes*?" Ren asked, fretfully. "That could be about spiders."

Arthur wasn't an arachnid expert, but he knew that the creatures had multiple sets of eyes. He also knew that creepy-crawlies were pretty much the only things Ren was scared of. "I guess we'll soon find out. But don't worry – if it *is* spiders, you won't be on your own."

Ren nodded, but he could tell by the set of her jaw that she was anxious.

Cloud's claws scratched the flagstones as the group skidded into the hall with the Bermuda Triangle. Questers filled the marble floor, walking to and from the column of light in the centre. It was obvious who had just finished a quest because they tended to have sweaty faces and torn clothes. Some wore exhausted but triumphant expressions; others trudged forwards with their shoulders down, looking defeated.

Ignoring the yelling paparazzi on the balcony, Arthur and the others zigzagged across the floor. Yesenia Colt was nowhere to be seen but Arthur caught a glimpse of Griffon, just before he disappeared into the Bermuda Triangle. "Griffon's just started his quest. The sooner we get to the Land of the Lost, the sooner we can start looking for him."

"Excuse me, Young Pipsqueaks?" A teenager, wearing a T-shirt with *Lone Wolf* printed on it in jagged letters, stepped into their path, holding a faze towards them. "I'm from *Lore of Legends*. Can you tell our readers how you feel abou—?"

"Sorry," Ren said, dodging aside. "We don't have time."

They ran to the edge of the triangle and stopped. Arthur took a deep breath and tried to steady his nerves. "No matter what's on the other side, we can do this," he told the others. "We have to."

As he stepped into the triangle, he was surrounded by bright light. He felt his body become weightless …

… and then everything went black.

"What happened?!" he yelped, reaching forward.

Cloud barked in alarm.

"Don't move!" Cecily shrieked.

Arthur had a terrifying vision of them all stumbling into a giant spider's web and went deathly still. His skin prickled as he listened out for sounds that might reveal their environment. Far off, he could hear the groan of large moving objects.

"There's something ahead of us," Ren warned, her voice unsteady.

As Arthur's eyes adjusted to the dark, shadows materialized around them. They appeared to be stood on a flat area of rock, about the size of a basketball court. Other platforms of rock moved backwards and forwards in different directions all around them, some disappearing into the mist below. In the distance, a city emerged. Pale-green light outlined cathedral-like buildings with soaring spires and long bridges. It was *Biringan* – Arthur recognized the design of the central tower from the quest-map. "It's only dark because it's night-time," he realized. "Yesenia said Biringan was seen on *moonless* nights, remember?"

Although he couldn't see or hear any drones, he knew they would be near by, watching. He wondered if they used heat vision to record what was happening in the dark or some other more advanced image-capture technology.

Cecily wrapped her arms around her. "This place is giving me all sorts of bad vibes. What do you think is below us?"

"All I can see is fog," Ren said, peering over the edge. "But I think it's safe to say we don't want to fall down there. Any sign of Griffon?"

Scouring the landscape for the Lone Wolf, Arthur noticed a handful of lights moving in short spurts in different directions. "I don't believe it," he muttered, as it dawned on him where they were. "I think this land is like a real-life platform game. Those lights must be our opponents."

"A platform game like *Super Mario*?" Cecily said, sounding anxious. "I've played that before. You have to make your character jump or run across different types of terrain in order to reach a particular destination."

Nodding, Arthur pointed to the tall black structure in the middle of Biringan. "On the quest-map, the Irontide helmet is at the top of that tower. Our quest must be to navigate our way across these floating rocks towards it. Our competitors probably have different destinations."

Ren squinted into the distance. "We'd better hurry. If Griffon is one of those lights, we need to catch up with him before he finishes his quest."

Arthur tried to hide his nerves. If this was anything like the platform games he'd played, it was going to take some serious skill to get across safely. The rocks would move in unexpected directions and at different speeds. Some would have traps. In the dim light, it would be easy to misstep.

"One of us should wear these," he said, taking the

Irontide boots out from under his armpit. "Whatever power they have, it might help us."

Cecily lifted her hands. "I certainly don't want them. It's going to be enough of a challenge trying to overcome my vertigo, without having to worry about whatever they might do."

"You should wear them, Arthur," Ren said, studying their surroundings. "You've played more platform games than we have. You'll probably have a better sense of how best to use them."

Arthur didn't share Ren's confidence, but he placed the boots on the ground, pushed his foot into the left one and shimmied his heel down hard. With a jolt, his trainer fit snugly into place. He pulled the right boot on and walked a few paces, wiggling his toes. Despite being made mostly of metal, the boots were as soft as slippers.

"Think you can run in them?" Ren asked.

"Actually … yes," he replied, surprising himself. As an experiment, he jogged to the opposite side of the platform. "Does it look like they're doing anything special? I don't feel any faster or stronger."

Cecily frowned. "Maybe the boots' power isn't that obvious? It could be something that we need to discover along the way."

They examined the first platform crossing. The gap was a couple of metres wide – too big to jump – and the opposite, smaller rock was moving side to side.

"Perhaps there's a bridge we have to unlock?" Ren guessed, adding with a shake of her head, "I can't believe we're in a platform game. This is so surreal."

Arthur cast around for inspiration. He couldn't see any buttons or levers anywhere, and there were no pressure pads in the ground. Testing an idea, he held his arm out over the gap, and was almost knocked back by a gust of wind. "There's an updraught here," he said. "It's probably designed to support our weight so we can jump to the next platform."

"Jump?" Cecily shrank back. "No, no, no. Running across a rope bridge is one thing, but I can't leap into open air."

Arthur remembered how much strength it had taken for her to cross a bridge in the Wonderscape. He knew this was asking a lot.

"Have you ever seen videos of people doing indoor skydiving?" Ren asked. "I've been begging my mums to let me try it for ages. It's where you get to fly in this big wind tube. Just imagine we're there."

With a whimper, Cloud poked his head out from under Cecily's jacket.

"Yes, but indoor skydiving will have safety measures," Cecily said, cuddling him closer. "This place could kill us."

Arthur couldn't argue with that. "Cecily, I know you can do this. Think of the confidence you had when you spoke to that hotel porter, or the merguard, or Lazarus Sloane. Try to channel some of that."

She sighed. "Yeah, OK..."

After a little more encouragement, she came closer to the edge. Arthur smiled at her. Her determination to succeed was one of the things he most admired about her. She refused to take no for an answer, even when she was asking questions of herself.

"Everybody ready?" he asked.

Ren nodded. Cecily's expression turned steely.

"We've just got to jump. The updraught should carry us across." It felt dicey to trust in the rules of the game, but what other option did they have? He waited till the opposite platform had slid closer. "All right. Ready, steady ... GO!"

Bending his knees, he leaped forward. A cushion of wind caught him from below and sent him sailing headlong towards the opposite rock...

He landed with a painful thump on his tail bone. The platform was moving faster than it had looked and he had to grapple with the surface to stay balanced. Cloud yapped as Cecily touched down beside him. Her jaw was trembling and her fists were clenched.

"Made it," Ren puffed, landing in a crouch. "Cecily, you've got this. Now we just need to speed up. If Griffon's one of those lights, he can't be that far away."

There were two options for the next crossing – a rock to the right that rose up and down, and another that moved in a square, connecting several different pathways. With Biringan's central tower as their guide, they chose the latter and jumped over three further platforms, before they reached a wide, stationary plateau.

Closer now, Arthur could see Biringan in more detail. The architecture was unlike anything he'd seen before, even compared to Atlantis. Skyscrapers tapered to needle-sharp points; rooftops curled up at the edges like burnt paper and delicate filigree bridges seemed to hover in mid-air, defying gravity. Everything was bathed in a hazy green light, like the steam from a witch's brew. He thought about what Yesenia Colt had said about seafarers claiming to have seen Biringan rising out of the sea. If this was the place they had described, no wonder its legend had endured.

As Cecily hurried towards the other side of the platform, a cloud of sparkling nano-particles burst out of the ground. "Wha—!" she shrieked, juggling Cloud as she hopped out of the way.

The particles converged into a stocky man with dark, bushy eyebrows. He looked identical to the trader they'd met in the Land of Outlaws, except he was wearing a long, black robe. "Can I interest you three in anything from the store?" he asked politely, waving a hand beside him.

Arthur couldn't see any store, but, remembering the invisible quest-map, he closed his eyes. A set of floating pale-green shelves appeared on the insides of his eyelids. They were stocked with all sorts of equipment, including ropes, head torches, spring-heeled shoes, grappling hooks and stilts. "Err, we'll take three head torches, please," he decided quickly, knowing they didn't have time to browse. His faze vibrated and when he opened his eyes, the trader was already handing the torches to Ren and Cecily.

"Shall we get anything else?" Cecily asked, pulling her torch on carefully over her hairdo.

"No time," Ren said, snatching Cecily's hand. "Look – I think that's Griffon!"

As they rushed to the edge of the platform, Arthur grabbed his head torch and dashed after them.

"Lovely doing business with you!" the trader called, over Arthur's shoulder.

Spotlit in Ren's torch beam, Griffon was sprinting across a crumbling platform a hundred metres away. Arthur's heart missed a beat as the isports champion leaped into the air and caught the edge of the next platform with his fingertips, heaving himself up with ease.

"If we continue in this direction, our paths will cross on *that*," Cecily said, pointing a shaking finger towards a circular platform covered in tall spikes. "We'll have to trap him there."

Arthur had no clue how they were going to achieve that, but they could think on the way. "I suppose to everyone watching, it'll look like we're trying to sabotage him. At least Lazarus Sloane said that wasn't illegal. Come on!"

He boosted Cecily and Cloud up to the next platform, which was blessedly motionless. Ren needed no help as she clambered up after them. Watching her, Arthur was reminded of their agreement that should he lose their hotdog-eating contest, he had to be her rock-climbing spotter for the rest of the summer holidays. It all seemed a million miles away now, but who knew...? If they could steal Griffon's faze and retrieve the time-key from his room, perhaps they could be home and safe in a matter of hours?

"Arthur –" Ren reached down towards him – "grab on."

Arthur stretched his hand up to meet hers. As he tried to get a foothold in the rock, his toes slipped and the Irontide boots struck each other, producing a pure, ringing note. Immediately afterwards, he heard a mysterious rumble in the distance. "Can you hear that?" he asked Ren.

"The music?" she replied, dreamily. "Yeah, it's beautiful."

"What?" Arthur strained to listen. He couldn't hear any music, just a strange drumming noise. It seemed to be coming from behind him.

And it was getting louder.

He did an about-turn, aiming his head torch back the way they'd come. A shadow was moving in their direction, sweeping up, down and over each platform like a blanket. As the beam of Arthur's torch fell over it, his skin turned to ice.

Caught in the light were *thousands* of writhing black bodies with twitching whiskers and whip-like tails.

Rats.

13

Ordinarily, rats didn't bother Arthur. But these were no ordinary rats.

Four platforms away, he could see them clearly. With hungry black eyes and gnarled yellow teeth sharp enough to pierce bone, they squeaked, hissed and chattered as they charged towards him, looking like they wanted to gnaw off his leg. Swirling around their feet was a haze of sinister red vapour.

A spasm of fear shot through Arthur and he launched himself up onto the platform where Ren and Cecily were. Cloud was barking loudly by Cecily's ankles.

"... *the shadows here have many eyes,*" he spluttered, recalling the clue on the quest-map. "It must have been talking about the rats – we have to run!"

It was only then that he realized Ren and Cecily had gone rigid. Tendrils of red vapour danced near their ears as they stared blankly into the middle distance.

"Ren?" Arthur batted her ear-wisps away.

Her kohl-lined eyes had a glazed look about them, like she'd been hypnotized. "Ren, can you hear me?!"

She didn't respond.

Arthur's chest tightened as he tried Cecily. Gripping her by the shoulders, he shook her hard. "Cecily! CECILY!"

But it was no use. The red vapour by their ears – the same stuff swirling around the rats – had done something to them. Ren had mentioned *music*. Arthur wondered if the vapour was making them hear things that had put them in this trance? He wasn't sure why he was unaffected...

The rats were getting louder. He knew he had to act before the three of them became the starter, main course and dessert in a rodent banquet. He removed Cloud's lead from Cecily's wrist and looped it around his own. "We've got to get Ren and Cecily out of here. I need your help." He moved to the opposite side of the platform to give Cloud some space, then crouched down to fiddle with his collar. As a dragon, Cloud could fry the rats with his fire breath and carry all three of them to safety on his back.

Arthur's fingers trembled as he fumbled with the beads on Cloud's collar. As he accidentally slipped past *Green-Winged Dragon* and on to *Corn Snake*, Cloud whimpered and pointed his nose over Arthur's shoulder.

Ren and Cecily had followed them over.

"Or maybe ... we could just lead them to safety," Arthur said, rethinking his plan. "Come on, we've got to hurry."

The next platform was too high to scale and there was no updraught to lift them over the gap, but when Arthur stepped closer to the edge, he discovered the ground was springy. Scooping Cloud into his arms, he bent his knees and jumped. To his relief, he landed on his feet, right where he'd been aiming. Ren and Cecily's torch beams flashed as they bounced up, after him.

He studied them worriedly. They were following him like lemmings, completely unaware of what was going on around them. Swallowing back his despair, he realized he was now responsible for saving everyone.

The rats were only three platforms away and gaining quickly. Arthur knew he couldn't outrun them, so he tried to think of another solution. Yesenia hadn't mentioned rats when she'd spoken of Biringan; they had to be part of another legend.

Rats ... music...

Racking his brains, he remembered he'd performed in a primary school play about the Pied Piper of Hamelin. It was a medieval legend about a piper who was hired to drive out the rats plaguing a German town. The piper had used a magical pipe to lure the rats into a river, but when the townspeople had refused to pay him for his services, the piper had punished them by leading their children away. Perhaps Ren, Cecily and the rats had all been ensnared by the music of a magical pipe?

But then why hadn't Arthur?

Testing a theory, he ran towards the next platform with Ren and Cecily in pursuit. When he stopped and changed direction, they copied him.

It's me, he concluded with a tingle of surprise. *Somehow, I'm the piper...*

Of course, he had no pipe, nor the musical talent to play one, but he *did* have a pair of Irontide boots. He examined them curiously. There was nothing about their appearance to suggest they were connected to the Hamelin legend, but when he checked the soles, he discovered a long musical instrument etched across the base – a medieval pipe. He remembered the clear, ringing note he'd heard when the boots had knocked together and wondered if he'd activated the pipe then. *Tread with care*, the quest-map had said. It hadn't been joking.

Grabbing the heel of one boot, he was about to yank it off – and hopefully disable whatever spell Ren and Cecily were under – when he noticed Griffon Ramsay tearing across a platform a hundred metres away.

Griffon was wearing his Irontide boots, but there were no rats chasing him so Arthur presumed he hadn't yet discovered what the boots did. Griffon was so agile and athletic he probably hadn't knocked them together once.

A risky idea occurred to Arthur. If he could get close enough, his boots might put Griffon under the same spell as Ren and Cecily. That way, Arthur would be able to steal Griffon's faze *and* trap him. The only major downside was that Arthur would have to keep his boots on, which meant towing Ren and Cecily around in a trance the entire time.

Oh, and … the rats would still be after them.

Full of uncertainty, Arthur checked the timer on his watch: only thirty-five hours remaining before they all turned into slime. It was worth the gamble. With renewed determination, he aimed himself in the direction of the spike-covered platform, and quickened his pace.

His boots bashed against the hard stone as he ran, sending vibrations through his calves. He dropped to another platform, hurtled through a short tunnel and scrambled up to the next, with Ren and Cecily following obediently behind. The rats shrieked and chattered, drawing closer.

By the time he reached his destination, his lungs were on fire and Ren and Cecily were both red-cheeked and puffing. He paused in a safe area to assess the spikes, which were each the size of goalposts. Some of them were immobile but others burst from the ground, ready to impale passers-by. The holes that the spikes fitted into were arranged in straight lines like the walls of a maze. At least a dozen of them were empty and loose spikes lay scattered across the ground.

"It's another puzzle. My guess is we have to complete the maze as we go," he wheezed to Cloud, wondering if there was a way to use the loose spikes to trap Griffon. He wrapped Cloud's lead a few extra times around his wrist, shortening the cord. "Stay close to me. This is going to be tricky."

His nerves jittered as he inched slowly around the edge of the platform, aiming for a gap in the spikes on the opposite side. It had to be the start of the maze. He tried to ignore the endless pit of fog below, but it was impossible. Ren and Cecily mirrored his footsteps, their blank faces beaded with sweat. Arthur promised himself that if they all survived this, he'd tell Cecily exactly what she'd achieved while under the pipe's spell. She'd never believe him.

In the beam of Ren's torch, he saw the rats were now two platforms away, and closing. Griffon was also drawing nearer. Arthur wasn't sure how to place the isports champion under the influence of the Irontide boots, so he tried striking them together as he had before, to produce a single, harmonious note.

The sound split the air like the toll of a bell.

Instantly, Griffon went stiff. His head snapped round and he came running in Arthur's direction.

"It worked!" Arthur told Cloud. But there wasn't time to celebrate.

With Griffon, Ren, Cecily *and* the rats now in tow, he started the precarious journey through the maze of spikes. The path was narrow and twisty. Every so often he heard the scrape of metal and flinched as a barb shot from the ground beside him.

Concentrate, he told himself. *You can do this.*

Trusting his gaming instincts, he collected the first loose spike he came across and fitted it into the nearest empty slot. The entire row of spikes immediately receded, clearing a new route through the maze. Blood pounded in his ears as he guided Ren and Cecily forward, hoping desperately that they didn't all get turned into human kebabs.

He soon turned into a clearing at the centre of the platform, where the holes formed a tight circle, big enough to trap Griffon. Arthur gathered a few loose spikes and pushed them into place. He had almost finished building a cage when Griffon caught up to him, stopping a few paces away.

Arthur shrank back. Despite Griffon's vacant expression, he looked as tough and as strong as ever. Arthur mumbled an apology as he gripped Griffon's chest armour and hauled him into the circle. Aware that the drones would be watching, he surreptitiously slipped Griffon's faze off his wrist before filling in any remaining holes in the cage with spikes.

Griffon just stood there, staring with milky eyes. He would be safe from the rats – they were following Arthur – but the thought of how furious he was going to be when he came round made Arthur's knees wobble. Still, Arthur couldn't focus on that right now. He had to get out of there, back to the hotel.

And that meant finishing the quest.

As the rats surged onto the maze platform, their yellow teeth glinting in the torchlight, Arthur gazed over at Biringan city, tugging on Cloud's lead. "Come on, boy, we've got to get to the top of that tower!"

14

Biringan's pavements glowed green, reflecting the eerie light that washed the city. Cloud's ears twitched as he and Arthur rushed through the deserted streets.

"I know," Arthur murmured, casting nervous glances in either direction. The place was as creepy as a graveyard on Halloween. It was deathly quiet; the windows in all the strange buildings were dark; and the air tasted dusty and stale, like in an attic.

Either no one had been there for a very long time, or the residents were all ghosts.

Arthur wasn't sure which option he preferred.

Still, at least there was no chance of him getting lost. The black tower dwarfed every other structure in the city, so it was easy navigating towards it. As he progressed, he reminded himself that he was on the home straight. The Irontide helmet had to be somewhere inside that tower. If he could find it, he and the others could get back to the hotel and search for the time-key in Griffon's room.

He glanced over his shoulder at Ren and Cecily, tailing him like hypnotized ducklings. They were relying on him. He couldn't let them down.

At the base of the black tower, an arched entrance led to a narrow, spiral staircase lit by flickering green torches. Arthur couldn't spy the Irontide helmet anywhere, so seeing no other way up, he took a deep breath and started to climb.

He counted the stairs as he went. After the first fifty, he heard an ominous chattering below, and knew the rats had made it to the tower. There was no turning back now.

His calves burned as he trudged higher and higher, on and on. Wiping sweat from his brow, he felt grateful he'd had that extra bowl of Zoorflakes for breakfast; he needed all the energy he could get. He wondered whether Ren and Cecily were in as much agony as he was, or if this all felt like a bad dream to them.

By the two hundredth step, his legs had turned to jelly and the insides of his thighs were chafing so badly, they felt red hot. Cloud barked and tugged at the bottom of Arthur's jeans, trying to spur him on.

"I can't do it," Arthur puffed. But even as he spoke, he found himself lifting one foot in front of the other.

Finally, when it seemed like the staircase would never end, a wooden door appeared in the wall. Arthur's knees buckled as he crashed through it, crumpling onto the flagstones of a small room. A familiar gong reverberated around the walls and in a burst of light, a golden helmet appeared floating in the centre of the room.

Tears watered in Arthur's eyes. He'd done it.

Now he had to free Ren and Cecily from whatever spell they were under. With one last burst of energy, he kicked off the Irontide boots and crawled towards the helmet. Behind him, the door creaked.

"Arthur...?" a voice murmured.

He glanced over his shoulder to see Ren and Cecily stood at the threshold of the door, rubbing their heads. Cloud bounded towards them.

"Hello, Fuzzball," Ren said groggily. "What's going on, Arthur? Where are we?"

"And why does it feel like I've just run a race?" Cecily added, rubbing her thighs.

Arthur couldn't help but smile, relieved and happy to have his friends back. "I'll explain on the way to the hotel. If one of you can carry the boots, I'll take the helmet. Griffon will have just woken up, so we don't have much time."

He snatched the Irontide helmet out of the air and the room dissolved into light. In seconds, they were all back in the hall at the Great Library. Arthur had barely a moment to think before a new quest-map materialized in front of them and fluttered to the floor.

Tucking the Irontide boots under her armpit, Ren picked up the map. She studied it for a second and then did a double-take. "Am I reading this correctly?"

The map was made of crinkly old parchment. Ren flipped it around so Arthur and Cecily could see. It showed an area of jagged coastline. Inland, the camps of two different armies were marked at opposite sides of a snowy valley with a pair of armoured gauntlets drawn between them. Scrawled in gloopy red ink at the bottom right-hand corner were the words:

LEGENDARI◊M
– *THE LAND OF BEARDS* –
**You will find your quest is ended
when the scars of war are mended.**

"The Land of *Beards*?" Cecily wrinkled her nose. "What's that supposed to mean? And yuck – is that written in *blood*?"

Arthur hoped they wouldn't need to find out. He slipped Griffon's faze out of his pocket, careful not to let anyone else see. As always, the media balcony was rowdy with photographers and there were all sorts of journalists milling around the hall. Arthur spotted a few people in *Lazarus Show* T-shirts hurrying towards them. "Come on, let's escape from here before we're asked any questions. If we're lucky, we can be in and out of Griffon's room before anyone notices."

Just as Ribbon promised, there was an autoshell waiting for them outside the Great Library, which they rode back to the hotel. On the way, Arthur explained to a dumbfounded

Ren and Cecily what had happened with the rats and the legend of the Pied Piper. They had no memory of anything, and seemed glad of it. At the hotel, after waiting for a maid to leave their corridor, they tiptoed along, checking to see which door responded to Griffon's faze. Eventually, the door at the far end clicked open and they slipped inside.

Griffon's room was neat and tidy. It had a similar layout to theirs, except there was only one bedroom attached to the lounge. Books covered the dining table and a swirling nano-particle mannequin stood beside the fireplace, wearing a set of Griffon's body armour. The holovision screen turned on automatically as they walked inside.

If Arthur hadn't been in a life-or-slime situation, he would have felt wrong being in there. Searching someone's bedroom without their permission was an invasion of privacy. As it was, considerations like that went out the window.

"Where do you think he's hiding it?" Ren asked, rifling through Griffon's mini-fridge.

"Not in there," Arthur answered. "It's got to be somewhere secure – a safe, or a locked box."

He caught sight of one of the books on the dining table and stiffened. It was titled: *What Happened to The Pipsqueaks?* The front cover featured the same humiliating image of the three of them as had been used for their holographic statue. "I think Griffon's trying to find out more about us," Arthur said, flashing the book at the others. "What if he suspects that we're not who we claim to be?"

"All the more reason for us to find the time-key and get out of here," Cecily said.

Cloud pressed his nose to the carpet and started sniffing around, twisting his bottom in different directions. While Ren and Arthur combed the lounge – exploring under the furniture, behind the sofa cushions and even in the fireplace – Cecily hunted through Griffon's wardrobe.

"These fashion labels have such weird names," she commented, sliding Griffon's hangers back and forth.

"Any sign of the time-key?" Arthur asked, checking behind the holovision screen.

She trudged into the lounge. "No, not in the bedroom or the bathroom. I rummaged through everything, even Griffon's pockets."

A cold, heavy feeling slipped through Arthur's body. If Griffon didn't have the time-key on him, and it wasn't in his room, then where was he keeping it?

"Err, guys…" Ren pointed a shaky finger at the holoscreen and Arthur angled his head so he could see. *The Lazarus Show* was showing live footage of Griffon Ramsay barrelling through the revolving doors of the Hotel Loch Ness, his face twisted in anger.

Arthur hastily stuffed Griffon's faze down the back of the sofa. He didn't want to get caught with it on him, and perhaps if Griffon found it there, he might think it had fallen off earlier. He grabbed Cloud off the floor. "Get out of here! Go!"

15

Arthur didn't think he'd ever felt so disappointed in his whole life. Had all that effort in the Land of the Lost really been for nothing? He checked his watch and saw they had just over thirty-two hours before their bodies became protoplasm. With every passing second, his desperation threatened to turn into panic. They were running out of time.

Back in their hotel room, he grabbed a can of the sugariest drink he could find in the mini-fridge – Novafuel – and flopped onto the sofa, wishing his muscles could take the rest of the day off.

A fire crackled in the hearth, filling the room with the scent of woodsmoke. The holoscreen above the mantelpiece was playing *The Lazarus Show* on mute. Its oh-so-scaly host seemed to be discussing the prospects of each remaining candidate with a panel of I-RAG analysts and experts. They replayed footage of Yesenia Colt somersaulting across a Biringan platform like a gymnast, and a clip of the three

Savage Strike guys being chased to the edge of a fiery pit by a swarm of rats. Arthur wanted to turn it off, but he couldn't see a remote and he was too tired to reach for the holo-controls.

"Where can Griffon be keeping the time-key if it's not in his room?" Ren said, slumping into one of the armchairs opposite. Cloud curled himself into a ball at her feet and started snoring.

"I don't know," Arthur replied. "If only we could trace his movements over the last twenty-four hours... Maybe he's hidden the time-key somewhere in Atlantis and is planning to retrieve it when he needs it?"

Cecily reached across the dining table to the fruit basket. "Wanna try one of these?" She was holding a strange cube-shaped fruit with a translucent red skin.

Arthur and Ren both raised their hands and she tossed them one each.

"Ribbon Rex might know more about Griffon's whereabouts," Cecily said, opening her faze display. "Isn't it her job to monitor all the tournament contestants?"

Arthur took a tentative bite into his fruit. The skin was smooth like a plum's and the flesh inside was soft and juicy. It tasted a bit like a satsuma with a hint of cinnamon. "Yeah, maybe." He watched Cecily swipe her finger through the air. "What are you doing?"

"Sending the UGP an enquiry. Ribbon told us to contact them if we have any questions."

"Aren't they going to think it's odd that we want to know everywhere Griffon's been?" Ren pointed out.

"Not necessarily." Cecily's face brightened. "Look – they've replied already!" But as her eyes raced across the screen, her shoulders fell. *"Thank you for your enquiry,"* she read flatly. *"One of our representatives will respond as soon as possible. We aim to answer all questions within forty-eight hours."*

"So much for that idea," Arthur mumbled. The time-key, he knew, could be anywhere by now. Griffon may have sold it on to someone else, or even returned it to Deadlock when he realized it wasn't the evader that he'd ordered. The chances of them getting back to the twenty-first century were shrinking. Fast.

Lifting his feet up on the sofa, he hugged his knees and thought of home. He pictured his dad, sitting alone at their dining table. "What if we never make it back?" he said quietly. "My dad's on his own. He doesn't have anyone else."

Cecily gave Arthur a forlorn smile. "My parents deal with every problem by trying to fix it. If we don't return ... well, there's no fixing that. I don't know how they'll cope."

"I know exactly what my mums will do," Ren said, staring into the middle distance. "Whenever they're sad or worried, they bake – muffins, scones, banana bread. They'll probably be round at both your parents', trying to force-feed them all cake."

"I thought you said they were terrible cooks?" Arthur replied.

She grinned. "Yeah. They are."

There was a pause and then all three of them burst out laughing. Arthur's belly hurt as he pictured his dad nibbling on a slice of burnt Victoria sponge. It felt good to laugh, even if the moment was tainted by sadness.

Just then, colours flashed on the holoscreen above the fireplace. Lazarus Sloane was hurrying through one of the corridors of the Great Library, followed by several members of his crew. A list of the Irontide teams was displayed at one side of the screen.

"It's the midday elimination," Cecily realized, reaching for the holo-controls to increase the volume.

It looked like every team had managed to complete their second quests and win an Irontide helmet because there was a golden helmet icon beside each team name. Yesenia Colt was at the top of the list, followed by Savage Strike. Arthur stared at *The Young Pipsqueaks* in third position, ahead of Griffon Ramsey. He'd guessed that they would have beaten Griffon's time, but he hadn't realized that would put them in third. At the very bottom, *The Ghost League* flashed red. Although they'd won an Irontide helmet, their time was more than an hour slower than Griffon's.

Arthur winced as Lazarus Sloane burst into one of the reading rooms of the Great Library, where the four members of the Ghost League were huddled around a table with their coach. Their faces went as white as their costumes as the lizard-headed presenter advanced towards them.

"This isn't over yet," Ren said, determinedly. "If we're still in the tournament, then there's still a chance we can find the time-key. We can't give up."

A graphic slid across the screen, flashing red:

BREAKING NEWS

Fiddling with an earpiece, Lazarus Sloane stopped where he was and turned around to face the camera. "We've just received some breaking news." His thin black tongue skimmed his lips. "Staff at the Hotel Loch Ness have reported a burglary at the property. One of the Irontide competitors' rooms has been ransacked!"

Arthur tensed. "Oh no. That's got to be about us. Griffon must have realized someone was there, rummaging around. What should we do?"

"We need to get our story straight," Cecily said, chewing frantically on a mouthful of cube-fruit. "If officials ask us what we've seen, we have to throw them off the scent."

At that moment, Cloud's snoring came to an abrupt stop. His right ear snapped up and a hologram projected out of it.

Milo Hertz was hurrying along an Atlantean street with his hood up and head down. The *Legendarium*-branded raincoat he wore must have been an impulse purchase because it clearly wasn't the right size – his muscles bulged in the sleeves. "Can't talk for long," he muttered, avoiding eye contact with whatever device he was using to record the call. "Something's come up and I'm not going to be able to meet you, as planned. You must be careful. D is in Legendarium."

And with that, his image evaporated. Cloud's ear went limp and he continued snoring as if there had been no interruption to his nap whatsoever.

Arthur hadn't even moved. "What was that all about?"

"D must be Deadlock," Ren said. "Milo was going to try to locate Deadlock's base; perhaps he succeeded?"

Before they could discuss it further, there was a knock at the door. "Young Pipsqueaks? I'm on my lunchbreak and saw your message. What's up?"

It was Ribbon. Arthur's gaze jumped from the door, to Cloud, to the holoscreen. Things were spinning out of control.

"Just coming!" Cecily called, staring worriedly at Ren and Arthur. "What are we going to say? It'll seem suspicious if we ask her about Griffon now."

As Cecily reached the door, Arthur desperately tried to think of another reason for them having contacted her.

"Survived again! Congratulations," Ribbon said, closing her faze display as she walked inside. "What can I do for you?"

Arthur hesitated. "Err … we wanted to thank you for your advice this morning, about proving everyone wrong."

"Oh." Ribbon blinked. "Well, I know how frustrating it is to be underestimated. I'm glad it helped." She signalled to the holoscreen. "To be honest, I thought you were going to ask me about the break-in. I've already had Savage Strike requesting to know what happened. They're worried it was raiders."

Arthur tried to stay cool. "Yeah, we just saw the report. Was anything stolen?"

"Yesenia doesn't think so. Apparently, the intruder just made a mess."

Arthur did a double-take. "Wait. Did you say *Yesenia*?"

"That's right. She was in the Land of the Lost when a hotel maid discovered her door hanging open."

"That's … horrible," Arthur said, trying to sound sincere. He gave Ren and Cecily a meaningful glance, wondering if they were thinking the same as him. Maybe the reason they hadn't found the time-key in Griffon's room was because it was *Yesenia* who had it. Whoever had broken into her room could have been looking for it…

They needed to question her.

"Does Yesenia seem OK?" he asked, probing for more information.

Ribbon snorted. "You have met Yesenia, right? It would take more than a mystery intruder to leave her shaken up. I only saw her a moment ago, in the lobby. She was leaving to start the next quest."

"In the *Land of Beards*?" Ren pulled the crinkled quest-map out of her pocket.

"That's right. She's obviously keen to get it over and done with. You all have until midnight to complete it, same as always." Ribbon checked her faze display. "Talking of which, I'm on duty at the Bermuda Triangle in half an hour. Can I help you with anything else before I go?"

"Yes, actually," Ren said, inspecting the map. "Can you recommend somewhere between here and the Great Library where we can buy thermal clothing? I think we're going to need it."

16

They'd been in the Land of Beards ten minutes and Arthur's toes had already turned numb from the cold. He gave them a wiggle to try to get the blood flowing, but it didn't seem to work. With the sun reflecting off the snow, he pulled down his new tinted goggles and gazed out at the landscape.

They'd emerged, via the Bermuda Triangle, on the shores of an icy wilderness. With the sea at their backs, a snowy valley lay ahead of them, surrounded by steep rocky mountains. The charred carcasses of several boats lay abandoned on the beach, along with the remains of splintered flagpoles, bloodied axes and smashed wooden shields, all dusted in fresh white powder. Wind howled eerily over the land, carrying with it a rotten stench.

"Well, this is grim," Cecily muttered, scooping Cloud off the ground. He was dressed in the only doggy-snowsuit they'd been able to find in the Quester's Supply Store in Atlantis – a Christmas-inspired red-and-white fleecy onesie with built-in goggles. "Careful where you tread."

Arthur stepped over part of a broken spear, frozen in a thick block of ice. "Some of these weapons look like they've been here a long time," he observed. "It's as if people have fought on the same spot repeatedly."

"Perhaps they have," Ren said. "If the battle that took place here is part of the game, it's probably reset over and over." She studied the quest-map, hanging in a waterproof pouch around her neck. They'd purchased it from the Quester's Supply Store, along with full thermal outfits, a pair of binoculars, a compass, a length of rope, a penknife and a rucksack in which Arthur was now carrying everything, plus their Irontide helmet. They'd left the Irontide boots back in their hotel room, deciding that their rat-controlling powers would be more of a hindrance than a help. Ren had tried the helmet on in the changing rooms, only to be informed by a passing shopper that gaming armour only functioned *inside* the quest-lands.

"We must be somewhere along this coast, which means the Irontide gauntlets are in that direction." Ren pointed in front of them, towards the centre of the frozen battleground.

Arthur peered through their binoculars, hanging around his neck. The mountains were jaw-droppingly tall, speckled with pine trees and sheer granite rock faces. High up in the cliffs, tents were erected at two different campsites on opposite sides of the valley. Each site flew a different set of flags, but Arthur was too far away to make out their details. Down below, several dark figures tramped through the wreckage. He recognized the crimson uniforms of the Savage Strike team, who had replaced their spears with climbing ropes. The other figure was dressed in a neon-yellow ski suit, plastered with logos. "Yesenia's heading inland, towards where the gauntlets supposedly are on our map. Savage Strike are here too but I can't see Griffon."

"He might be planning to start his quest later," Cecily said. "Do you think Yesenia has the time-key on her?"

"Maybe. Or it was stolen by whoever broke in." Arthur dropped the binoculars in order to adjust the straps on the rucksack. "We'll have to convince her to tell us what she knows. We'll be slime in under thirty hours and we still have no idea if we're on the right track, so every minute counts."

Cloud growled, like he thought that convincing Yesenia was a bad idea.

"I hear you, Fuzzball," Ren said, under her fur-lined hood. "Yesenia's too ruthless to help us. We need something to bargain with, something we can offer her in exchange for information."

"Like what?" Arthur asked.

Ren's breath fogged the air. "Don't know. We've got to come up with something."

As they shuffled through the frozen slush, Arthur tried to ignore the aching in his legs. They were still sore after his tower workout and the energy bars he'd gobbled on the way to the Great Library had done little to help. Still, the crisp, clear air sharpened his mind, even if his body felt drained. "Do anyone else's muscles feel like jelly?" he asked.

"Yep," Ren said. "Everywhere hurts. No wonder isports players train before every tournament."

"That's exactly why Yesenia hates us," Cecily commented, "because we're still here, despite not doing the training. Ribbon's right: it does make Yesenia look bad." She stopped in her tracks. "Wait. Maybe *that's* what we can offer Yesenia? We could promise to complete our quest slower than she completes hers – to purposefully sabotage our place."

"That'll only work if we can prove that we're on target to do it faster than her," Arthur pointed out, "and we haven't even worked out what the clue from the quest-map means."

"You will find your quest is ended when the scars of war are mended," Cecily repeated. "The 'scars of war' could refer to this area of land, damaged by the many battles that have taken place here. Perhaps we have to repair it somehow?"

"Or the scars of war might be actual scars," Arthur said, with a thought. "The quest could be to gather a rare ingredient in order to craft a healing potion. I've done *loads* of side missions like that in games before."

They all gazed up at the mountains as they drew closer. Bulky figures moved around both campsites. One was populated by dark-clothed individuals with wide hats and long jackets. In the other, soldiers were dressed in heavy furs and large helmets.

"Can I borrow the binoculars?" Cecily asked. Handing Cloud to Ren, she took the binoculars off Arthur and peeked through them. "Interesting... One camp is flying a skull and crossbones. Do you think they're pirates? The other camp's banner is triangular with tassels on. It has the image of a bird – a raven." Lowering the binoculars, she bit her lip. "I think the raven is a Viking symbol. My parents did the hair for a Viking-inspired fashion show once, and there was raven-patterned stuff everywhere."

Arthur hadn't expected the fact that Cecily's mum and dad were famous hair stylists to be so helpful. He glanced over his shoulder at the shrinking beach. Some of the burned-out boats were the right shape for Viking longships and others might easily be the remains of small rowing boats that could have cast off from a pirate's galleon, moored further up the coast. "Perhaps it's Vikings versus pirates? The boats and weapons seem to fit."

"I wonder who's up there," Cecily said, squinting at the distant camps. "I've heard of a few legendary pirates – Anne Bonny, Calico Jack. Maybe this place is like the Land of Outlaws and we have to decide who we want to side with: the pirates or the Vikings."

Arthur wondered if "neither" was an option. He didn't know much about legendary Vikings, but he was pretty sure they all had names like Eric the Bloodthirsty and Ivar the Bonecrusher – not the kind of people they wanted as enemies *or* allies.

As they trekked towards Yesenia, they passed the openings of several caves in the base of the mountains. The ground around them was impacted by hundreds of muddy footprints and some caves had flags posted outside – either a skull and crossbones, or the raven banner. "Do you think the two armies appear out of those caves?" Ren asked, warily. "They might lead up to the clifftops, where the camps are."

Despite wearing a coat as warm as a duvet, Arthur shivered. He hoped they were back in Atlantis when the next battle commenced. Turning into slime might actually be favourable to being sliced in half with a Viking axe. "Let's just get the information we need and get out of here," he said, treading faster.

In her luminous yellow outfit, Yesenia was like a beacon against the snow. She was sat on an upturned Viking shield as they approached, studying her quest-map through what looked like a pair of X-focal sunglasses. Her pale hair had been pulled into a neat bun and the apples of her cheeks glowed rose pink. Snowflakes dusted the Magmaflo-3000 holstered at her hip. "Can't you three find another patch of ice to clown around on?" she asked, keeping her gaze fixed on her map. "You're ruining my view."

"We need to talk to you," Cecily said, earnestly. "It's important."

"*This* is important. Anyway, I've got nothing to say to you."

Arthur tried to bite back his frustration. "Look, we know what you were keeping in your room, and why someone came looking for it," he chanced. "We want to strike a deal."

"I honestly don't know what you're talking about," Yesenia responded, glancing at something to her left. "As I explained to the UGP, nothing was taken from my room. Most likely, the intruder was a fan who wanted a picture."

"And would that fan's name be *Deadlock*, by any chance?" Cecily asked. Arthur couldn't see Yesenia's expression behind her sunglasses, but her neck tensed. "We know that three of Deadlock's raiders delivered a device to you yesterday, before the tournament opened."

Yesenia shot another look to her left, crushed her quest-map in one hand and pushed up her X-focals. "What do you want?" she snapped, glaring at them.

"The device they gave you belongs to us," Cecily lied. "We want it back. We propose a deal: if you tell us where the device is, we'll guarantee you survive the next elimination by completing our quest slower than you complete yours."

Out of the corner of his eye, Arthur glimpsed the outline of a drone hovering to Yesenia's left. It was covered in some sort of reflective material that made it almost impossible to spot, but Yesenia must have noticed it. That was why she kept looking in that direction.

"Ha!" Yesenia barked with laughter. "What's to say that won't happen anyway? I'm a thirteen-times isports champion. I have nothing to fear from the likes of you."

"If you'd figured out how to complete your quest, you wouldn't still be sitting here studying your quest-map," Arthur observed. "We already know how to win our Irontide gauntlets." He remembered Yesenia telling Lazarus Sloane that she prides herself on her reputation and added, "All your fans are watching. Do you really want to give them cause to doubt you?"

Irritation flashed in Yesenia's eyes. For a moment, Arthur thought she might reach for her gun and blast him, but the corners of her mouth twitched. "Fine. I'll tell you about the device you're seeking in there, away from Savage Strike." She nodded to a nearby cave.

There was no flag posted outside, and no footprints stamped around the entrance, so Arthur didn't think it could be used by the pirates or Vikings. He glanced at Ren and Cecily, who nodded. "All right," he agreed. "Quickly."

The cave was small and empty. The temperature inside was a few degrees warmer than out on the battlefield, and, bizarrely, the air smelled of vanilla and fresh lilies. Arthur, Ren and Cecily positioned themselves just inside the entrance, while Yesenia stood opposite, with her hands on her hips and her back to the battlefield.

"I don't know how you survived the first two eliminations," Yesenia admitted. "But somehow you're still here. Do you know what that means?"

"That we're better questers than you thought we were?" Cecily hazarded.

Arthur shrugged, wishing Yesenia would just hurry up and tell them about the time-key.

"It means you're making me look average," Yesenia continued. "And when I win this tournament – which I inevitably will – it won't feel as satisfying. There's no glory in defeating children." She lifted her chin. "The only way to salvage any kind of respect is not just to beat you, but to crush you. To annihilate you."

Arthur sensed her change of tone too late. Before he could do anything to stop her, she skidded outside, snatched her Magmaflo-3000 from its holster and aimed it at a spot above the cave entrance. The weapon fired an unbroken stream of sizzling molten rock that struck the mountain with a loud hiss.

Thunder rumbled as the entrance collapsed and a choking cloud of steam and snow filled the air.

"Get further back inside the cave!" Cecily shouted, grabbing Cloud. "Go!"

17

The wind outside fell silent. Coughing snow out of his mouth, Arthur swung the rucksack off his shoulder and fumbled through it in the pitch black, searching for a head torch.

"Is everyone OK?" Cecily asked breathlessly.

"Still alive," Ren sputtered. "Arthur?"

"Yeah. Just." His fingers finally found a torch, and he twisted on the bulb.

His heart crumpled when he saw their surroundings. The cave entrance was *gone*. In its place stood a monstrous barrier of rock and ice, dribbling crumbs of snow. Judging by the height of the ceiling, they'd retreated at least ten metres inside the cave, and yet the wall blocking their exit was only a few steps away ... which meant it had to be as thick as a double-decker bus.

Ren's face paled. "We can't dig our way out of that!"

"I should have known Yesenia would double-cross us," Arthur said bitterly, feeling annoyed with himself for trusting her. "We should have suspected foul play when she agreed to our trade. She's our opponent; of course she deceived us."

Cloud gave an uppity bark that sounded a lot like, *I told you so*, and chose that particular moment to shake the moisture off his coat, covering them with icy droplets. Arthur felt they probably deserved it.

"It's done now," Cecily muttered, glancing at a drone hovering beside her. It must have been damaged during the blast because part of its reflective coat was missing. "We still have to remain in the tournament if we're to have any chance of retrieving the time-key. Come on, let's find a way out of here."

Pushing aside the Irontide helmet, Arthur rooted around in their bag for the other two head torches and passed them to Ren and Cecily before putting on his own.

Illuminated by their three torch beams, the cave grew in size. It was roughly as big as their school library, with dark granite walls and a ceiling of jagged stalactites that reminded Arthur uneasily of the rock blasters in Deadlock's warehouse. The impact of the explosion at the entrance had revealed a metal door at the back, labelled *STAFF*. It was hanging open and sparks flew from the handle.

"That way, I guess," he said. As he went to shoulder the rucksack, Ren stopped him.

"I'll carry that. It's your turn to take a break."

He gave her a grateful smile and helped her put it on.

Venturing through the door, they found themselves in

a long, carved tunnel. The rocky walls were covered with wire mesh, and electric lights sputtered on overhead as they passed.

"Hey, look," Cecily said, pointing behind them. "I don't think they can follow us in here."

The drone that had been watching them was hovering beyond the doorway. "Maybe because this is an area for staff, *The Lazarus Show* doesn't have permission to film here?"

Cecily led the way as they proceeded towards the other end of the tunnel. Out of the wind, it felt warm enough for them to remove their gloves. Arthur rubbed his frozen cheeks, trying to get the blood back to them. His nose was so cold he was surprised he could still smell the scent of vanilla and fresh lilies in the air. He wondered what was causing it.

At the end of the tunnel, they came to a T-junction. Cloud whimpered.

"It's all right, buddy," Arthur said, reaching down to stroke him. "These corridors must lead somewhere. We'll find a way out."

Shining her torch on the ground, Ren stiffened. "Actually, I don't think that's what the Fuzzball is worried about – look."

There were wet footprints on the floor.

Big ones.

Arthur spread his hand next to one of them. The impression was at least twice as wide and three times as long. "There's only one legendary creature I can think of that lives in the snow and has feet this huge," he said, swallowing.

He caught a strong whiff of vanilla and fresh lilies and then a deep voice at his back growled, "That's right. A *yeti*."

His blood froze. He spun around and came face to belly with a three-metre-tall grey, hairy beast. It had long arms that hung past its knees and a row of razor-sharp incisors that protruded over its black lips. A terrified squeak left Arthur's throat.

"RUN!" Ren yelled.

They all pumped their arms as they sprinted away, but Arthur soon realized he couldn't hear the yeti pursuing them. A glance behind told him the creature hadn't moved. It was just stood there, watching ...

... and it was wearing clothes – a pink velour tracksuit monogrammed with the initials *TD*. Arthur must have been too terrified to notice before.

Slowing down, he called to the others, "Wait, I don't think it wants to eat us!" As they came to a twitchy stop, Arthur waved at the yeti. "Err ... hello?"

The yeti smiled, revealing a mouth of impeccably white teeth. "Hello! You must be lost!" Its voice was gruff but well enunciated. "You're going the wrong way if you want to get out of here. That's a dead end."

Arthur had to pinch himself. He was talking to a yeti. "I don't suppose you could show us the way out, could you?"

The yeti sniffed the air. "You're humans?"

"That's right..." Arthur said uncertainly. "My name's Arthur. This is Ren, Cecily and Cloud."

The tunnel trembled as the yeti stomped towards them. Arthur had to fight the urge to run.

"I'm Teréze Dufour!" the yeti announced. Closer, Arthur saw that her shaggy fur was styled into delicate curls around her face. "You might have heard of me? I won a Golden Ragger for my portrayal of a clay monster last season."

Arthur tried not to stare at Teréze's huge claws. "Umm, we don't know what a Golden Ragger is. Sorry."

"You don't? Oh, well, the Golden Raggers are only *the* most prestigious awards for performances in I-RAGs!" Teréze explained, batting a furry hand through the air.

"Performances?" Arthur frowned. "You mean, you're an actor?"

Teréze beamed. "You thought I was a *real* yeti? Oh, how fabulous! No, in Legendarium, human roles are portrayed by mimics, but the creature roles are always played by actors. Come on, I'll tell you more about it on the way. It's a long walk out of here."

And so with Teréze Dufour as their guide, the group hiked back past the T-junction and along the left-hand tunnel, forging deeper into the mountain.

"If she's an actor, is she wearing a costume?" Ren whispered in Arthur's ear. She cocked her head, as if looking at Teréze from a different angle might make everything clear.

"I don't think so," Arthur said, keeping his voice low. "I think people from her planet are just big and hairy like that."

Up ahead, Teréze smoothed down her tracksuit. "Sorry about the loungewear – you caught me on a break. The yeti isn't scheduled to appear for another hour. When I heard you in the tunnels, I thought I'd investigate." She guided them around a corner into a wider passageway. "It'll be quicker if we cut through my dressing cave. This way."

They entered a large ice cavern with glowing blue walls. An ornate gold-framed mirror hung over a table on one side with a yeti-sized chair tucked underneath. All manner of curling, brushing and volumizing hair tools were strewn on top, along with several bottles of the same perfume. Arthur could smell the fragrance already – vanilla and fresh lilies.

"Are these your awards?" Cecily asked, passing several shelves cut into the icy wall. A collection of glittering statuettes – both real and holographic – were on display. Arthur skimmed a few of the trophy bases:

Best Beast 2491

Scream of the Year Runner-Up 2490

Queen of Monsters Silver Medal 2487.

Teréze brushed a lock of silvery hair away from her face. "That's just a few of them. I mostly get cast as monsters, although my dream is to play a hero."

Arthur wondered if she'd ever seen *Shrek*.

"I think you'd make a great hero," Cecily told her earnestly.

Teréze beamed. Her gaze fell on the quest-map swaying around Ren's neck. "Here, let me show you where you're going to reappear outside." Ren lifted the map closer and Teréze pointed with one of her claws. "There. Right at the heart of the Viking camp."

"The V-Viking camp," Arthur stuttered. "Are you sure there's no other exit?"

"Afraid not. That's the only one."

As Teréze guided them out of her dressing cave and into another tunnel, Arthur wondered how they were going to complete the quest and get back to Atlantis. He noticed on the quest-map that the Irontide gauntlets had been drawn clasping each other. Perhaps it was a clue. *"You will find your quest is ended when the scars of war are mended,"* he repeated. "Maybe to win a pair of Irontide gauntlets, we have to *stop* the war between the pirates and Vikings? Make them shake hands?"

"That could be it!" Ren said. "But how? We all saw how much battle debris there was. The two sides must have been fighting for ages."

"Conflict resolution is about getting both sides to see things from the other's perspective," Cecily said sagely. "We just have to help them understand."

Arthur remembered that their Irontide helmet would be working now they were in a quest-land, and wondered if it could prove useful. "Ren, slow down. I want to try something." He unfastened the top of the rucksack and retrieved the helmet. "All right, now tell me if anything weird happens when I put this on." After slipping off his head torch, he tugged the helmet over his head. It felt tight at first but just like with the Irontide boots, it seemed to adjust until it was a perfect fit. "Well?"

Cecily studied him carefully. "Nope, nothing. You look exactly the same."

But *Cecily* didn't look the same.

True, Arthur could see her as normal, but he could also see another version of her shimmering above, like a mirage. The new version was dressed in a sharp navy-blue suit and carried a small box with a distinctive gold medal inside. Arthur knew what it was because he'd seen one before in the Wonderscape. A Nobel Peace Prize.

"The helmet has ... done something to my vision," he told them, trying to make sense of it. "I can see ... I don't know what exactly, but Cecily's holding a Nobel Peace Prize."

"I am?" Cecily stared at her hands.

"Maybe the helmet shows the future?" Ren guessed. "I can imagine you winning a Nobel Peace Prize someday."

Cecily's cheeks flushed. "I doubt it. Nobel prizes are awarded to people who do great things that have a huge impact on the world."

"You shouldn't doubt yourself, little human," Teréze remarked, coming to an abrupt halt. "You have the power to achieve whatever you want, if you try hard enough." She tapped Arthur on the head. "What do you see when you look at me?"

Teréze's mirage was wearing a floaty pastel-blue evening gown and clutching a star-shaped trophy with the words *BEST ACTOR IN AN I-RAG – HERO* etched on the base. "You've won an award for best hero," Arthur described. "The trophy looks like a star."

"Really?!" Teréze squealed and jumped, landing with a resounding *thud*. "That's a Golden Ragger statue! I'm going to get my wish!"

Arthur surveyed Ren, but her mirage was blurry. He tried to adjust the fit of the Irontide helmet, but it didn't improve things.

"Is there something wrong?" she asked.

"I'm not sure. I can't see your future for some reason; it's all foggy."

A line appeared on Cecily's brow. "Pass the helmet here. Let me take a look." Wearing the helmet, she examined them both. Arthur squirmed under her gaze, uncomfortable with what she might see.

"I don't think the helmet shows the future," she decided. "I think it just shows what we hope for in the future – our dreams, ambitions and goals."

"Oh." Ren's shoulders fell. "Yeah, that makes sense. It's what I've been arguing about with my mum – my goals. I told her I don't want to do work experience at the garage because I have no interest in being a mechanic, but when she asks me what I am interested in, I draw a blank." She sighed. "I just don't want to disappoint her."

Teréze patted Ren on the shoulder. "I wouldn't worry about that, youngling. Not everyone knows what they want to do when they grow up. I thought I wanted to be a chef when I was your size."

Ren peered up at her. "How old were you when you were my size?"

"Only three, but years are different on my planet." Teréze shook her shaggy head. "The point is, it's OK to feel lost sometimes. You'll get to where you're meant to be in the end. Especially with the support of friends like these."

Cecily pulled off the Irontide helmet and stuffed it back into the rucksack. "I've just had a thought about how we could use the helmet to stop the war," she said. "What if we try to convince the Vikings' leader to wear it? That way, they'll be able to see the hopes and aspirations of all their warriors. The warriors must be tired of the endless fighting. Perhaps if the leader realizes that, it will persuade them to make peace?"

"What if we don't get a chance to give the leader the helmet?" Arthur said. "They might try to kill us on sight!"

Cecily hesitated. "Well, then we're in trouble."

Light flickered up ahead. Arthur heard noise drifting into the tunnel – booming voices and the stomp of heavy feet.

"The exit is down there," Teréze explained. "I'd better return to my dressing cave – I'm on set in thirty minutes. If there are any Irontide competitors still out on the battleground, they're about to get a fright." With a wink, she reached into her pocket and pulled out a wedge of signed photographs. "Please, have one of these. It was a pleasure to meet you."

While Cecily remarked on how lovely Teréze looked in her headshot (her hair was set with pin curls and she was wearing glittery blue lipstick), Arthur slipped the photo into their rucksack. After bidding Teréze farewell, they set off.

"When we emerge in the … uh, Vikings' camp, we stick to Cecily's plan," Arthur said. He could feel his blood pressure rising as he tried to mentally prepare himself. The Vikings might not enjoy having uninvited guests. "Find the Vikings' leader and persuade them to wear the Irontide helmet."

A battle horn blared in the distance and the ground trembled, making Cloud whimper.

"And what if that goes wrong?" Ren asked, fiddling nervously with the straps on the rucksack. "How will we escape?"

Arthur swallowed. He doubted they'd be able to outrun a horde of trained warriors.

"You heard what Teréze told us," Cecily said, gathering Cloud into her arms with a determined frown. "We have the power to achieve whatever we want, if we try hard enough. That means we can do this."

Ren had to force their rucksack ahead of them as they wriggled through a narrow hole and surfaced beside the snow-dusted canvas of an A-frame tent. Evening had fallen and the Vikings' camp was lit by flaming braziers. The air was clouded with smoke, and freezing wind whistled through the tents, carrying the stench of cooked meat. Brawny male and female warriors tramped purposefully in all directions, carrying longswords and round wooden shields. A few were busy dressing themselves in chainmail armour or affixing leather scabbards to their belts. They *all* had magnificent beards.

Seeing the size of some of their weapons, Arthur almost crawled back inside the tunnel. "I don't think they've spotted us yet," he hissed, yanking off his head torch and stuffing it in his pocket.

"Good," Ren said, staring at an enormous axe resting against a nearby tent. "I hope it stays that way."

Cecily placed a hand on Arthur's shoulder, pushing him into a crouch. "Maybe if we keep our heads down, we'll be able to move around unnoticed? They seem too busy to pay us any attention."

Cecily was right. Everyone was focused on their tasks with a hurried purpose, like they were running out of time. It wasn't till Arthur heard the sound of pounding drums that he realized what was going on.

The fighting was about to begin.

18

Drums boomed all around, making the tents tremble. With renewed speed, the Vikings rushed to finish their battle preparations, pulling on helmets and grabbing swords.

Arthur, Ren and Cecily flattened themselves into the shadows as a line of warriors stomped past, snorting into the frigid air.

"How are we going to find their leader?" Ren whispered.

Arthur's heart beat out of his chest as he hoped they weren't spotted. "I don't know. Maybe they're in a special tent, making plans for the battle? We'll have to look around."

"We'll stand out too much if we try sneaking about in these clothes," Cecily said, pulling on the collar of her thermal coat. She signalled to an abandoned tent across from them, with animal skins drying outside. "Over there – let's get a disguise."

They waited till the coast was clear before dashing across a muddy footpath and hurrying inside the tent. Various animal furs and strips of hide were hanging over a cold stone brazier filled with charcoal, in the centre. The place reeked of leather and cooking oil. Cecily unhooked a couple of grey wolf furs and tossed one each at Ren and Arthur. "Put these on."

Arthur guessed the fur was artificial because it was incredibly light and had a fluffy texture that reminded him of an old dressing gown. "Do you really think this will help us blend in?" he asked, draping it over his shoulders.

"That, and the beards," Cecily said, running her finger around the sooty edge of the brazier. "Come here and I'll smudge one on you. If we keep to the shadows, the Vikings shouldn't notice a difference."

She rubbed charcoal over Arthur's chin and upper lip, then did the same to Ren. Arthur was worried that they'd both end up looking like messy toddlers who'd just eaten chocolate cake, but Cecily had done such a good job of shaping Ren's beard that it actually looked passable.

"If we somehow manage to survive all this," Cecily said, applying soot to her own face, "I don't *ever* want to be reminded of this moment."

"Wouldn't dream of it," Arthur said, trying not to grin.

Cloud tilted his head to one side, inspecting them all.

"I don't think he knows what to make of us," Ren observed. "That's probably a good thing. Come on, let's find the leader's tent."

Cecily bundled Cloud into her arms (there was no way to disguise him) and they ventured back outside.

Around the camp, the noise and activity had intensified. The stomp of heavy boots sounded in all directions and shouting filled the sky. Without warning, a bullish warrior with a plaited blond beard shoved past Cecily, almost knocking her over. "Ouch!" she muttered, rubbing her arm.

But the warrior paid her no attention.

"Our disguises seem to be working," Ren said. "Which way?"

Arthur glanced in either direction. Ten metres to their right, the tents ended perilously close to the cliff edge. The battleground beyond was a wide expanse of darkness, and on the opposite side of the valley Arthur could see the fires of the pirates' camp flickering against the mountains. "This way," he said, turning left. "Let's aim for the centre of camp."

They waded as fast as they could through the mud and ice, darting into the shadows whenever necessary to avoid Vikings. The site was easily as big as a football pitch and because it had been constructed on the side of a mountain, you occasionally had to climb a ladder or scramble up a boulder to get into the next area. Through a few open tent flaps, Arthur spotted straw-filled beds, wicker baskets stuffed with grain and fish being smoked over hot coals. He wondered if this was how real Viking warriors had lived, all those years ago.

At one point, the group came across a tent that looked different from all the others. Steam rose through a hole in its straw roof and there was a stone-built well outside. Ren pulled back part of the canvas and poked her head in.

"Anything?" Arthur asked, as a cloud of vapour escaped from inside.

Ren drew her head back quickly. "Vikings," she said, her eyes wide. "Big, hairy half-naked ones."

They all shuddered.

"It must be a sauna," Cecily said. "Let's keep searching."

Eventually, they spotted a prominent red tent with a pair of spear-wielding guards stood outside. Both of them had curly ginger beards decorated with iron beads. "That looks promising," Arthur said. "Let's check it out."

They snuck around the back to search for a way in. Cecily kicked at one of the tent pegs. "We'll have to take this out and crawl under..."

But her voice died as one of the guards appeared around the side of the tent, pointing his spear. "Oi! What are you doing by the king's tent?"

The king? Arthur made a panicked about-turn, only to find the other guard had crept up behind them. "You're not going anywhere," he said, poking Arthur's wolf fur with the end of his spear. "*Theft* is punishable by death."

Arthur edged away, his stomach doing somersaults. He looked frantically for escape routes but they were surrounded by tents and the guards were blocking the only exits.

Cecily pushed back her shoulders and said in a steely voice, "We need to talk to your king urgently. We have a proposition for him that might prove useful in the upcoming fight."

The nearest guard considered her through the eyeholes of his riveted iron helmet. "Very well. But if you are lying, you will face the king's axe."

After the guards had ripped away their fur disguises, they marched them around to the front of the red tent and pushed them through the entrance. The air inside stank of mud and sweat, reminiscent of an unwashed PE kit. They shuffled past several racks of wooden bows and gleaming swords until they came to a large, round table spread with a more detailed version of the quest-map. A Viking the size of a grizzly bear stood with his back to them. His wiry blond hair hung in braids over the shoulders of his chainmail coat and an enormous axe hung from his thick leather belt. "There had better be a good reason for this interruption," he growled.

His voice was so deep and hoarse it made Arthur's ribs shake.

"There is," Cecily said, squeezing Cloud's lead as she stepped forward.

"Well?" the king boomed. "You've got yourself an audience with the great Ragnar Lothbrok, now out with it!"

Ragnar's name didn't ring a bell, but Arthur assumed he was a legendary Viking king. As Ragnar turned around,

Arthur noticed two things. First, despite Ragnar's weathered skin and scarred face, he was ruggedly handsome. He had piercing green eyes, a thick blond beard and an ornate chest plate decorated with the image of a serpent. Second – and most interesting – there were several locked cages resting on the floor behind him. Sat inside one of them, with her hands and feet bound by thick ropes, was *Yesenia Colt.*

When Arthur met her gaze, Yesenia scowled and turned away. Whatever she'd done to try to complete her quest must have gone horribly wrong...

Cecily noticed Yesenia, too. "Change of plan?" she hissed to Arthur and Ren. "Maybe we can get Yesenia to tell us where the time-key is, after all?" She lifted her sooty chin to address Ragnar Lothbrok. "Your Majesty, we've come to offer you a trade. We are in possession of a fabled helmet that grants the wearer clear-sightedness in the heat of battle."

The king stroked his golden whiskers, looking intrigued. "A trade, you say?"

Arthur winced, hoping Cecily hadn't just condemned them all to a fate inside one of Ragnar's cages.

"Yes," she said. "In return, we ask for that prisoner."

When Cecily signalled to Yesenia, Ragnar chuckled. "A friend of yours, is she?"

"Something like that," Cecily answered drily. She lifted their Irontide helmet out of the rucksack so the king could inspect it.

Ragnar Lothbrok ran his hands over the helmet's smooth gold skull. "A fine piece of craftsmanship, but I already have a legendary shirt that makes me invincible." He tugged at the silvery fabric under his chainmail. "It was made by my wife, Áslaug. Why should I give up the prisoner for a helmet I don't need?"

Arthur wasn't sure how Cecily could convince him. He wished they knew more about Ragnar's legend.

Cecily's attention fell on the king's mighty axe. "Legend has it that only the most fearsome warrior may wield the helmet's power," she said in a dramatic voice. "If you wear it, you will prove to your men that you are the mightiest of all."

Temptation flickered in Ragnar's gaze. Arthur knew what Cecily was doing: trying to appeal to the king's vanity.

"Why don't you test the helmet's powers?" she ventured. "Put it on and walk around the camp. If you aren't satisfied with the results, then we will leave."

Ragnar laughed, pushing out his huge chest. "Child, if I'm not satisfied with the results, I shall take you three as my prisoners. Guards!"

Something sharp prodded Arthur between the shoulder blades, and he turned round to find one of the guards' spears pointing directly at his chest. A cold sweat broke out at the back of his neck. Apparently, the deal was done.

"This could be exactly what happened to Yesenia," Ren hissed as they were led outside. "What are we going to do if the helmet doesn't convince Ragnar to end the war with the pirates?"

"I don't know," Arthur admitted, glancing warily at a few of Ragnar's men. "If we try to make a run for it, we'll be caught."

Ragnar tramped into a muddy clearing beyond his tent and brusquely tugged on the Irontide helmet. Watching from a few metres away, Arthur held his breath.

The camp was still a frenzy of activity as warriors prepared for war. Weapons clashed, armour clinked, fires hissed and sizzled. Ragnar surveyed the scene slowly. As his gaze passed over his guards, he did a double-take.

"What's this, Einar?" he asked, gruffly. "You appear to be holding a plough instead of an axe. And is that a basket of cabbages at your feet?"

The guard's cheeks went the colour of rhubarb. "I…"

Ragnar gave a deep, hearty laugh. "This must be a jester's helmet! Helgi, you're covered in flour and wearing an apron!"

The king's other guard studied his feet, the tips of his ears going pink.

"How will this foolishness help me in battle, girl?" Ragnar demanded.

Cecily stepped forward nervously. "The helmet allows you to see people's wishes for the future," she explained. "It shows you what *could* be if you weren't all here, fighting."

"Not fighting?!" The king stuck out his chest. "Einar, what is she talking about? Speak up!"

Einar cleared his throat. "My father runs a cabbage farm back home. It's beautiful there. I've always harboured the ambition to have one of my own someday."

"You *have*?" Ragnar frowned. "And you, Helgi? Your hope is to be a baker?"

"Bread is my life," Helgi replied firmly.

Ragnar grew more flustered as he looked around. "Do none of you dream of being mighty warriors? Of charging onto a battlefield with fire in your heart and blood in your mouth?"

A chorus of clinks and clatters filled the camp as Ragnar's warriors downed tools and conversations hushed. One of them – a woman with a fluffy grey beard who was wielding a longsword – shuffled forward and dug the point of her blade into the earth. "I've always wanted to be a jewellery-maker," she admitted.

"A cloth merchant," said another.

"A shipbuilder!"

"A fisherman!"

Ragnar's shoulders dropped as, one by one, his men and women declared what they'd rather be doing with their lives.

Cecily gazed at him, her eyes shining with hope. "They dream of peace, Your Majesty. And you can give it to them."

"Aye," Ragnar said, a quiver of emotion in his voice. "And they are good and loyal. They deserve happiness." He peered up at the dark sky. "Perhaps we have lingered here too long. Truth be told, I can't remember why we started fighting the pirates in the first place. It would be good to go home, to see my family." With a heavy sigh, he nodded at Cecily. "You have told the truth: your helmet *does* give the wearer clear-sightedness." He signalled to Einar and Helgi. "One honourable deed deserves another. Give them their prisoner."

Cheering erupted around camp. Axes were hurled into the air and warriors started singing. Arthur crumbled with relief.

"Wait!" Cecily said, as the guards headed back into the tent. "Don't release her just yet. We have some questions for her first."

"What will you do about the pirates?" Arthur asked Ragnar, curiously.

"Those scurvy dogs?" The Viking king pulled off the Irontide helmet and stroked his beard. "I suppose I'll have to negotiate peace with Blackbeard. Perhaps I'll offer him your helmet…"

Maybe it was just Arthur's imagination, but as the king marched off towards the pirates' camp, his steps seemed lighter.

Cecily grabbed Arthur's sleeve. "Come on – we've got to talk to Yesenia. As soon as Ragnar and Blackbeard shake hands, the quest will be complete and we'll return to the Bermuda Triangle."

They rushed back inside the red tent, where they found Yesenia trying to wriggle out of her ropes. "I bet you're loving this," she said. "But don't think for a second that this makes you better than me. This was just a fluke."

Cecily smiled sweetly. "I think Lazarus Sloane will call it a 'major upset'."

As much as Arthur wanted to relish their reverse of fortunes, he knew they didn't have time. "We'll release you on one condition: tell us where the device is that the raiders gave you."

"I *can't*," Yesenia said. "I don't have it any more. It wasn't working properly."

No surprises there, Arthur thought. He wondered what Yesenia would have done if she'd realized her evader was actually a time machine. Nothing good, probably.

"So, what did you do with it?" Ren asked, kicking the corner of Yesenia's cage.

Yesenia shot her a hateful look. "I complained to Deadlock. I was about to return the device and collect a refund when it was stolen from my room."

"So … it could be anywhere by now," Arthur realized. Panic rose in his chest as he combed back through Yesenia's story. "You said you complained to Deadlock. How?"

Yesenia shifted on her bottom. "I wrote a message on a slip of paper. Three words. All capitals. I tucked it inside a popcorn box and left it in Seat 645a of the Kraken stadium. That's how Deadlock communicates."

Before Arthur could process the information, the sound of a gong travelled through the air, making the tent walls vibrate.

There was a rustle as one of Ragnar's men poked his beard in. "There's a pair of gauntlets floating in the middle of camp, right near the hog roast," he grunted, sounding annoyed. "Ragnar says they belong to you."

19

Paparazzi pushed and shoved on the balcony overlooking the Bermuda Triangle. "Young Pipsqueaks, over here!" one shouted. "Why did you help Yesenia Colt? Have you struck a deal?"

Arthur barely heard them. With his arms hung limply at his sides and snow melting off his thermal layers, he felt as miserable as he probably looked. "What are we going to do?" he whispered. "Whoever stole the time-key from Yesenia's room could be anywhere in the Known Universe by now."

Cloud whined and flopped onto the floor, symbolizing how they all felt.

"Here comes the next one," Ren said as a quest-map materialized a metre away in mid-air. Arthur reached over and caught it before it landed in one of the puddles at their feet.

The map was made of linen and hand-drawn in rust-red ink. After brushing a few grains of sand off the surface,

Arthur saw it depicted a rocky desert landscape with a canyon to the west and dunes in the south. Scrawled at the top were the words:

LEGENDARIⓋM

– *THE LAND OF SLEEPING KINGS* –

**Answer well the one who calls
and you shall find the hidden walls.**

Cecily peered over his shoulder. "I can't think of a legend to do with sleeping kings. What do you think those notes are about?"

There were annotations written around the edge of the map, with arrows connecting them to different areas in the desert:

Trekked to these mountains, but no sign of Z.

Could Z be here?

Trader reports seeing Z from here.

"Sounds like whoever wrote them is searching for this Z." Arthur noticed that the next component of Irontide armour – whatever it was – wasn't marked anywhere on the map and wondered if it was located wherever Z was hidden.

"It's them!" a voice called, from across the hall.

Arthur thought at first that a Young Pipsqueaks fan had found them, until he saw Milo Hertz dashing towards them, juggling three paper-wrapped bundles and a monster-sized bag of fried seaweed crisps. Archimedes jogged at his side, balancing a cup-holder filled with three *Nice as π* mugs.

"You're all right." Milo's eyes shone with relief as he reached them. "Any injuries?"

They all shook their heads. Cecily held up the Irontide gauntlets that they'd collected from the middle of the Viking camp. "We did a thing."

Archimedes smiled and handed them each a mug. "In that case, these can be your rewards. Hot chocolate from the coffee machine on the third floor – my own secret recipe."

"And this is brain fuel," Milo said, allocating the paper-wrapped bundles and bursting open the packet of seaweed crisps.

The bundle was soft and warm. Inside, Arthur found what he suspected was a twenty-fifth-century burger. It had a fluffy white bun dusted with diamond-shaped grey seeds, a crispy green patty and a sticky brown sauce that smelled like cold Chinese takeaway. Hungry, Arthur took a tentative bite. It tasted surprisingly good.

"What happened in there?" Milo asked, lowering his voice. "It looked pretty tense between you and Yesenia Colt."

Ren glanced left and right, checking no paparazzi were within earshot. She warmed her hands on the mug of hot chocolate, letting the steam rise into her face. "We discovered the raiders delivered the time-key to Yesenia

Colt," she relayed with a heavy sigh. "She was due to return it to Deadlock when it was stolen earlier today."

"Stolen by who?" Archimedes asked.

Arthur was about to tell Archimedes that they didn't have the foggiest, until he realized that wasn't strictly true. "I suppose that's what we've got to work out. Deadlock could have just stolen it back to avoid giving Yesenia a refund."

"I'm not so sure," Milo said, with a shake of his head. "Breaking into the hotel seems too risky with all the cameras and UGP around. It would be far safer to let Yesenia return the device."

"I guess one of the raiders could have stolen it for themselves?" Cecily ventured. "Although ... they all seem terrified of Deadlock, and none of them really knew what the time-key was."

Ren drummed her fingers against the side of her mug. "There's only one other person who's definitely aware of the device's existence – the engineer who built it."

"That's if Deadlock didn't build it themselves..." pointed out Arthur.

"Right, but say there is another engineer, why would they steal it back?" Cecily said. "If they wanted the device for themselves, they wouldn't have given it to Deadlock in the first place."

Milo shrugged. "Perhaps they realized too late that someone like Deadlock shouldn't have a time-key?"

He was talking from experience, Arthur knew. It was only after inventing the time-key that Milo had understood how dangerous it was. Maybe the new time-key engineer felt the same. Arthur took a sip of his hot chocolate – which was caramel-sweet with just a hint of spice – and thought carefully. "Our next move should be to investigate Yesenia's break-in. Hopefully, whoever stole it wasn't a very good thief, and they left behind some clues."

"Excellent plan," Milo said, opening his faze display. "We've still got twenty-three hours before … well, you know. Did you get my message earlier? I've narrowed down the location of Deadlock's base to somewhere in Legendarium. I still can't pinpoint where it is exactly, but I'm working on it."

"I don't know if this will help, but Yesenia told us how Deadlock communicates," Arthur said and relayed the details.

Milo took notes on his faze. "Yes, that's useful. I can send a drone to stake out that part of the Kraken in case someone comes sneaking around. You never know, they could lead me right to Deadlock's base."

Out of the corner of his eye, Arthur spied Griffon Ramsay watching them from across the hall. He must have just escaped from the Land of Beards because he was wearing a thick black ski jacket and clutched a pair of Irontide gauntlets in his right hand. Arthur's nerves bristled as he shuffled closer to the others for protection. Griffon must know by now that Arthur had trapped him in the Land of the Lost, and probably wanted retribution...

"Come on," Ren said, downing the last of her hot chocolate. "We should get back to the hotel and search the crime scene."

"I don't think so," Milo voiced, in a tone reminiscent of Arthur's dad. "There's still an hour till the midnight elimination and you three need to get some sleep before you collapse. I'll do some digging into the break-in. You can meet me outside my hotel room at 8 a.m. tomorrow and I'll let you know what I find out."

Ren opened her mouth to argue, but seemed to lose the will. Arthur could see the tiredness in her eyes. "Yes, coach."

"While you're all asleep, is there anything *I* can do?" Archimedes asked, gathering everyone's empty mugs.

Being a mimic, Archimedes didn't need to sleep. Arthur handed him the quest-map for the Land of Sleeping Kings. "If it's within the rules, maybe you could find out what Z is?" he suggested. "If we're to stay in the tournament past midday tomorrow, we'll need to know."

20

Arthur woke to the feel of a smooth, wet tongue being dragged up his cheek. He lifted open one eyelid to find Cloud panting in his face. The dog's breath smelled like car exhaust, but Arthur figured that was normal for a mimic.

For a blissful second, he wasn't sure where he was – the four-poster bed, the pine-green carpet, the tartan curtains...

Then a humped shadow snaked over the wallpaper and, with a shudder, everything came back to him:

He was in a Loch-Ness-monster-themed hotel, *inside* an in-reality adventure game, more than four hundred and seventy years in the future.

He pushed himself up on his elbows and saw his faze display was still open in front of him. He'd been watching news reports about Yesenia Colt's break-in before he'd dozed off.

Footsteps clomped outside his door, then a knock. "Arthur? Are you awake?"

Cecily. She sounded tired.

"Yeah. You OK?"

She sighed. "I can't sleep."

"OK, gimme a sec." His legs wobbled as he slipped them out of bed and stood up. After all the trekking and stair-climbing yesterday, his muscles felt like glue. He pulled on one of the complimentary Hotel Loch Ness dressing gowns he'd found in his wardrobe, and headed into the lounge area of their suite.

Cecily was pacing up and down in front of the fireplace. A bleary-eyed Ren sat watching her from one of the armchairs. *The Lazarus Show* was playing on mute on the holoscreen above the fireplace. The clock read 7.06 a.m.

"Yesenia made it through to the next stage of the tournament," Ren said. "The Savage Strike team were eliminated at midnight, so it's only Griffon, Yesenia and us remaining."

"You haven't been watching holovision since midnight, have you?" Arthur asked, feeling unexpectedly guilty for actually getting some sleep.

Ren yawned. "No, they repeat the tournament headlines every hour and we've been up since the last one." She nodded to a room-service trolley in the corner. "We ordered breakfast. The skullfruit muffins taste all right, but don't try the merberry marmalade. It's nasty."

Arthur wasn't particularly hungry, but given that he didn't know what they might face in the next thirteen hours, he decided to eat something. He lifted up a silver cloche on the trolley to find pink-iced muffins, pastries shaped like little bows and steaming porridge swirled with something dark and glossy, which he presumed was the merberry marmalade.

"Any thoughts on how we're going to find Yesenia's thief?" Cecily asked, biting a fingernail.

Arthur took one of the pink-iced muffins and sat on the sofa to eat it. There was a skull-shape baked into the top, so he presumed it contained the skullfruit Ren had mentioned. "I watched the news reports again last night. Yesenia's room was found broken into at 10 a.m. yesterday, so the thief must have arrived at some point before that. Perhaps the receptionist saw them sneaking around?"

"Or one of the other guests," Ren voiced. She got up to study the *Emergency Fire Safety and Evacuation Instructions* displayed near their room door. "According to this, the only way in or out of this corridor is via the main stairwell. That means, the thief either travelled up from the lobby or came down from the roof."

Arthur wasn't sure what the hotel roof was like. Perhaps it was connected to an adjoining building that the thief had used to make an escape. "After we've knocked for Milo, let's quiz everyone in the lobby and then explore upstairs. Someone must have seen something."

"We should ask Ribbon, too," Cecily suggested. "The UGP might know more about the theft by now."

Once they'd showered and dressed, Arthur stuffed

the Irontide gauntlets into their rucksack and they set off. Ribbon's room, Number 167, was before Milo's in the coaches' corridor, so they decided to pay her a visit first.

Arthur knocked on her door. "Ribbon, it's Arthur, Ren and Cecily. We need to talk to you…"

But as he did so, Ribbon's door swung inwards. Arthur frowned at the others before poking his head around the side of the door. "Ribbon? Are you OK?"

When nobody replied, they all tentatively walked in.

Ribbon wasn't there. Her bed was roughly made; her wardrobe doors were hanging open, and her bathroom mirror was still foggy. "She could have only just left," Arthur realized. "Perhaps she had to rush off on UGP business?"

"It seems odd that she wouldn't shut the door properly, though," Cecily remarked. "Especially given that the hotel has just had a burglary."

Ren flipped through the folders on Ribbon's desk, all stamped with the UGP's logo. "I'm sure she's OK. The UGP would know if something had happened to her. Do you think we should search around for more information about the break-in? There might be some secret UGP stuff Ribbon can't tell us."

Arthur glanced at the door. He didn't feel right about searching through someone's personal belongings *again*, but with Slimeageddon fast approaching, he decided Ribbon would understand. "OK, but we need to shut the door and be quick. If anyone catches us, we'll be in trouble."

While Ren examined the documents on Ribbon's desk, Cecily searched through Ribbon's bathroom and wardrobes. The task of rifling through the waste-paper bin fell to Arthur, who cringed as he shook out a few empty Novafuel cans and a brown apple core.

There were also a few scraps of paper with words typed on them, but they had to be torn from a larger sheet because they made no sense on their own:

IS THIN / FINISH / PATIENCE / DO NOT / YOU WILL / QUESTION.

"Anything about the break-in in those folders?" he asked Ren.

"Nah, just some designs Ribbon's been working on for the UGP. She's got to be a genius, because they're seriously complicated. Gadgets to stop cheaters, I guess."

Arthur remembered Chief Inspector Doveton saying Ribbon had "unquestionable" talent. Perhaps this was why.

Perching on the end of Ribbon's bed, Cecily swung her legs. "Maybe we should go? We haven't found anything and we've got to meet Milo soon."

But then the heel of her shoe hit something hard under Ribbon's bed and, with a groan, she got down to examine what it was. She dragged a small, black briefcase out into the room. As she tested the clip-locks on the front, Arthur was surprised when they snapped open.

He didn't know what he was expecting as she lifted up the lid; it wasn't red-and-white-striped, flat-pack popcorn boxes.

"Why would Ribbon keep *these* hidden away?" Cecily muttered, flicking through the stack.

It wasn't till Arthur spotted the sea-monster logo on the side of the boxes that it dawned on him. "Those are the popcorn containers they use at the Kraken," he realized. He felt the back of his neck tingle as he remembered Yesenia's instructions for communicating with Deadlock: "Three words. All capitals. I tucked it inside a popcorn box..."

"I think..." He almost couldn't say it. "I think Ribbon's been talking to Deadlock."

Ren dropped the folder she was holding. "No way."

Arthur snatched back the waste-paper bin and fished out the torn scraps of text. They could be either fragments of draft messages *to* Deadlock, or actual messages *from* Deadlock. Spreading them on the floor, he matched their ripped edges together like the pieces of a puzzle:

DO NOT QUESTION / YOU WILL FINISH / PATIENCE IS THIN.

As he read them, he tried to understand what Ribbon and Deadlock had been talking about. "I think these might be from Deadlock. It sounds like they're not happy with Ribbon... They've told her to finish, but finish what?"

Cecily frowned. "Is Ribbon in trouble? Maybe that's the reason she left here in such a hurry?" Her pupils flitted left to right. "You don't think... Could *Ribbon* be the time-key engineer?"

"She's definitely got the brains for it," Ren said, tapping

the files on Ribbon's desk, "and breaking into Yesenia's room would have been easy – that's means and motive."

Cecily shuffled the popcorn boxes back inside the briefcase and snapped it closed. "Come on, we've got to tell Milo."

Leaving Ribbon's door open behind them, they raced along to Milo's room. A bearded man in pale brown cords and a wine-red jumper was stood outside, examining his faze display.

"Archimedes?" Arthur said, as they approached.

The scholar looked up, his cheeks flushed. "Have you heard from Milo? Have you seen him?"

"We're supposed to be meeting him here..." Cecily said uncertainly.

"Then, it's as I feared." Archimedes' bushy brows drew together. "Last night, Milo sent a drone to stake out that seat at the Kraken. When the machine unexpectedly lost power, he went there to investigate." The scholar opened his faze screen and tapped on the surface. "He called me from the stadium. Watch this."

With a flick of his finger, Archimedes flipped around his faze screen. On the surface was a video of Milo sitting in one of the stands of the Kraken. The stadium was dark, with only a few lights illuminating the chairs and exits. Resting on the seat beside Milo was a small, mirrored drone, similar to the ones that had been filming Arthur and the others in the quest-lands.

"Whoever shot this down used cybernetic weapons," Milo was saying. "Archimedes, you know what that means—"

Just then, the camera shook and fell to the floor. Milo gave a muffled shout as heavy footsteps pounded the stands. A pair of buckled black boots appeared in the corner of the frame before everything went black.

Cecily gasped. "Those were raiders' boots! What have they done with Milo?"

Archimedes shook his head. "I don't know, but I've already checked the stadium and there's no trace of him or the drone."

"Deadlock's ruthless," Ren said, worriedly. "If they've discovered that Milo was searching for their base, then Milo's life could be in danger."

Arthur began to feel sick. Not only was Milo their friend and their only way home, he was also the only person capable of stopping Deadlock. "We've got to find out where the raiders have taken him. Without Milo to prevent Deadlock using the time-key, the whole universe is in trouble."

Cecily glanced back along the corridor towards Ribbon's room. "We have to find Ribbon. If she's working for Deadlock, she might have some idea where Milo is being kept."

"Ribbon?" Archimedes looked puzzled.

"We suspect *she's* the time-key engineer," Arthur said.

"What?" Archimedes scratched his beard. "I just saw her at the Great Library. She was on UGP business, heading into the Land of Sleeping Kings."

Arthur glanced at his watch – under twelve hours and counting. "We'll have to follow her. Archimedes, can you keep trying to locate Milo? Ask around the Kraken – I know it was late, but someone might have seen the raiders leaving."

The scholar nodded and reached into his pocket for the tatty linen quest-map they'd given him yesterday. "You'll need this. I think Z refers to Zerzura, a lost oasis somewhere west of the River Nile. A fifteenth-century camel-driver gave a mysterious account of it to the Emir of Benghazi and the legend grew from there."

"Anything else we should know about it?" Arthur asked.

"Yes," Archimedes said. "Apparently it's guarded by giants."

21

The air felt hotter than the inside of an oven. Sweat trickled under Arthur's T-shirt as he pulled down the peak of a YP cap to shade his face from the baking sun.

He'd seen a desert in the Wonderscape, but the scenery in the Land of Sleeping Kings was different. Rather than soft, rolling dunes, a flat sandy plane studded with rocks and prickly grass stretched all the way to the horizon. In the distance, tabletop mountains rose through the shimmering haze, like the sawn-off trunks of giant trees.

It seemed as though they'd arrived in the middle of nowhere until a drone slipped out of the air, watching them.

While Cloud rolled around in the dirt, Ren twirled her ponytail into a bun. "We've got to find Ribbon quickly," she said, securing her hair with an elastic band. "Not only for Milo's sake, but also because the amount we're sweating, we're going to need to drink. And we've only got three bottles of water."

"Where do you think Ribbon is?" Arthur asked. "We haven't seen any UGP officers in the quest-lands before."

"Her job is to stop players cheating, so she's probably stationed near where an important part of a quest happens – like where some Irontide armour appears," Cecily said, unshouldering their rucksack and dumping it on the ground. She retrieved the quest-map from a side pocket. "*Answer well the one who calls and you shall find the hidden walls.* Do you think 'hidden walls' refers to the lost oasis Archimedes told us about – Zerzura?"

Arthur considered the handwritten notes around the map. It sounded like they were written by an explorer searching for Zerzura. "The Irontide armour is probably somewhere inside the oasis. That would explain why it isn't marked on the map." He wasn't sure what the rest of the clue meant – *Answer well the one who calls* – they'd have to work it out on the way.

"That's our task, then: find Zerzura and we'll likely find Ribbon." Ren fished a pair of binoculars out of their bag. As she lifted them to her eyes, the air shifted. There was a loud *crack* and a towering column of light materialized a few metres away. Arthur jumped as a hulking figure in black stepped out of it, wearing a pair of armoured golden gauntlets.

"Griffon…!" Arthur immediately wished he had something to hide behind.

The isports champion gave Arthur a fierce glare, but said nothing. Other than his trademark body armour and energy-baton, he was travelling light, with only a rope and grappling hook dangling from his belt. Adjusting his sunglasses, he surveyed the terrain, pausing for a moment in a southerly direction. He checked his quest-map and broke into a full sprint, heading west, towards the tabletop mountains.

Watching him go, Cecily sighed. "I'd better put on our Irontide gauntlets. Griffon's wearing them already." She reached into her bag and pulled them out. They'd decided not to bring along their Irontide helmet and Irontide boots, figuring that each component was only designed to be used in the next quest.

"Griffon looks like he knows where he's going," Arthur remarked, as Cecily pushed her hands into the gauntlets. Just like with the other components of Irontide armour, the gloves resized to fit her perfectly. "Do you think we should follow him? His quest might have something to do with Zerzura, too."

"Maybe, but if he realizes we're tracking him, he'll only lead us into a trap," Cecily said, marvelling at how dainty-fingered the gauntlets now looked. "You must have noticed how closely he's been watching us – it's like he's plotting revenge."

Arthur remembered the *What Happened to the Pipsqueaks?* book they'd found in Griffon's room and how Griffon had glared at them when they'd arrived back from their first quest. Arthur wasn't sure what the Lone Wolf was planning, but one thing was certain: they couldn't trust him.

Facing south, Ren lifted her binoculars. "I wonder what caught Griffon's attention over here—" Suddenly, she started shaking.

"What is it?" Arthur asked.

"S-sand…"

"Yeah, we can see the sand."

"No, sand*storm*! Coming this way!"

Arthur grabbed the binoculars. No wonder Griffon had sped out of there. A billowing yellow cloud the size of the Kraken shifted on the horizon. It was difficult to judge how fast it was moving because it was so far away, but it was definitely getting bigger. "We need to move – now!"

The sand gave way under Arthur's feet as he ran, making it difficult to stay balanced. Cloud scurried alongside, his ears flattened in panic.

"Put these on," Cecily yelled, tossing Arthur the same tinted goggles he'd worn in the Land of Beards. "They'll protect your eyes if the storm reaches us."

Arthur caught the goggles in mid-air and pulled them over his head. Cecily was being optimistic when she'd said, "if". He could already feel the wind picking up around them. "We need to take cover," he told her. He scanned the landscape. Griffon had vanished and there was no sign of Yesenia, but a small herd of brown-and-white goats were sheltering at the base of a rocky outcrop. In another direction, a figure with a long stick was shepherding a few strays together. "What about over there, under those rocks?"

They altered direction and hurried towards safety. Arthur lifted his knees, trying to pick up speed, but the storm was faster. The wind howled and burning sand spat at his arms and legs.

Ren fetched a rope from the rucksack. "Mountaineers connect themselves to one another with ropes so they don't lose each other in low visibility," she explained, tying the middle of the cord around her waist. She'd just about managed to fasten one end of the rope to Cecily and Cloud when the light dimmed and the air turned brown with dirt.

Wind whipped and snarled around them like a wild animal. Sand blasted Arthur's body, exfoliating any bare areas of skin to baby-smooth levels. He drew his T-shirt up over his mouth, coughing dust from his lungs. He couldn't see more than an arm's length in front of him and briefly wondered how the drones were managing to film anything.

"Ren? Cecily?" He tried to wipe his goggles clean, but in seconds they were filthy again. Panic filled his chest. Without Ren's rope to guide him, he had no idea where the others were, and no hope of finding them again.

But then…

"Arthur!"

It was Ren. He felt her hands patting his back, trying to feel where he was.

Slowly, she threaded the rope around his waist and knotted it securely.

"The rocks are this way," she called, yanking on the rope. "We're almost there. Come on!"

Arthur started to follow the rope when he heard a bleating noise.

Bahhh...

It had to be one of the goats he'd spotted earlier, and it sounded distressed. He remembered what Teréze Dufour had told them, that all animals in Legendarium were real. "Wait!" he cried. "We have to go another way!"

Bahhh! The goat's cries came again, more anguished this time.

"Why?" Ren yelled.

"Just trust me!" Without waiting for an answer, Arthur pulled Ren and Cecily in the direction of the bleating. He didn't want to put his friends' lives in danger, but he couldn't leave the animal to the mercy of the elements – that was just cruel. When they heard the goat, he knew they'd understand.

Bahhh! Bahhh! The goat sounded louder and more desperate than ever. Arthur plodded through the gloom until a shadow appeared in front of him: a mound of rocks, slowly being buried by sand. A small amber-eyed goat with a fuzzy white beard was trembling beside it.

Bahhh, it cried, feebly.

It was only as Arthur got closer that he saw the goat's

hoof was jammed in a fissure between three rocks. "No wonder you're crying," he said, as soothingly as possible. "Don't worry, I'm going to get you out of there."

Arthur examined the rocks with his hands, trying to determine which he needed to move in order to free the goat. He decided the problem was the largest boulder, but it was too heavy for him to lift on his own.

"Arthur, what's going on?" Ren shouted, appearing out of the fog behind him with Cecily and Cloud in tow. Coated head-to-toe in sand, they looked like a family of weird gravel monsters.

"Its foot is stuck," he explained, gesturing to the goat. He couldn't see their expressions behind their sand-masks, but he got the sense they understood. "Can you help me lift this?"

Ren wrapped her arms around the boulder and, with Arthur gripping it from the other side, they both tugged. When the rock didn't budge, Arthur clenched his jaw. "Cecily, we need you, too."

He shuffled aside to give her room. She clasped the boulder with the Irontide gauntlets and they all heaved.

Immediately, something felt different. With a judder, the rock broke free and lifted into the air without Arthur having even to strain. It was like it suddenly weighed no more than a ball of newspaper! He couldn't understand what had happened until he noticed Cecily's Irontide gauntlets *glowing*...

"Whoa!" she cried, her goggles fixed on her hands. "I think these have given me super-strength!"

Arthur and Ren let go of the boulder and Cecily carried it away and put it down. With its hoof released, the goat bleated and stumbled away from the rocks.

And then something incredible happened.

The wind disappeared and every single grain of sand froze in mid-air, like someone had pressed pause on the sandstorm. With a long, dry hiss, the sand fell to the ground in a shower of gold.

Wobbling with shock, Arthur pushed up his goggles.

Stood before them were the dazzling white walls of a city. Palm trees poked over the top and flocks of brightly coloured birds flitted between them.

It could only mean one thing.

They had found the lost oasis of Zerzura.

22

Further along Zerzura's walls, a man wearing a loose cotton tunic, sandals and a white head wrap was patting the neck of a familiar amber-eyed goat.

The man's cool brown skin was weathered with deep wrinkles and in his free hand he carried a long bamboo stick. "Over here, friends!" he called, as he saw them. "Come, have some water! I must thank you for saving my favourite goat!"

Arthur reached for Cecily's shoulder to steady himself. The sandstorm had been so intense, he could barely believe it was over. *"Answer well the one who calls,"* he said, coughing dirt out of his mouth. "The map must have meant the goat. We answered its cries for help – that's why the walls of Zerzura have appeared."

Several other goats were stood chewing at a patch of grass near by, so Arthur guessed the stranger in the sandals was a goatherd. A spout protruded from the wall beside him and water gushed out, glittering in the desert sun. Arthur's mouth felt like sandpaper. He didn't need to be asked twice to have a drink.

The three of them took it in turns to slurp the water. It was cool and clear and tasted as delicious as if it had burst straight from a mountain spring. Once they'd had their fill, they washed the sand off their hands and faces. Arthur was certain that if they ever made it home, he'd be finding grains in his ears and nostrils for weeks. After they were finished, Cloud took a few mouthfuls of water to help cool his inner circuits and Ren did her best to rinse his fur clean under the running stream.

"You don't happen to be a trader, do you?" Cecily asked the goatherd, dusting down her jumpsuit.

"Only if you're interested in goat's milk," the man answered cheerfully. With his laid-back smile and calm tone of voice, he put Arthur at ease instantly.

Accompanied by a herd of goats, he obviously wasn't a quester, which meant he had to be a mimic.

"Are you a *legend*?" Arthur questioned, thinking there must have been some reason they'd needed to save one of *his* goats to find Zerzura.

The goatherd gave a bashful shrug. "Some think so. My name's Kaldi."

"*Kaldi…?*" Cecily frowned. "I swear I've heard that name before."

Arthur extended his hand. "I'm Arthur. This is Ren, Cecily and Cloud. Pleased to meet you."

While Kaldi shook Arthur's hand, Cloud tentatively sniffed at one of Kaldi's sandals.

"Hello there," Kaldi said, reaching down to tickle Cloud under the chin. "You're a curious little chap, aren't you?"

Arthur knew from their experiences in the Land of Outlaws that not all legends were good, but Kaldi didn't strike him as someone they needed to be worried about. "Maybe you could help us, Kaldi? We're looking for a UGP officer named Ribbon Rex. She's a bit taller than Ren with spiky black hair."

"Ribbon Rex…" Kaldi scratched the stubble on his chin. "I don't know the name, but I think I've seen an officer fitting that description. She was in the north-west quarter of Zerzura, by the Sleeping Kings."

The Sleeping Kings… Standing on tiptoes, Arthur gazed over the walls of the oasis, wondering what the city was like. In the midst of the barren desert, it already seemed like something out of a dream.

"I can lead you there if you like," Kaldi offered. "My goats quite enjoy a walk through the oasis – there's always lots of interesting things for them to nibble on."

"Thank you, that would be great," Arthur said. "We're, err, in a bit of a rush, though?"

Kaldi swung his bamboo stick forward and started walking. "Better get going then."

So with Cloud trotting happily among his new goat friends, Kaldi guided the group around Zerzura's walls, towards some large iron gates. They were flanked by a pair of colossal sandstone warriors dressed in heavy armour. It was only as Arthur craned his neck to look up at them, that he remembered Archimedes saying that the oasis was guarded by giants.

"Stay alert," he muttered to Ren and Cecily, suspicious that the statues might come to life. But as they walked between them, the sandstone warriors remained still. Arthur wondered if it would be the same for Griffon or Yesenia, should they pass by...

Through the gates, Zerzura was as idyllic as Arthur had imagined. Pristine white pavements lined the streets; fountains splashed and glittered and birdsong filled the sweet-smelling air. Colourful geometric murals decorated all the walls and every building had a mosaic doorstep crammed with potted flowers. Mimics dressed similarly to Kaldi strolled to and fro, carrying baskets of fruit or freshly folded laundry. It seemed more like a five-star luxury holiday resort than a legendary lost oasis.

Cecily retrieved the quest-map from their rucksack and shook it clean of sand. "Look – Zerzura's appeared on the map now, and so, too, has the Irontide tunic."

Sure enough, a white-walled oasis was visible to the west, in a valley between two mountains. An armoured gold tunic was drawn inside.

As Kaldi guided them around a corner, Arthur's nostrils filled with the aroma of coffee. It reminded him of weekday mornings, when his dad drank espresso while making Arthur's packed lunch.

Gazing along the road, he saw it was full of different coffee shops. Some had shaded balconies where baristas were pouring steaming black coffee from long-spouted golden pots; others served frothy cappuccinos at indoor bars. The shopfronts were all decorated with national-flag bunting, presumably so you could tell which country's coffee they served. Most of the designs Arthur had never seen before, but he recognized the flags of India, Kenya and Colombia. It was like the best coffee houses in the Known Universe had set up residence there. Archimedes would have loved it.

"And I thought having a Starbucks, Nero and Costa in our local high street was over the top," Ren commented, as Kaldi tried to coax one of his goats away from a row of patio plants.

"Strange ... I haven't heard of those companies before." Kaldi shook his head. "It's my fault these places are here. It's my legend."

Cecily's eyes widened. "Now I remember where I've heard the name Kaldi – it's the brand of coffee beans my parents use! Is your legend something to do with coffee? Did you *invent* it?"

The goatherd studied his sandals. "I wouldn't say I invented it, more like I *discovered* it. I noticed that when my goats chewed on the berries of a particular plant, they started bounding around, full of energy. I thought there might be something special about the berries, so I took them to my local monk." His expression tightened. "He said the berries were dangerous and threw them into a fire..."

They all stopped to allow a waiter past, holding an enormous tray of coffee mugs.

"Then what?" Cecily asked.

"The fire roasted the berries," Kaldi recalled, "and the monastery filled with the most wonderful smell. The monk and I raked the roasted berries out the embers, ground them up and added hot water." He added with a nonchalant shrug, "That was the first cup of coffee. It was around AD 850."

"That's amazing," Arthur remarked, glancing back along the road at all the national flags. "I wonder how many people in the universe grow coffee now because of you."

Kaldi looked pensive. "Yes, it's strange to think that one small action can have such an enormous impact."

"See," Ren said, elbowing Cecily. "Little things *do* make a difference. You never know how everything you're doing to fight climate change might influence someone else. Those make-up recycling bins in the toilets, for instance, could encourage other students to recycle more at home. Really, you need to multiply everything you do by twenty to understand how powerful it is."

Cecily smiled and glanced at the Irontide gauntlets. "Yeah … I suppose I do have a super-power. It just isn't as obvious as super-strength."

Just then, a car horn blared behind them. Kaldi's goats bleated and bounded aside as an open-topped four-by-four came hurtling past, throwing up dust from its tyres. Arthur spotted a skull and crossed spanners on the side. "Raiders!" he exclaimed. "What are they doing here?"

"Maybe they've discovered that Ribbon stole the time-key from Yesenia and they've come to take it back?" Ren blurted.

Arthur tensed. They couldn't let that happen. "Thanks for the help, Kaldi," he said, hurriedly, "but we've got to go."

Waving a quick goodbye to the goatherd, the team set off after the raiders. Despite being slower than the four-by-four, they tracked the vehicle easily, following the flocks of green parakeets that exploded into the air whenever it hurtled past.

Soon enough, they caught up to the four-by-four parked in a secluded courtyard at the back of several buildings. The area was bordered by palm trees and potted shrubs, and in the centre stood a magnificent carved stone tomb. Arthur had seen its kind before in old churches. Sculpted on top were the figures of two crowned men, lying with their hands steepled in prayer over their chests.

Sleeping Kings.

"This was where Kaldi said he'd seen Ribbon!" Ren hissed, as they all darted behind the largest shrub they could find and watched three raiders dismount from the four-by-four. Arthur's stomach plunged as he saw who it was: Vorru, Tide and Rultan. Tide had a devious grin on her face; Rultan was fiddling with the cybernetic modification in his arm; and Vorru – as huge and muscly as ever – lumbered after them both, his shoulder-cannon clattering.

A small figure in UGP uniform suddenly sprang up by the Sleeping Kings' tomb.

"Look – there she is!" Arthur whispered. He noticed her turning her head in all directions, like she was looking for a way out. "She's got nowhere to run. We have to help her escape or else the raiders will get the time-key." He wasn't sure how they were going to extract her. If they all rushed into the square, Vorru would likely obliterate them with his cannon live on holovision.

Cloud wiggled his bottom like he was about to charge.

"No, boy," Cecily said, pulling on Cloud's collar. "I've got super-strength, remember? I'll use the gauntlets to distract the raiders while you three help Ribbon."

She gave Arthur and Ren no chance to argue with her, as before they could open their mouths, she was on her feet.

"You three, over here!" Cecily roared, sprinting towards the raiders with her golden fists pumping. There was an expression of reckless determination on her face, and Arthur felt a little surge of pride that she was his friend.

Rultan gawped with surprise. "What the—?" He shouted

at Tide and Vorru, "Well don't just stand there! GET RID OF HER!"

Flames blazed from the bottom of Tide's jetpack as she blasted into the air. Vorru's shoulder-cannon whirred and started to glow red, like it was warming up. Even with super-strength, Arthur wasn't sure how long Cecily could survive against them.

Ribbon was still stood by the tomb. With the raiders distracted, Arthur saw their chance to help her. He gathered Cloud into his arms. "Now, go!" he told Ren.

They dashed out from behind the shrub and hurtled towards the Sleeping Kings. Rultan, meanwhile, was tampering with his arm mod.

"Ribbon!" Arthur yelled, waving.

"Arthur! Ren!" Ribbon gave the raiders another concerned glance, before running over to him.

"We're here to help," Arthur sputtered, sliding to a stop in front of her. He wasn't sure how much he should reveal, only that he needed to get her attention. "The raiders are after the time-key. You need to get to safety."

Ribbon went ashen. "The *time-key*?"

"That's what we call it," Ren explained. She quailed as the roar of cannon fire erupted around the courtyard.

Arthur's ribs trembled with the force of the blasts. He checked on Cecily, who was cowering behind the raiders' four-by-four as Vorru bombarded it with fireballs from his shoulder-cannon. The windscreen shattered; two tyres exploded; and molten metal spewed up from the bonnet as one of the fireballs melted right through the cover.

As Vorru paused firing to recharge his shoulder-cannon, Cecily seized the chance to strike. She punched the ground with her gauntlets, fracturing the paving slabs into large chunks. One by one, she ripped them up and hurled them at Vorru and Tide.

Arthur had seen Cecily compete in the heptathlon on sports day. Her second-best event was the shot-put, and it showed.

Up in the air, Tide careened all over the place, trying to dodge the chunks of stone. Vorru was too cumbersome to avoid being hit. One of the slabs crashed into his leg, making him howl.

Ribbon's face flushed as she followed the chaos with panicked eyes. "I..." Fumbling with her faze, she opened the display and entered a few commands. "I've alerted the UGP. Reinforcements will be here right away."

"We need to take cover." Arthur scanned the courtyard and pointed to a large mosaic trough brimming with flowers. "Over there!"

As they took off, there was a burst of light behind them and Arthur saw that Rultan had opened another light-portal.

"Time to go," Rultan barked. "UGP are incoming!"

Smoke trailed from the bottom of Tide's jetpack as she landed on the ground and joined Vorru, running towards the light-portal. Arthur's ankles almost gave way as he skidded into a crouch behind the trough, his blood pounding. He was relieved to see Cecily still in one piece, sheltering at the rear of the four-by-four, but there was also another figure watching everything from the courtyard entrance. Arthur could tell by the outline of the head and shoulders that it was Griffon Ramsay.

"You kids really don't know who you're messing with!" Tide cackled as she reached the light-portal.

Ren snorted in Arthur's ear. "Who's she calling *kids*? She can't be more than two years older than us."

As Tide and Vorru disintegrated into the column of light, Rultan lifted his chin. "A piece of advice," he yelled in their direction, "Deadlock isn't patient. If you ever want to see Milo Hertz alive again, I suggest you return the device you've stolen, Ribbon, before it's too late."

23

As the raiders' light-portal dissolved, Arthur, Ren and Ribbon staggered out slowly from behind the mosaic trough. The courtyard was covered in scorch marks and smoking craters, and masonry dust billowed through the air.

"They're going to kill him," Ren said, breathlessly. "They're going to kill Milo!"

Arthur's blood ran cold, replaying Rultan's threat: *If you ever want to see Milo Hertz alive again...* He imagined their friend tied up somewhere, fearful and alone. They couldn't let him die.

Cecily came hobbling over through the wreckage. Her chin was grazed and the fabric of her jumpsuit had been torn open over one knee, revealing a bloody gash in her left thigh. Arthur hurried over and placed his arm under her left shoulder, trying to take some of the weight off her injured leg. "What happened?"

She winced. "I'm not sure. It was all so fast."

Arthur wondered how much had been caught on camera, and if Lazarus Sloane was trying to make sense of it all for his viewers.

"You were amazing," Ren stated. "You didn't allow Tide or Vorru the chance to come after us."

"It was all the gauntlets," Cecily replied, dismissively.

Ribbon gazed at Cecily's wound. "Here, let me see to your injury…" She fetched a small silver tool from her satchel and aimed it at Cecily's leg.

Cecily glanced at it warily. The instrument had a cross marked on one end and a glowing blue tip.

"It's just a cell-regenerator," Ribbon explained. "You might not use them on the outer rings of Navagool, but they're standard here. I'll simply scan the wound and press 'repair'."

The cell-regenerator had to be the twenty-fifth-century equivalent of a first-aid kit. Cecily studied the instrument a moment longer, then nodded.

Tiny blue dots appeared on her skin as the cell-regenerator got to work, healing her wound. Arthur watched with interest, but was soon distracted by multiple columns of light materializing around the courtyard. UGP officers strode out of each portal, some carrying weapons and lanterns; others tapping urgently at their faze displays.

Their arrival seemed to be Griffon Ramsay's cue. He sprang into the open and sprinted towards the Sleeping Kings, powerful as an Olympic athlete.

As he clambered onto the tomb, he turned to look in Arthur's direction. Arthur swallowed, feeling like a baby gazelle who'd just been spotted by a lion, but Griffon's expression seemed more thoughtful than angry. After a moment, Griffon produced a small tin from his pocket. Flipping open the lid, he sprinkled a measure of bright-red dust onto the faces of the Sleeping Kings.

The ground immediately rumbled and the leaves shook on all the trees and shrubs. A solemn gong reverberated around the courtyard and a shaft of light appeared over the Sleeping Kings. Rotating inside it was a gleaming gold tunic.

Griffon didn't hesitate in reaching for it. As soon as his fingers made contact, there was a loud clap and he disappeared in a shaft of light.

"We still need to find our Irontide tunic before we can get out of here and return to the Great Library," Ren realized, fishing their quest-map out of a side pocket in the rucksack. "Maybe there's another clue on here? We've answered the call and found the hidden walls ... now what?"

Arthur examined the map carefully, but couldn't see anything that might help them.

"I'd tell you the answer if I could," Ribbon said shyly, "but only senior UGP officers are briefed with that information."

"That's all right," Arthur said half-smiling. "Are you OK?"

Brushing dirt off her uniform, Ribbon nodded. Although the colour had returned to her cheeks, her movements were a little shaky. "I'll be all right, but your coach is in danger. I can't talk now with so many other officers around, but I'll find you when you return to the Great Library. I promise."

As Ribbon jogged off towards the nearest UGP officer, Cecily rocked forward on her tiptoes. "Hang on," she said, peering over to where she'd been sheltering behind the raiders' four-by-four. "When I smashed one of those paving stones, there was a hollow space beneath it – a chamber, of sorts. What if the 'hidden walls' in the clue aren't just the walls *around* Zerzura, they're also the walls *underneath* it?"

They hurried across the dusty courtyard as UGP officers continued arriving in bright flashes. "There," Cecily said, pointing. "Can you see it?"

Part of a wooden roof beam was visible through a jagged hole in one of the flagstones. Arthur dropped to his knees and used a head torch from their bag to help him see inside. "Cecily's right," he said, feeling a burst of hope. "There's a huge room down here that extends under the whole courtyard." Mosaic walls twinkled at the room's edges and, through a forest of stone pillars, Arthur spotted an empty plinth in the centre, directly beneath the statue of the Sleeping Kings. "I think I can see where an Irontide tunic might appear, but how are we going to get down there?"

Ren was already pulling a rope out of their bag. "I've got this. They don't just teach you how to go *up* during climbing lessons. I also know how to get down." She tied one end of the rope to a bar on the raiders' four-by-four and threw the other end into the hole. Her expression didn't flinch as she sat on the edge and, gripping the rope between her knees, pushed off.

"Be careful," Arthur called, as Ren slid into the cavern.

He watched her dismount and land in a crouch on the floor below. As her feet touched down, a gong echoed around the underground chamber and light burst in the centre of the room.

"You were right, Arthur!" Ren cried, dashing towards the plinth, where a glowing gold tunic now hovered above it.

As Ren reached for the tunic, the courtyard dissolved into blinding light and Arthur's body turned weightless. He knew at once that he'd been flung into the Bermuda Triangle and Ren must have claimed the Irontide tunic. As gravity returned to his limbs, he found the ground with his toes and took a tentative step forward ...

... into the hall of the Great Library of Alexandria.

He swayed, adjusting to the sudden change of environment. The hall was much cooler than Zerzura and bristling with members of the press. Tense voices echoed all around him and drones whizzed like dragonflies above his head. Ignoring a handful of people rushing towards him, he spun around to check on the others.

Cloud's shiny black nose emerged through the Bermuda Triangle first, followed by the rest of his body. He was covered in sand and dust, but his eyes were bright and his tail was wagging. He was tailed swiftly by Ren, who stomped out ahead of Cecily, now walking unaided. Arthur had to pinch himself when he caught sight of her wound. It was little more than a dark line across her thigh, the skin closed and blood gone.

He wanted to ask her how it felt when a clamour of voices yelled, "Young Pipsqueaks!" and his neck tightened. If he somehow survived all this, he hoped he never had to hear that name again.

"Young Pipsqueaks, what happened with those raiders?" a journalist with a slicked-back ponytail asked.

"Do they have anything to do with the break-in at the Hotel Loch Ness?" another quizzed.

Arthur tried to ignore the shouts and tricky questions, but his mind was racing. They still didn't have the time-key; Milo's life was hanging in the balance; and time was running out before they spontaneously turned into slime.

"UGP business, stand aside!" Ribbon yelled, elbowing her way through the crowd. She lowered her voice as she drew closer. "Let's talk in one of the reading rooms. It'll be quiet there and the press aren't allowed in."

As they all hurried out of the hall, Cecily murmured something in Ren's ear and then sidled closer to Arthur. "I just told Ren – Ribbon's only going to let us use the time-key if we give her a *seriously* compelling reason."

"Like the truth," Arthur said, following Cecily's train of thought. "It's a big risk. What did Ren say?"

"She said we don't have any other choice."

There were no free tables in the first reading room they came to, so they proceeded to the next one along. It was daunting in size, with a vaulted ceiling and dark mahogany bookcases that scaled the walls. Questers floated up and down on small drones, moving from shelf to shelf.

They found a quiet area near the back of the room with a large rectangular table. Ribbon grabbed an armful of books and spread them across it, presumably so they'd look like they were discussing a quest. Arthur and Cecily took positions opposite Ren and Ribbon, with Cloud sat on a chair between them.

Once they'd all double-checked no one was listening, they huddled closer.

"So how do you three know about the – what did you call it – *time-key*?" Ribbon asked.

Arthur glanced at the others for approval before answering. "We're from the twenty-first century. The time-key is what brought us here."

Ribbon lost her breath. *"What?"*

"But we're not saying any more until you tell us the truth about who *you* really are," Ren said. "And what you're doing working for Deadlock. Aren't the UGP meant to stop people like them?"

A line appeared on Ribbon's brow. "Regarding Deadlock, I had no choice." She rolled up the sleeve of her uniform to reveal a faded tattoo on the inside of her elbow: a skull and crossed spanners. "Raiders snatched me from my parents when I was a baby and raised me as part of Deadlock's crew. When I was old enough, I ran away to carve a new life for myself. That's how I ended up working for the UGP. I hoped by fighting to protect others, I could put my past behind me."

Ribbon had been a raider? Arthur shuddered. He could only imagine the kind of harsh childhood Ribbon must have had, growing up alongside people like Tide, Vorru and Rultan. She probably felt like her whole life had been stolen away from her. At least she'd managed to escape before Deadlock had given her a cybernetic mod.

"So, what happened?" Ren asked, gently.

Ribbon took a long sigh. "A year after I received my commission to join the UGP, Deadlock found me."

"Do you know who Deadlock is?" Arthur asked.

"No idea," Ribbon said, huffing. "Whoever they are, they're smart enough to keep their identity a secret. They never communicate face to face, only with paper messages that can easily be destroyed. When Deadlock discovered I was working for the UGP, they threatened to reveal my criminal past to my new employer, unless I built them that *thing* – the time-key." Reaching into her satchel, she retrieved a small black disc, the same size as a hockey puck.

Arthur's heart almost stopped. He'd been searching for the time-key for what felt like so long, it took all of his strength not to snatch it out of Ribbon's hand.

Ribbon regarded them with hooded eyes.

Rather than place the time-key down on the table, she kept it locked between her fingers. "You know how dangerous this is, don't you? It could give someone the power to rearrange history to suit their will."

"Is that why you stole it back from Yesenia?" Arthur asked, carefully. "Because you didn't want Deadlock to have it?"

Ribbon glanced at the lantern logo on her uniform. "I've fought hard for my position at the UGP and I don't want to lose it," she said firmly. "That's why I built the time-key – because I was scared of Deadlock destroying everything I'd worked for. But I can see now that this is bigger than all that. I created the time-key. It's my responsibility to make sure it doesn't fall into the wrong hands."

She sounded a lot like another inventor Arthur knew. "Our coach, Milo Hertz, engineered the original time-key. He wants the same as you – to stop his technology being misused. He thought he had ... until Deadlock came along."

"It must have been a technical drawing of Milo's design that they gave me, then," Ribbon realized. "Deadlock wanted me to recreate it, but I couldn't resist adding a few improvements of my own. I suppose I got carried away. You said the time-key brought you here?"

"Not through choice," Cecily uttered. "We were minding our own business in Ren's back garden when a mist-portal opened and swept us up."

"Then we found ourselves in Deadlock's warehouse,"

Ren continued. "We think a raider triggered the time-key by accident, after it was stored there. But we still don't know why it opened a portal to where we were."

Ribbon scratched her head. "It must have something to do with the anchor."

"The *anchor*?" Arthur repeated.

She fetched a stylus from her satchel and used it to scribble a series of calculations in the air. The lines showed up like pale white threads. "The time-key should work perfectly, but no matter how many different portals I try to open, the device will only connect me to one particular year in the twenty-first century. It's like there's something anchoring it there. The last few weeks, I tested the time-key repeatedly before I eventually sent it to Deadlock and explained the problem. Deadlock was furious and stored the time-key in their warehouse while they decided what to do with it. It wasn't until I saw Yesenia trying to use the device that I realized something had happened…"

"But how can anything in the twenty-first century be connected to the time-key?" Ren asked.

As soon as she said *connected*, Arthur's memory flashed back to something Cecily had told them about Cloud's strange behaviour over the past few weeks. "What if *Cloud's* the anchor? That would explain why he disappeared through the mist-portal before us – because it opened at his exact location. And Ribbon's testing of the time-key might account for why Cloud's been freezing."

Cloud's ears pricked up. Cecily reached over and scooped him into her arms. "I don't understand. Ribbon's time-key has nothing to do with Cloud, so how can they be connected?"

"I'm not sure," Arthur confessed. "Ribbon's time-key was based on Milo's old designs, and he also designed Cloud. We'd probably need to ask him."

Ren's eyes widened as she stared across the table at Cloud. "Oh no... If the time-key can only open a portal to wherever Cloud is, then ... it'll only take us right back here!"

Arthur felt like he'd had the wind knocked out of him. Ren was right. So long as Cloud *and* the time-key were both in the twenty-fifth century, there would be no way for them to get home. Perhaps that was why the time-key hadn't worked when they'd first arrived in Deadlock's warehouse, because Cloud was there, too. Arthur's gaze fell to his watch. The glass had been so badly scratched by the sandstorm that it was practically frosted, but he could still make out the glowing green numerals underneath. "In that case, we've got eight hours to find a way to disconnect Cloud and the time-key. Ribbon, could you do it?"

"I, err..." Ribbon swiped her hand through the air, erasing her calculations. "I'm sorry, but it would take months of study just to identify *how* they are connected, let alone separate them."

Arthur tensed. "Then Milo is the only one who could help. We could never live with ourselves if we left him as Deadlock's prisoner. We need to focus on rescuing him."

"Why only eight hours?" Ribbon looked puzzled.

"In eight hours, the universe..." Arthur couldn't say the words without his throat closing up. He clenched his jaw, trying to focus. "In eight hours, our bodies are going to break down into protoplasm."

Everyone's fazes simultaneously vibrated. Arthur opened his display to find Chief Inspector Doveton sat smiling at him from behind a desk. Ribbon hastily rolled down her sleeve and stuffed the time-key back in her satchel.

"Bad luck, Young Pipsqueaks," the chief inspector said robustly, "Yesenia Colt and Griffon Ramsay won their Irontide tunics faster than you. As such, you've been eliminated from the tournament. Your portal permits have been rescinded and you've been checked out of the Hotel Loch Ness. A courier drone will deliver your belongings to you shortly."

The message ended abruptly and the faze display went dark.

Arthur had barely enough time to process the inspector's message before the door to the reading room thudded open, shattering the quiet. Dressed in a fuchsia-pink suit, Lazarus Sloane came strutting in, his tail swaying behind him. A gaggle of crew scurried around, juggling cameras and clipboards.

"Young Pipsqueaks!" he cried, gleefully. "Eliminated right before the final quest – you must be devastated!"

Ren closed her faze display with an irritated scowl. "The last thing we need is another interview with that creep. Let's get out of here. We've got to save Milo."

"I could be of assistance there," Ribbon offered. "I know how raiders operate. Will you let me help?"

Arthur nodded. If they were going up against Deadlock, they needed all the advice they could get.

As they all raced for the other exit, Lazarus called after them. "Fleeing so soon? Don't you have anything to say to your fans?" There was a hint of irritation in his voice, which left Arthur feeling mildly satisfied. He supposed it didn't look good for Lazarus's viewers to see them running away and avoiding interview.

"Seeing as we can't return to the hotel, do you know somewhere in Atlantis we can go to wash off this sand?" Cecily asked, scratching under her armpit. "It's so itchy I can't focus."

"What about the *Flying Dutchman*?" Ribbon suggested. "You can get changed, grab something to eat and we can discuss plans in quiet. That place is always dead."

The Flying Dutchman... Arthur had heard that name before. "Sounds good. Now let's hurry. We've got a rescue mission to organize."

24

The *Flying Dutchman* was a colossal old warship with tattered linen sails, moored in a canal west of the Great Library. Rusty cannons protruded from her barnacled hull and the faded red, white and blue colours of the Dutch flag flapped atop each of her three masts.

As soon as Arthur saw the vessel, he understood why Ribbon had described it as *dead*. Every timber of the hull glowed with an eerie green light and behind a cross-hatch of rigging, you could see semi-transparent crew members floating across deck.

The *Flying Dutchman* was a *ghost* ship.

Cloud flattened his ears as they approached.

"Are you *sure* we should go in here?" Ren asked, reaching down to give Cloud a reassuring stroke. "I'm pretty sure the *Flying Dutchman* was in one of the *Pirates of the Caribbean* movies. Legend has it, the ship was never able to make port and its crew were doomed to sail the seven seas for ever."

"I know it's a bit spooky," Ribbon acknowledged, "but the phantom sailors are only mimics and the ship is used as a shopping mall now. There's an American diner on one of the gun decks that's always really empty."

It didn't take a lot of imagination to wonder why. Still, Arthur didn't mind where they went, so long as they got something to eat. He needed brain fuel.

After coaxing Cloud forward, they boarded the *Flying Dutchman* via a seaweed-draped gangplank, and then climbed down a ladder from the main deck to access the second gun deck. A creepy soundtrack was playing inside the hull – a combination of crashing waves, crying gulls and ghostly voices. Arthur had to remind himself that he was in a twenty-fifth-century shopping mall and not a horror movie.

As they proceeded through a set of galley doors, he got a whiff of grilled meat and greasy fries. To starboard, a sailor in a chef's apron floated up and down behind a grill, flipping blue-yolked eggs and black-swirled buns. The deck was dotted with mostly empty tables, each with a holographic menu rotating above it. Diner-style booths had been built around the cannons, giving customers a view through the gunports at the passing Atlantean crowds. Λ giant holovision screen shimmered above the bar, playing *The Lazarus Show*.

"There's a gym two decks below this," Ribbon said, navigating her way to one of the booths. "Once the courier drops off your belongings, you can use the changing rooms to wash and get out of those clothes."

Sand scratched Arthur's thighs as he slid into the booth next to Cecily and Cloud. Ren and Ribbon sat opposite. The menu featured a plant-based burger named after Lazarus Sloane, various legend-themed snacks and an assortment of weird shakes. After a quick peruse, Arthur selected a "Fountain of Youth" omelette, fries and salad; Ren opted for "El Dorado" waffles; and Cecily and Ribbon chose a "King Arthur" toasted sandwich. They all ordered skullfruit shakes.

"So," Arthur began, passing round a pot of napkin-wrapped knives and forks. "If we're going to rescue Milo, we first need to find out where the raiders are holding him."

"In Deadlock's warehouse?" Cecily guessed, pulling out a set of cutlery.

"It's not really a warehouse," Ribbon told them. "It's more like a base. Deadlock's whole business is run out of that building. It's the most secure place the raiders use – that's why Deadlock was storing the time-key there. I guarantee Milo will be in there somewhere. Trouble is, the entrance moves and I have no idea where it is now."

Arthur jerked his head. "The entrance *moves*?"

"The entrance is a type of portal," Ribbon elaborated. "An illegal one. Deadlock moves it around every week in order to keep the base secret. It isn't easy to find unless you know where it is because it looks like a thin veil of light; barely perceptible."

Like a force field, Arthur thought. It could be anywhere. A ghoulish waiter in ragged sailor's clothing drifted over, balancing all four dishes and milkshakes on one arm. He placed them gently on the table and then gave everyone a creepy smile before departing.

Ren stabbed one of her waffles with a fork. "Milo said he'd narrowed the location of Deadlock's base to somewhere in Legendarium. He must have been tracking the moving entrance, but where is it?"

As they chewed the problem over, the galley doors swung open and a large cardboard box glided through the diner towards them. It wasn't till it got closer that Arthur heard the whir of an engine and saw that the box was being carried by a small, Frisbee-shaped drone.

"Young Pipsqueaks," the drone buzzed. *"Delivery from the Hotel Loch Ness."*

Arthur took a quick slurp of his milkshake before getting out of their booth and lifting the box onto the floor. It felt surprisingly light.

"Looks like that's the only one," Cecily commented as the drone whirred away. "Perhaps our mysterious 'concerned benefactor' has had all our merchandise returned to them?"

"Mysterious benefactor?" Ribbon smirked. "You mean you haven't worked out who that is? Think about it: who

profits if the three of you appear to be a more professional team?"

Arthur gave it some consideration. If the Young Pipsqueaks looked more qualified, they'd probably get more fans tuning in to watch them. "Lazarus Sloane?" he guessed. "His ratings will be better, so he'll be able to charge more for advertising."

"Bingo," Ribbon said, pointing.

Arthur opened the cardboard box. Neatly folded inside were the clothes they'd each been wearing in Ren's garden, three days earlier: Cecily's summer dress, Ren's jeans and hooded tank top, and Arthur's shorts and *The Mandalorian* T-shirt. As he distributed them, he imagined how it would feel to be back in Ren's garden, with their parents inside making lemonade and the whole of the summer holidays still lying ahead of them. It seemed like a hazy dream.

"Even if we do find the entrance to Deadlock's headquarters, how are we going to bypass its defences in order to get inside?" Cecily wondered, stirring her milkshake.

"And then battle the raiders," Arthur added glumly. If only they had a group of heroes to fight alongside them, like they'd had in the Wonderscape. They could always ask Archimedes for help but Arthur doubted he'd be much use against the raiders. What was he going to do, hurl equations at them?

Just then, the galley doors banged open.

"*There* you are," snarled a voice. "I've been searching everywhere for you."

Arthur froze as Griffon Ramsay came weaving through the dining tables towards them. In place of his usual body armour, he wore his gold Irontide tunic, which fit snugly around his ripped torso. Alongside his energy-baton, several new tools hung from his belt.

This is it, Arthur thought, his legs shaking under the table. *He's come for revenge!*

But rather than attack them, Griffon slid onto the bench next to Ren, who hastily shuffled along.

"W-what are you doing here?" Ren asked nervously. She gestured towards the holoscreen where *The Lazarus Show* was still playing. "Shouldn't you be in the next quest-land?"

"I don't know. Maybe." Griffon scowled. "I had to lie to my coach. No one knows I'm here." He gave Ribbon a cautionary look before continuing. "I finally recognized your coach this morning. He's Milo Hertz, isn't he? One of the founders of the Wonderscape?"

"Err ... yeah," Arthur said, figuring they had nothing to lose by telling the truth.

"And he's been kidnapped by Deadlock?" Griffon asked.

Arthur's mouth twitched, uncertain how to respond.

"I overheard what that raider said to you in Zerzura," Griffon continued. "Every isports champ knows about Deadlock. We get offered illegal equipment all the time – there are notes slipped under doors, whispers in the training rooms – the Dark Market is always there, bubbling under the surface." He flared his nostrils. "But I'm no cheat. Those rumours Lazarus Sloane mentioned came about after I *refused* to do business with a couple of raiders. I believe Deadlock started them. That's why I'm here to help you."

"To *help* us?" Arthur said, astounded. He wasn't sure he'd heard correctly. "I thought you were here to confront us – about what happened in the Land of the Lost."

A line wrinkled Griffon's brow. "After you survived the first elimination, I grew suspicious that you might be cheating – I've never seen inexperienced players do that well. So, I kept you under close scrutiny. I'll admit I was planning to take my revenge in the Land of Sleeping Kings, but then the raiders showed up and I realized you weren't the cheats I thought you were."

That's why he's been watching us, Arthur realized. *He thought we were cheats.*

"But how can you help us with the tournament still going on?" Cecily questioned.

Griffon shrugged his huge shoulders. "I'm runner-up now, no matter what, and fighting Deadlock is more important. I *care* about my sport. Crooks like Deadlock are out to ruin it. They need to be stopped."

Arthur swallowed back a bubble of guilt, remembering how quickly he'd assumed that Griffon was a cheat. But still, could they really trust him? He was the Lone Wolf. Out for himself.

"If you're here to help, you can start now," Ren said. "Milo's being held inside Deadlock's base. We think the entrance is somewhere in Legendarium..."

As she filled Griffon in on what they knew, Arthur's gaze was caught by something on the holoscreen. *The Lazarus Show* was streaming live footage of Yesenia sprinting along a dark, sandy passageway lit by fiery torches. In a flash, she ran past a golden sun-shaped statue, stood in a recess in the wall.

It took Arthur a split second to remember where he'd seen the statue before. "Where is Yesenia?" he asked Griffon, tapping him on the shoulder.

Griffon glanced at the holoscreen. "Somewhere in the Land of the Hidden Sun, I guess. It's where the final quest in the tournament takes place." He withdrew a quest-map from his pocket and spread it on the table. The map showed an area of dense rainforest with a river meandering through. A golden shield was marked in a clearing in the trees and around the edge of the map was written:

LEGENDARI♥M

- THE LAND OF THE HIDDEN SUN -

Write your legend in the sand
to move the shield to your command.

"Why d'you want to know?" Griffon asked.

Arthur took a deep breath, trying to straighten his

thoughts. "Because I've seen that sun statue before – outside the doors of Deadlock's base."

Ren leaned closer. "Are you sure?"

"He's right," Cecily said, excitedly. "I remember it, too." She slammed her hand over the quest-map. "So, the entrance to Deadlock's headquarters must be in the Land of the Hidden Sun!"

All at once, the three of them rose from their seats and started to shuffle out of the booth. Arthur felt a sliver of hope. They could do this. Deadlock didn't know they were coming, which meant they would have the element of surprise. If luck was on their side, they could sneak into Deadlock's base, break Milo out and be back to the twenty-first century before they all turned into puddles of slime.

"Wait – you don't understand!" Ribbon said, grabbing Arthur's arm. "You three can't travel through the Bermuda Triangle – your portal permits have been rescinded."

"What?" Arthur slumped back down. "Can't you just issue us a new one?"

"Not unless you're in the tournament," Ribbon replied. She tightened her jaw. "Deadlock's clever. The Land of the Hidden Sun is the last place the UGP would look because it's right under our noses."

Griffon ran a finger around the neck of his Irontide tunic. "I can't believe I'm saying this, but ... you three could rejoin the tournament as members of *my* team."

"Is that allowed?" Cecily asked.

Ribbon opened her faze display and tapped impatiently at the surface. "You can compete in teams of four, so, technically, Griffon has three empty places on his squad. Yes, look – it's been done once before, in Silverstar '79, so it should work in this tournament, too. I can contact Lazarus Sloane now with the changes."

Arthur smiled sheepishly at Griffon, knowing it must feel uncomfortable inviting three strangers into his normally solo outfit. "Apart from losing the green clothes, is there anything you need us to do?" he asked.

Griffon frowned. "Just keep your mouths shut. With all *The Lazarus Show* crew in the Land of the Hidden Sun, you're bound to get asked questions, and I need to protect my reputation. Let me do the talking."

"*Lazarus Show* crew?" Arthur queried.

"The final quests aren't timed like the others," Ribbon explained. "The remaining two teams are assigned the same quest and whoever claims the Irontide shield first, wins. Rather than being transported immediately back to the Great Library, the champion stays in the quest-land, where they participate in a special episode of *The Lazarus Show*."

"Yesenia already has a head start on the quest," Griffon said. "But that shouldn't affect us finding Lazarus's base. Just follow my lead, and maybe I won't regret this."

25

Arthur couldn't believe that in the last two days he'd hiked along a frozen coastline, survived a sandstorm in a desert and was now trekking through dense, lush rainforest. But hey, that was isports for you.

He pushed through the fronds of a giant fern, following single file behind the others. Ribbon had joined them soon after they'd arrived in the quest-land. Arthur wasn't sure what viewers would think about a UGP apprentice tagging along with their team, but they could come up with an explanation later. "So where exactly are we?" he asked, lifting his voice above the din of birdsong around them.

The air was hot and sticky and smelled like the inside of a greenhouse. Moss grew up the poker-straight tree trunks and delicate white orchids swayed from branches. At the head of the line, Griffon thrashed his energy-baton through a curtain of creepers, which sizzled and fell to the ground. "I'm not sure what planet this is, but if my research is correct, the Land of the Hidden Sun is inspired by the legend of the lost Inca city of Paititi. It's believed to be somewhere in the remote rainforests of Peru."

Arthur had studied the Inca empire at school. They were a civilization of people who lived hundreds of years ago in parts of western South America. As well as building temples to worship their gods, he remembered with a shiver that they also made *human sacrifices.* "Is that where you think we saw Yesenia? In Paititi?" Arthur didn't like the fact that Griffon hadn't offered up any information about where they were going. Perhaps it was because he wasn't used to working with others, but it still left Arthur feeling distrustful.

"That's right," Griffon said. "And if my theory is correct, the entrance to the lost city should be somewhere around here."

"What theory's that?" Ren asked, jumpily.

Trudging behind her, Arthur could see how tight the muscles in her back and neck were. He knew she must be finding it difficult to stay focused with the loud hum of insects in the air. "You're doing great," he muttered, patting her on the shoulder.

"It's about the phrase *hidden sun,*" Griffon voiced. "There have been countless failed expeditions in search of Paititi, and I think the designers of this quest-land are offering a possible explanation: because Paititi can only be found in a place where the sun is hidden."

Arthur tried to puzzle through Griffon's meaning.

"The sun touches everything on the surface of the planet, so ... Paititi is underground?"

"Uh-huh." Griffon came to a stop and gestured to a set of rough-hewn stone steps, sloping into a dark hole. "And behold – I was right."

Cecily took one look at the hole and fetched their head torches from the rucksack. With the devices deployed, the group slowly descended.

The deeper they went, the danker the air became. At the bottom of the steps, a long ashlar tunnel stretched ahead of them, full of cobwebs and scuttling shadows. Plants sprouted through crevices in the floor and creepers dangled from the ceiling.

Ren leaned in to Arthur's ear. "If anything jumps, flies or crawls onto me, can you get it off?"

"Don't worry," he said. "I've got you."

As they proceeded into the tunnel, he checked the timer on his Casio. They had five hours left in which to rescue Milo and get home. If they failed, they might never see daylight again.

"The Irontide shield will probably be somewhere in the centre of the city," Griffon said. "Yesenia must have been trying to reach it when we saw her in that tunnel. If we want to locate the statue that she ran past, we should aim for the shield, too."

Arthur wondered nervously what challenges they should expect along the way. He repeated the quest-map advice in his head: *Write your legends in the sand to move the shield to your command.*

"There's bound to be raiders here," Ribbon warned. "They'll all be disguised, so keep your wits about you. Don't trust *anybody*."

They came to a T-junction. Arthur shone his torch along the right-hand passage and something glinted. "Look!" he cried, rushing over. A gold disc surrounded by gold isosceles triangles stood in a recess in the wall – the sun statue. "It's the same as the one I saw outside Deadlock's base, I'm sure of it!" He ran his hands over the opposite wall, looking for a thin veil of light, like Ribbon had described.

"There's another sun over here," Cecily said, projecting her beam into the left-hand tunnel. "Actually ... there are a lot of them."

Arthur's enthusiasm faded as he saw there were sun statues set into the walls every few metres.

"Well, that's just great," Ren said. "If these are decorating every tunnel in the city, then Deadlock's base could be anywhere. It could take us hours to search them all!"

Griffon peered thoughtfully in both directions. "Inca architecture was all about symmetry. I wouldn't be surprised if these two tunnels both lead to the same place, just with mirroring routes. If we divide into two teams, we can take both paths. That way, we should cover everything in our search and all meet up at the end."

Arthur studied Griffon's face, wondering if they were

right to follow his lead. Splitting up would certainly save them time, but there was strength in numbers and in this deep, dark maze, who knew what might be waiting around the next corner. "I'm not sure. What does everyone else think?"

"Griffon has a point, but I think the three of *us*," Cecily drew a triangle between herself, Arthur and Ren, "should stay together. Perhaps Griffon and Ribbon should search one tunnel and we can check the other?"

Ribbon nodded in agreement. "Maybe Griffon and I should take Cloud with us? That way, if we find Milo, he'll know he can trust us." She added under her breath, "If he sees my tattoo he might think otherwise."

"Err…" Arthur wasn't keen on parting with their fluffy companion, but Ribbon made a valid argument. With time running out, they needed Milo to trust her and Griffon immediately. "Can't you contact us via our fazes and we can explain everything to Milo?"

"That function doesn't work inside quest-lands," Griffon said, shaking his head. "Once we part ways, we won't be able to communicate until we meet up again. You need to hurry up and make a decision."

Ren turned her back on Griffon and lowered her voice. "Maybe, since Ribbon has the time-key, it makes sense for her to have Cloud, too? That way, if she finds Milo first, he can start disconnecting them."

With a sigh, Cecily crouched down towards Cloud.

"You're right. Every second counts." She scratched Cloud between the ears. "Be a good boy. We'll see you soon."

"Good luck, Fuzzball," Ren said.

Ribbon took Cloud's lead, and she and Griffon set off at a brisk jog. Arthur watched as they disappeared into the shadows, wondering if they'd made the right decision.

"Come on," Ren said, turning in the opposite direction. "Let's find the entrance to Deadlock's warehouse and then rescue Milo before he gets hurt."

As they progressed, the tunnels of Paititi changed. The dank smell faded and the air turned cool and dry. Torches appeared on the walls, filling the passageways with flickering amber light. Every corner they turned Arthur hoped to find what they were looking for. He could almost feel time slipping away with each step.

"How do you think the others are getting on?" Cecily asked, removing her head torch now there was no need for it. "Do you think they've found the entrance?"

Arthur scanned the walls carefully, checking for signs of a shimmering force field. "Maybe. They've got to be having better luck than us."

He walked round a corner, and before his brain had time to send his body a warning, he lifted his foot over the edge of a precipice. "Wha—!" he yelped, windmilling his arms to try to avoid falling.

"Arthur!" Cecily yanked on his T-shirt, pulling him away from the edge.

His heart was thudding as he staggered back against a wall. "Thanks," he gasped.

Cecily's eyes widened as she gazed at their surroundings. They'd turned into a large, rectangular chamber with a gaping hole in the floor. A woven rope bridge connected a narrow strip of ground on either side. Six hessian sacks of grain rested against the wall closest to them: three green and three red. On the other side of the hole, a set of scales were attached, via a system of cogs and pulleys, to a closed stone door.

It appeared to be the only way out.

Ren walked over to the rope bridge and gave the handrail a shake. "Feels strong enough to bear our weight..."

But as she lifted her foot to step on it, Cecily yelled, "Wait – look at the ceiling!"

Arthur tipped his head back. The roof of the chamber was divided into thirds, each painted with a scene set in the very same room. In the first, an Inca warrior carrying two green bags of grain had fallen through a hole in the rope bridge. The second scene was identical, except the warrior was clutching one green bag and one red bag. In the third instance, the warrior was holding no grain at all.

Elements of the paintings seemed familiar. Arthur racked his brains. "I think this is a river-crossing puzzle," he told the others.

Ren looked confused. "*River*-crossing?"

"It doesn't have to be a river, but that's the general name for them," Arthur elaborated. "You basically have to move objects or people across a river or bridge according to certain rules." He pointed to the scales, opposite. "We probably have to fill the scales with all six bags of grain in order to open the door. The paintings tell us what we can and can't transport over."

Examining the ceiling, a line appeared on Cecily's brow. "So, the bridge will break if we move over two green bags at once; or one green and one red bag; or no bags." She shook her head. "That makes no sense."

"We just need to figure out the correct order to move the grain," Ren said. "It's tricky because we can't return over the bridge empty-handed. Perhaps the first step is for one of us to cross with two red sacks? That way, there'll be something for the next person to carry back. Cecily, do you want to get the bridge crossing over and done with?"

Cecily groaned. "I suppose so."

After a few words of encouragement from Ren and Arthur, Cecily crossed the bridge, holding two red sacks of grain. "Now what?" she called, dumping them on the floor on the other side.

Arthur thought ahead, trying to plan their next few moves. "Ugh, my brain feels like mush," he admitted. "I can't keep track of what we're carrying each time we cross the bridge, and if we make one bad decision, we'll end up down there." He peered over the edge of the floor, into the endless pit of darkness. That was a fall you wouldn't recover from.

"I think it's a bit like playing chess," Ren said, biting her lip. They watched as she looked between the ceiling and bridge, puzzling out the answer. "I've got it: Arthur and I should carry over a green sack each and return using both of those red ones. Then I will bring over the final green sack and stay on that side with you, Cecily. Arthur can then carry over two reds, leaving one with us, and then return to collect the final red."

"I have no idea what you just said," Cecily called over. "But let's go with it."

Arthur repeated Ren's solution in his head, double-checking it would work. The bridge wobbled as he set off, but his nerves held firm. Once he and Ren had deposited their green sacks on the other side, Cecily heaved them onto the scales.

"I'm glad one of us knows what we're doing," Arthur told Ren, as they crossed back with a red sack each. "These kinds of puzzles make my head go fuzzy."

"Yeah, but I wouldn't have known it was a puzzle without you. You've got a sixth sense about these things. That's exactly why you're going to be a brilliant video games designer one day."

As they reached the other side, Arthur's steps faltered. "How do you know I want to be a video games designer?"

"Because I told her," Cecily hollered. "I saw it through our Irontide helmet."

Arthur's cheeks flushed as he collected another red sack. It was true that he'd played enough video games to know intuitively where to search for hidden clues or when a boss might be lurking in the next room. "Well, it's not like it'll ever happen. You have to be really good at physics and computing."

"All things you *are* good at," Ren pointed out, replacing her red sack for the remaining green one.

With a shrug, Arthur tried to push the matter to the back of his mind as they crossed back to Cecily. But when they got there, she was stood with her hands on her hips, staring at him.

"Arthur, you seriously need to start believing in yourself," she said, sounding like one of his teachers. "You spotted this puzzle, you understood exactly what the Land of Outlaws was all about and you single-handedly saved Ren and me in the Land of the Lost."

"And you outwitted Griffon," Ren added. "That's no small feat. You're going to be a great video games designer. You'll probably win more trophies than Teréze Dufour."

Arthur cracked up laughing as he hefted one of the red sacks back across the bridge and collected its final remaining twin.

"If we make it home, you should really reconsider signing up for that video games workshop," Cecily called. "You'll have a major advantage over everyone else – you've literally seen the future of gaming."

"Yeah, maybe," Arthur said.

Cecily cleared her throat. *"Maybe?"*

"All right, definitely. *If* we survive."

By the time Arthur had made it back, Ren and Cecily had already lifted the third green sack onto the scales. As he helped them dump the three red sacks, he thought more about what they'd said. They were right, of course. Arthur was just as capable as any of the other students who'd signed up.

As the last sack fell onto the scales, the pan sank to the ground, pulling a chain. There was a series of clicks and rattles as the system of cogs and pulleys burst into action. The walls juddered and, with an echoing groan, the stone door slid open.

Behind it was another corridor with a gold panel on one side, decorated with Inca symbols. Arthur moved closer to inspect it. "You don't think *this* could be the entrance to Deadlock's base, do you?" he said, running his fingers around the edge.

"Doubt it," Cecily said. "According to Ribbon, the entrance is nearly invisible."

Arthur found a notch along one side of the panel and flicked it down. There was a soft click and the panel slid away, revealing a small room filled with crates. They were all stamped with the reptilian-eye logo of *The Lazarus Show*.

"What's all this doing here?" Ren asked as they weaved through the boxes. "Have we stumbled into another staff area?"

Cecily edged around a particularly tall crate. "If we have, then we're not being filmed any more."

On the opposite side of the room was a heavy metal door. Arthur tested the handle and it swung open to reveal a massive sound stage fitted with lights and cameras – just like the one they'd visited at *The Lazarus Show* studios in Atlantis. Golden sun statues ran along the walls and an open door at the back peeped into another sandy passageway. The set of *The Lazarus Show* was arranged in the centre of the room, including the twinkling Atlantean night-time backdrop and Lazarus's green suede chair. Arthur thought it was strange that he couldn't see any of the show's staff loitering around, because the amber "standby" lights were glowing on all the cameras.

"This must be where Lazarus intends to interview the tournament champion," Cecily said as they all wandered in. "I suppose that means Yesenia hasn't won the Irontide shield yet. As soon as she does, they'll rush her through make-up and onto that sofa."

With a gasp, Ren ran over to a holoscreen floating beside one of the cameras. "Look – it's Griffon!"

Arthur rushed closer. *The Lazarus Show* was streaming live footage of Griffon *flying* around inside a chamber of identical size to the one they'd just escaped from. Here, though, there was no rope bridge or sacks of grain. Instead, a trio of skeleton archers dressed in feathered Inca armour were shooting arrows at Griffon from the floor.

Arthur winced as one sailed past Griffon's head. "His Irontide tunic must have given him the ability to fly. I can't see Cloud or Ribbon. Where are they?"

Cecily searched the screen and yelped. "What if one of those skeletons got them?"

"We shouldn't have split up," Arthur realized, annoyed with himself that he'd agreed to it in the first place. "Now we've got to save Cloud *and* Milo."

Ren turned back the way they'd come. "Should we go and find them? The entrance to Deadlock's base obviously isn't in here. I think Lazarus's staff would have noticed."

But as Ren spoke, a cog started turning in Arthur's head. He remembered Ribbon's warning that there were bound to be raiders in Paititi, in disguise. The thing was, other than UGP officers and Yesenia Colt, there was only one group of people who even had access to the Land of the Hidden Sun – the staff of *The Lazarus Show*.

He considered the number of storage crates used to transport the show's equipment from I-RAG to I-RAG, everywhere the Dark Market traded, and was struck by a chilling thought:

Could Lazarus Sloane be Deadlock?

26

Cecily lifted a hand to her mouth. "You might be right," she uttered, after Arthur had shared his theory. "That producer told us that *The Lazarus Show* travels all over the Known Universe – he could transport illegal goods without raising any suspicion."

"And Lazarus Sloane has the perfect disguise," Arthur said. "No one would suspect a charming holovision host is the brains behind a Dark Market empire."

Ren surveyed the sound stage. "Maybe we *should* check around here for the entrance to Deadlock's base after all. But what about Cloud and the others?"

Glancing at the holoscreen, Arthur felt torn. Choosing between two sets of friends was an almost impossible choice.

He didn't want to abandon anyone, but rescuing Milo was the only way they were going to get home, and time was running out. "Griffon is a pro; I'm sure he can despatch those skeleton archers himself. As for Cloud and Ribbon –"

his heart tugged – "we've just got to hope they're OK and that we meet up with them later."

Cecily set her jaw. "Come on, then. Let's find this entrance."

They headed off in different directions to examine the sound-stage walls. Arthur trod carefully over wires, pulled aside boxes and squeezed behind crates. His eyes were tired, so he made sure to check each area twice for any sign of a hidden force field. When he reached the far wall, he turned a corner and heard people talking.

"Is everything ready to go in the temple?" someone asked.

Arthur waved to catch the others' attention, then gestured for them to hide. He ducked behind the nearest crate as five people in baseball caps and black T-shirts printed with *The Lazarus Show* logo lumbered into the sound stage, carrying heavy reels of cable.

"Sound is set up and cameras are on standby," one of them said. "As soon as one of the questers opens that chest to retrieve the shield, the microphones will start recording and the broadcast will automatically go live. Viewers will be able to see and hear the winner's reactions."

"Great," said another. "I'll prep Lazarus."

One of the staff had a large rucksack and hung back from the others. Arthur spotted a tuft of red hair poking out from under their baseball cap and as they turned around, he froze.

It was *Tide*.

So he was right: Lazarus Sloane *was* Deadlock – Tide was a raider disguised as a member of his staff. Tide darted behind a crate, hiding from the other staff members. She waited for the rest of the crew to leave, then she crept out from her hiding place and scanned the room. Arthur rounded his shoulders and tucked his arms in, trying to make the smallest shape possible. If she spotted him, he'd never discover what she was up to.

But her gaze travelled over where he was cowering, towards an area of wall he hadn't reached in his search. She marched towards it and rolled aside a few wheeled crates.

Arthur drew his breath. A barely perceptible film covered the wall, shimmering with rainbow colours like the surface of a bubble. He checked opposite, to where a golden sun gleamed in the alcove of a sandy wall. Although not as dark and torchlit, it was the exact same view he had glimpsed from inside Deadlock's base – which meant it could be the entrance they were looking for!

Tide ran her hands around the edge of the portal and the film wobbled, distorting the ashlar behind. Arthur heard the groan of a heavy door opening and glimpsed a dark gap beyond. Tide gave the sound stage one last shifty glance before stepping forward and disappearing *into* the wall.

A split second later, footsteps sounded at Arthur's back and he turned with a jump.

"That's got to be the entrance to Deadlock's base!" Ren exclaimed, running over. "We need to get inside before it closes."

As Cecily came to join them, Arthur approached the entrance cautiously. Ribbon had told them that it was an illegal portal, which meant it was probably dangerous. His arm trembled as he pushed his fingers through.

"Well?" Ren asked.

"It *feels* like they're still attached to my body..." Arthur replied, worriedly.

"We'll just have to risk it," Cecily decided. "There's no time."

They simultaneously all took a deep breath and then strode into the portal.

The journey was instantaneous. As soon as they'd left the sound stage, they found themselves walking into Deadlock's base, on the other side of its massive doors.

The place was just as Arthur remembered it – cold and dusty, and filled with floor-to-ceiling shelving units where the blue, red and green crates were being stored. The dim spotlights had all been turned off, except for one in the far corner. Tide was nowhere to be seen.

"Where do you think they've got Milo?" Ren whispered, sneaking forward.

"Not sure." Arthur checked the balcony but there was no light spilling out from under any of the doors. "Let's see what's in that corner."

As they passed the area where they'd first appeared three days ago, Arthur noticed the scorch marks were gone, along with the damaged crate that had once contained the time-key. He wondered if Lazarus had discovered what had happened and punished the raider responsible for triggering the device. As they drew closer to the lit area, Arthur began to hear voices. He signalled for Ren and Cecily to speed up, and quietly as they could, they padded towards the noise.

"... Deadlock's got everything they need," a boastful voice was saying. "Which means they no longer have a use for you."

Tide. Arthur recognized her unusual accent. He flattened his back against a crate and peeped around the corner.

Tide was stood in a spotlit clearing between the shelves. A red crate rested on the floor beside her with its lid hanging open. Sat hunched in a chair opposite was a dishevelled Milo Hertz. He had a bloody lip and swollen eye, but although his hands and feet were fastened with plastic ties, there was a defiant look in his eyes. "Deadlock's got nothing," he growled. "The technical drawing is gone and the time-key will be destroyed."

Tide wiggled her fingers casually over the red crate. "That's not for me to worry about; I'm just here to follow orders. Now, what to choose?" She reached in and selected what Arthur recognized as a rex-claw – one of those daggers with a dinosaur-claw handle. Tide pointed the blade at

Milo, her lips curling into an evil grin. "This looks sharp enough for the job…"

Arthur jolted, realizing Tide intended to *kill* Milo. Without thinking, he rushed into the clearing and rugby-tackled her.

They crashed to the ground, Tide's jetpack clattering against the concrete.

"Get off me!" she yelled, punching Arthur in the chest.

Tide's knuckles smashed into his ribs, knocking all the air from his lungs. "Not … until … you drop that," he croaked, straining to wrestle the rex-claw off her. Adrenaline dulled the pain spreading through his chest.

The slap of feet echoed as Ren and Cecily sprinted out behind him. Ren grabbed another rex-claw from inside the red crate and hurried over to free Milo, while Cecily reached for something else.

As Arthur struggled against Tide, he heard the whir of charging machinery and a red target appeared on Tide's forehead.

"Drop the dagger!" Cecily shouted, in a tone angrier than Arthur had ever heard her use before. The rock blaster in her hand trembled. "Or you'll feel the full force of … whatever this is."

Tide went cross-eyed as she tried to view the target on her head. "You can't shoot that in here!"

"Well, I will," Cecily said, brashly. "Unless you drop the weapon and move away from my friend."

Tide snarled and threw away the rex-claw, then loosened her grip on Arthur's arms. "Fine."

Arthur scrambled back before Tide could push him. Ignoring the pain in his ribs, he limped over to Milo. "Are you OK? What happened?"

As Ren sawed through the last of Milo's ties with the rex-claw, Milo rubbed the marks on his wrists. "Raiders snatched me at the Kraken and brought me here. I initially managed to escape and sneak into an office upstairs, where I was able to access Deadlock's mainframe and delete all copies of the time-key technical drawing." He glowered at Tide. "Unfortunately, someone caught me again before I could leave."

"You really deleted *all* the copies?" Ren asked.

Milo smiled tiredly. "Every one. Now all that's left is to destroy the time-key itself. Do you have it?"

"No, but we know who does," Arthur answered. "We also know that Deadlock is otherwise known as Lazarus Sloane."

"Lazarus?" Milo frowned. "No—"

But before he could continue, the ruby pendant hanging around his neck flashed and a hologram of Ribbon Rex projected out of it.

Arthur stumbled back. *"Ribbon?"* The UGP apprentice was stooped over a long table, strewn with bits of wire and flasks of swirling metallic particles. A pair of X-focals nestled in her spiky black quiff and in one hand she held a tool with a glowing red-hot tip. The time-key glinted on one side of the table and at the edge of the hologram hung a pair of limp white paws. "Where are you?" Arthur asked anxiously. "Are you OK? Is that Cloud?"

Ribbon jumped. "Arthur?!" She placed the red-hot tool down and fiddled with something outside the hologram. "What are you doing? Where are you? Is that Milo Hertz with you?"

There was something *off* about her tone. Arthur had expected her to be happy to see them; instead, she sounded irritated.

"This is what I was about to tell you," Milo said, jabbing a finger at the hologram. "It was *Ribbon* who caught me before I could leave here. The raiders take their orders from her; she's running the whole operation. *She's* Deadlock."

27

Arthur went numb. Ribbon couldn't be Deadlock. It made no sense. She'd been helping them. She was their friend.

But the stern look on Milo's face said otherwise.

"What have you done to Cloud?" Milo shouted at Ribbon's hologram. "You must have tampered with his internal systems for this call to have been triggered."

"Cloud, no!" Cecily brought a hand to her mouth, almost dropping the rock blaster.

Tide bent her knees like she was considering making a run for it or even firing up her jetpack.

"I've done no permanent damage to your precious mimic," Ribbon sneered. "I've only severed the connection between it and the time-key."

Ren scowled. "You said you'd need months to do that!"

"Well, I lied."

Arthur felt like he'd been winded. If Ribbon had lied about that, then everything she'd ever told them could be a lie.

Tide laughed, noticing the look on Arthur's face. "I told you before: you kids don't know who you're messing with."

Ribbon called to someone outside the hologram. "I can hear Tide! They're at the base." Reaching forward, she dragged Cloud's body across the table. Arthur's heart wrenched at the sight of Cloud's floppy legs and dull fur. His eyelids were closed like he might be asleep, but Arthur knew Ribbon must have switched him off.

"I'll be seeing you very soon," Ribbon snarled.

And with that, the hologram cut out. Arthur's mind whirred, trying to make sense of everything. He checked his watch. There were only three hours left before they turned into protoplasm. "What do we do now?" he asked the others. "Ribbon still has the time-key and we've got to rescue Cloud."

"We'll stand no chance against her and her raiders," Milo said, taking the rock blaster off Cecily. "For the moment, there's only one thing we can do: run."

They wrestled Tide to the floor and, using part of one of Milo's recycled ties, fastened Tide's hands to a warehouse shelf, before racing back to the base doors. Heat coursed through Arthur's veins as he ran, his mind in a whirl at how Ribbon had manipulated them. When they'd parted ways in the tunnels, it was Ribbon who had suggested Cloud join her and Griffon. She'd orchestrated everything so she could snatch Cloud and disconnect him from the time-key.

Perhaps she would have stolen him earlier if Griffon hadn't turned up...

Just as they reached the base doors and saw that they were still open, voices echoed behind them and the spotlights flickered on, flooding the building with light.

"Ribbon's here!" Ren called, as the roar of Tide's jetpack reverberated off the walls. Another raider must have freed Tide. "Hurry!"

They charged through the doors, into the portal and back onto *The Lazarus Show* sound stage. Arthur looked left and right. There were two exits – the padded metal door through which they'd first entered, and another, through which Tide and Lazarus's staff had appeared. He considered which way to go. Glancing at a camera, he had a flash of inspiration. "We need to head for the centre of Paititi, as if we're trying to complete the tournament quest. I've got an idea." He only hoped it worked...

They left the sound stage and advanced along the same fiery-lit passageway they would have followed, had they not been diverted behind the gold panel.

"I can't believe Ribbon's been Deadlock all along," Ren said, panting. "How did we miss it?"

Cecily shook her head. "It's not our fault. She fooled everyone – including the UGP."

Stinging with Ribbon's betrayal, Arthur replayed everything that had happened in the last three days, trying to pinpoint where they'd gone wrong. They'd been too quick to assume that those messages in Ribbon's hotel room were replies she'd received from Deadlock. They could just as easily have been messages she was drafting to send *as* Deadlock. And in the Land of Sleeping Kings, they'd jumped to the conclusion that the raiders were there to seize the time-key from Ribbon. In reality, perhaps Ribbon had staged the whole thing just to win their trust? Or was there something else they'd missed?

As they continued along the tunnel, the air started to smell putrid, like rotten eggs. Cecily pulled the neck of her dress over her nose. "Eww, what *is* that?"

"Sulphur," Milo said, ominously. "We must be close to the next part of the quest."

Up ahead, the air was hazy near an archway in the right-hand side of the tunnel. The stink of sulphur grew stronger as they ventured closer and turned right, through the archway, into an enormous cavern. A glassy black path ran down the centre, bordered on both sides by a lake of undulating lava. Crackling and rumbling, the lava threw off waves of intense heat that made Arthur's skin roast and his eyes water. On the far side of the chamber, the path banked up to the steps of three Inca temples. One was hewn from white marble, another from a semi-translucent red rock and the third from yellow sandstone. The steps leading to the sandstone temple had a jagged section missing.

"Young Pipsqueaks!" a voice called from above. Yesenia Colt was balancing on top of a floating hunk of sandstone, the same shape as the hole in the temple steps. Her face glistened with sweat; her hair was pulled loose in several different places and the logos on her catsuit had started to melt. "I thought you were eliminated!"

Arthur briefly considered giving Yesenia an explanation, but decided in the end that he didn't owe her anything. If she'd survived until now, she could wait there until this was all over. However it concluded.

He scanned the place for Griffon, but saw no sign of him. Wherever the isports champion was, Arthur hoped he was OK. Arthur realized now that Griffon had been honest with them this whole time, and all of Arthur's misgivings about trusting him had been wrong.

Ignoring Yesenia completely, Cecily gave the lava a nervous glance. "Arthur, you'd better share this plan of yours..."

"Right." Shielding his face from the searing heat, Arthur pointed to the temples. "One of Lazarus's staff mentioned they had cameras and microphones set up in a temple, and as soon as someone opened a chest to get the Irontide shield, the equipment would start recording and the broadcast would go live. I think activating the equipment is our best line of defence – if the UGP sees and hears what's happening on live holovision, they'll be here in a flash."

Ren coughed gas out of her lungs. "Good plan, but how do we get the time-key off Ribbon—?" She broke off as footsteps thundered along the passageway behind them.

Milo turned around and readied his rock blaster. "Go!" he said, shooing Arthur and the others away. "I'll try to hold them back long enough for you to trigger the broadcast."

There wasn't time to discuss it. Leaving Milo at the mouth of the chamber, Arthur, Ren and Cecily charged along the central pathway towards the temples. Every breath Arthur drew felt like burning acid, but adrenaline pushed him forward. Cecily hitched up her dress so she could move easier; Arthur imagined that with the amount they were all sweating, it must have stuck to her like cellophane. After a few strides, he had to wrench his feet up from the floor because the rubber soles of his trainers were sticky.

"Which temple is it?" Ren asked, as they approached the end of the path. "Yesenia must have chosen the yellow one, but she was clearly wrong. We've got to make the right decision or we'll end up like her."

Arthur strived to unpuzzle the answer. "Each temple must represent something different. What do the colours yellow, red and white stand for?"

"That's not the only difference between them," Cecily observed. "The white temple has a small doorway; the yellow one is a little bigger and the red one is huge."

Different doorways, different colours, different temples...

Despite the rumbling lava, noxious air and blazing heat, Arthur tried to clear his mind and focus. "Maybe each temple was built for a different Inca god and we have to choose the right one?"

"But surely that would be the god of the sun, and wouldn't that be yellow?" Ren said.

Thinking of the sun, Arthur had another brainwave. Like all stars, the sun had a life cycle that took place over billions of years. He tried to picture the diagram he'd drawn for his physics homework last term. "Perhaps each temple represents a different phase in the sun's life cycle? At first, the sun is a yellow star, burning steadily. Then, when the hydrogen in the core runs out, it will become a red giant. And finally, when the core collapses, it will become a white dwarf."

"The giant and dwarf part fits with the door sizes," Cecily said, the lava reflected in her eyes. "But which one do we pick?"

"I'm not sure. Maybe because this is the Land of the *Hidden* Sun, it's the white dwarf?" Arthur said. "That's what will happen when the sun dies."

They approached the white steps cautiously. Cecily's leg trembled as she placed a foot on the bottom stone. "It feels OK, but let's take it slowly, just in case."

Suddenly, a crash sounded behind them and dust crumbled from the cavern walls. Over his shoulder, Arthur saw Milo firing jets of green flames from the rock blaster into the passageway outside.

"On second thoughts," Cecily said, "run!"

They bolted up the temple steps two at a time. Arthur was so focused on his speed, it wasn't till he reached the summit that he realized none of them had been lifted into the air like Yesenia, and so he must have made the right decision.

Ren gave him an appreciative slap on the back as they ducked through a small doorway, into the white temple.

Inside was a large, square room with no other openings. Orangey-red light seeped through multiple slits in the ceiling, creating an Inca-inspired geometric pattern on the sand below. Although it felt blissfully cool, Arthur knew that was only compared to the boiling lava cavern outside. In the centre of the sandy floor rested a rectangular stone chest. Its lid was at least ten centimetres thick and carved with a shield.

"The Irontide shield must be inside that," Ren said, rushing over.

Arthur scoured the walls for cameras and microphones, but couldn't see any. It didn't worry him too much; the cameras were probably hidden here, too. "The lid looks too heavy to lift. We'll have to try pushing it off."

They all got into position along one side and, on the count of three, drove their shoulders against the stone.

"It's not budging," Ren noted through gritted teeth. "Do you think there's another way to open it?"

Watching the sand shift under her feet, Cecily's face brightened. *"Write your legends in the sand to move the shield to your command,*" she muttered, repeating the clue on the quest-map. "That's got to be connected to this! In order to move the shield on the lid, we have to write our legends in the sand."

"But *we* don't have legends," Ren pointed out. "We're thirteen. We haven't lived long enough for people to tell stories about us."

Arthur shrugged. "I don't know – there is that statue of us outside the Kraken…"

Cecily examined the shield on top of the chest. "Didn't Archimedes say that the word *legend* has several different meanings? I'm pretty sure a legend can also be the motto on a coat of arms. They're drawn on shields, aren't they?"

"Yeah…" Arthur tried to remember what a coat of arms looked like. "Medieval knights displayed their coat of arms on their armour to show which noble family they came from. The mottoes were things like: *Fortune favours the bold*, or *For love, life and honour.*" He could hear the thunder of fighting outside. "Come on, we'd each better think of our own quickly. It's got to be something that represents us."

He dropped to his knees and held his finger over the sand. If he was a knight riding into battle, what would the legend on his coat of arms be? He reflected on everything he'd learned about himself in the last three days. He thought of how he'd found the strength to climb that tower in Biringan in order to save Ren and Cecily, and how he'd managed to stay focused enough to rescue Kaldi's goat while in the middle of a sandstorm. He didn't consider himself to be anything like the heroes in the video games that he played, but all the qualities that they possessed – bravery, quick-thinking, determination – they were inside him, too. He'd just never realized it before.

With a deep breath, he pushed his finger into the sand and wrote *Courage and confidence.* Three days ago, he might have chosen something different, but his experiences in Legendarium had taught him exactly who he was and what he was capable of.

He glanced over at Ren and Cecily, wondering what they were writing. He understood Cecily felt powerless sometimes, but she was the most formidable person he knew. She'd had the skill to convince a bloodthirsty Viking king to stop fighting, and she'd single-handedly defended everyone from the raiders in Zerzura. Ren worried a lot about other peoples' expectations, yet whether she was abseiling into an underground cavern, battling through a sandstorm or riding a robot-horse, she always risked her own safety to help others. She was anything but disappointing.

"Your legend seems accurate," Cecily commented, peering over Arthur's shoulder.

He got to his feet to survey her offering. *"The power to achieve,"* he read, with a broadening smile. "It suits you perfectly. What did you go for, Ren?"

"Nothing to prove," she said with a shrug. "It makes me feel like as long as I'm myself, that's good enough."

"We're in a team with Griffon. We should probably write a legend for him, too," Cecily said, kneeling down. "Any ideas?"

"How about *Truth above all*?" Arthur suggested. "Griffon sacrificed his chance to win the tournament in order to help us rescue Milo and fight Deadlock. I think he'd appreciate that."

Ren gave a firm nod and Cecily scrawled the legend in the sand. The words they'd written immediately started to glow, and as the fighting outside grew louder, the lid of the stone chest dissolved into a glittering cloud of nano-particles. Arthur flooded with relief as the sound of a gong reverberated around the temple walls.

They'd done it. They'd completed the challenge – which meant they'd also activated the hidden microphones and live broadcast. In a burst of golden light, a kite-shaped shield materialized above the stone chest …

… and then a hole exploded in the side of the temple.

28

Heat swept in from the lava chamber as the temple masonry collapsed, crashing into the sand below. Coughing dust out of his lungs, Arthur squinted through the haze. Whatever had blown a hole in the wall had left the stone glowing red-hot.

Dark figures stormed inside, clanking and rattling. *Raiders.*

The Irontide shield was still rotating in mid-air. Thinking quickly, Arthur reached up and snatched it.

"Down here!" Ren yelled, on the other side of the chest. The shield was made of the same lightweight metal as the other components of Irontide armour and as Arthur slipped the strap over his arm, he felt it adjust to his size. He darted around the chest and crouched next to Ren and Cecily.

Shadows climbed the walls as the temple filled with bodies. With his back pressed against the chest, Arthur took ragged breaths, wondering why they hadn't already been surrounded. Then he heard an icy voice.

"If I'm not mistaken, there's only an hour or so remaining before the three of you go splat."

It was Ribbon. Arthur snuck a look out from behind the chest. She was surrounded by a gang of grimy, trench-coat-wearing teenagers, each modelling their own horrific cybernetic modification. Some of them had jet-propelled wheels fused to their feet or rocket launchers attached to their heads; others had propeller blades growing out of their shoulders.

Among the sneering faces were three that Arthur recognized: Tide, Vorru and Rultan.

Milo, Cloud and Griffon were nowhere to be seen.

"Trouble is, if viewers watch you spontaneously turn into slime, they'll start asking questions," Ribbon said, "and I can't risk anyone learning about the time-key or they might try to stop me. Better you die now." She signalled to her raiders. "Get rid of them."

Arthur dodged back behind the chest, his heart hammering. What did Ribbon mean by "stop me"? Stop her from doing what? He looked around but there was nowhere for them to run to. They were trapped. Hearing the hum of charging weapons, he leaped to his feet. "Wait!" he shouted, waving his arms around like a lunatic. If nothing else, maybe he could confuse the raiders long enough for Ren or Cecily to formulate a plan.

"Ignore him," Ribbon said, tiredly. "He's stalling."

"No!" Arthur had to improvise. "If you kill us now, you

won't learn about the other side-effects of time travel, not until it's too late."

Ribbon folded her arms. "What side effects?"

"The universe doesn't just turn you into protoplasm," Arthur lied hastily. "When you move forward in time, other things happen, too."

"Is that so?" Ribbon's tone was doubtful. "Well, that's not something I need to worry about. I won't be going forward."

It was then that Arthur recalled something Ribbon had mentioned in the Great Library. She'd said that the time-key could give someone the power to rearrange history to suit their will. "That's what you're planning, isn't it?" he realized, panic rising through him. "To go back in time and rewrite history in your favour."

Ribbon only smirked.

"But you can't!" Arthur blurted. "You'll destroy the lives of millions of people! Time isn't something to be messed with."

"You sound just like my father," Ribbon said with a tone of contempt. "He was Deadlock before me, and made me join the UGP as a double agent. He was always so unambitious. He knew the time-key technical drawing was powerful, but he didn't understand how to read it. After he died, I inherited the technical drawing, and with it, the opportunity to carve out my own reputation as a Deadlock more powerful than any other that had come before me."

Arthur could feel himself quaking with emotion – anger, panic, despair – but he tried to keep his expression neutral. Clearly Ribbon had forgotten that this was all being broadcast live with sound – she'd just announced her true identity to every viewer watching!

But that wouldn't save Arthur and the others from being killed. He remembered it had taken six or so minutes for the UGP to arrive in Zerzura. Arthur just had to keep Ribbon talking long enough…

"We thought Lazarus Sloane was Deadlock," Arthur said, hoping Ribbon would enjoy correcting him. "We saw Tide disguised as a member of his crew."

His statement provoked a few sniggers from the raiders. Ribbon snorted. "Lazarus Sloane can't even decide his own wardrobe. He couldn't run an empire like mine."

It seemed to be working, but Arthur's stomach danced with nerves. *Courage and confidence,* he told himself. "In Zerzura, we thought we were rescuing you from the raiders. When they came after you, was that all for show?"

Rultan, Vorru and a few of the others chuckled. "Of course it was," Ribbon snapped. "Despite my raiders' best efforts, Milo refused to talk after we captured him. So, I decided to find out how much you three knew about the time-key, in the hope you might be able to help me fix it. In order to win your trust, I left the door to my room open so you might find those messages and believe I was reluctantly working for Deadlock. I offered to help you find

Milo so I could stay close and wait for a good moment to snatch Cloud. I could have taken Cloud by force earlier, but it would have meant exposing my true identity and losing a valuable position at the UGP."

Arthur tightened his jaw. He couldn't believe how well Ribbon had manipulated them. It was like she'd left a trail of breadcrumbs for them to follow, and they'd never once questioned it.

He was just planning his next comment when Cecily sprang up beside him, her fists balled. "We *trusted* you! We thought you were our friend!"

Ren rose to her feet, shaking with anger. "If you've hurt Cloud or Milo, I swear I'll—"

Ribbon laughed, cutting her off. "I told you not to trust anybody. Friends aren't *real*. I was only nice to you initially because I was trying to figure out whether you'd be potential clients."

All of a sudden, Rultan pointed at the walls and shouted, "I think there's microphones here, boss! This is being broadcast live!"

Ribbon flared her nostrils. "Scarper, all of you!" she yelled. She snatched a rock blaster off a departing raider and aimed it at Arthur and the others. "You'll pay for this."

In the same split second that she fired her weapon, Arthur instinctively drew the Irontide shield in front of him. And then something unexpected happened.

In a puff of nano-particles, the shield transformed into a shining energy field that enveloped Arthur, Ren and Cecily in a giant bubble, lifting them off the sandy floor.

Arthur's body turned weightless – like he was moving through the raiders' light-portal again – only this time, he could see everything around him.

Streaks of green light diffused throughout the bubble as Ribbon's shot reflected off the surface and catapulted straight back towards her. Ribbon ducked just in time but Rultan, fleeing behind her, wasn't so lucky. The blast hit him square in the backside, sizzling a hole through his trench coat and trousers, and leaving a smoking red burn on his bottom.

"Arrgh!" he cried, reaching round to fan it.

A few of the raiders witnessed what happened and started firing over their shoulders as they bolted. Among them was Vorru, who aimed a blast from his shoulder-cannon directly at the shield. Arthur flinched as it came careering towards them, crackling through the air like a firework...

But it bounced off the energy field like a rubber ball and rocketed straight into a group of raiders, causing chaos among the fleeing mob.

"What are you doing, you big idiot?" Tide shouted down. Flames spurted from the base of her jetpack as she circled overhead. "Next time, THINK!"

She was so busy rebuking Vorru that she didn't notice Yesenia Colt, balancing on a floating chunk of stone a few metres away. Yesenia's eyes flashed hungrily, sensing an opportunity to get back down to the ground. She waited till Tide was closer and then leaped onto Tide's front, grappling to keep hold.

"Get off me!" Tide yelled, punching and kicking. Her jetpack sputtered, struggling to keep them both in flight.

Meanwhile, Ren's bun came loose and her hair drifted into Arthur's face as she did a roly-poly through the air beside him. "Look – it's Griffon!" she exclaimed, pointing.

Still wearing the Irontide tunic, the isports champion was zooming around under the cavern roof, zapping raiders left, right and centre with his energy-baton. Blood seeped from a wound in his shoulder, and his mouth was drawn into a tight grimace, but he'd obviously survived those skeleton warriors and come back to help them.

Arthur spied Ribbon hurrying down the temple steps, tapping her faze display. In the centre of the chamber, a column of green light rose from the floor. "Ribbon's escaping with the time-key!" he realized. "We've got to stop her!"

He wasn't sure how to operate the energy-shield, so he tried kicking it. As his shoe made impact, the force field disintegrated into a haze of nano-particles, which re-formed on his arm as the Irontide shield. Gravity returned to his body and he fell to the sand.

He landed awkwardly on his ankle, but adrenaline dulled the pain and he pushed himself to his feet. He and the others scrambled through the hole in the temple wall.

Smoke and chaos filled the lava chamber. Green, red and blue blaster-shots hurtled in all directions as the raiders battled Griffon and Yesenia. The heat stung Arthur's eyes so much he had to squint to see Ribbon. She wasn't far away from the light-portal.

"Come on – we can catch her!" Ren yelled, breaking into a sprint.

They raced down the temple steps, but as Arthur reached the cavern floor, his ankle gave way. He cried out, only just managing to stop himself from falling. Suddenly Cecily was there, pulling Arthur's arm around her shoulder, supporting him under the armpit. "Don't stop now!"

Clenching his jaw, Arthur hobbled on as fast as he could. The pain was blistering, but he focused on Ribbon. They couldn't let her get away with the time-key.

As they gave chase, Ribbon started to draw away from them.

"No!" Cecily screamed.

Arthur didn't want to give up hope, but Ribbon was only a few metres from the light-portal and even with Ren charging at full speed, it was obvious she wouldn't reach her in time. "No, this can't be happening..." he said in a hollow voice. Ribbon was going to disappear, along with their only means of returning to the twenty-first century.

To home.

To his dad.

Tears rimmed Arthur's eyes as he limped forward. He was never going to see his dad again. They'd never play football together in the back garden, or laugh while watching movies, or have snowball fights, or cook pancakes...

"This is it, isn't it?" Cecily sobbed, starting to slow. "We're going to end our lives as miserable puddles of slime, in this stinking lava cavern."

Arthur glanced at his reflection on the shiny, black floor. It had all been for nothing. Everything they'd achieved, everything they'd learned about themselves; it would make no difference. Their futures were over.

He heard Ren shouting and found the strength to lift his head. As he did so, Cecily seized his arm. "Look," she said, breathlessly. "Look!"

Ribbon was a step away from the light-portal, but there was a shadow inside it, growing darker...

Ribbon screamed as an enormous tiger with a red collar pounced through the light, knocking her to the floor. Its thick rust-red fur was streaked with black and there were white patches on its brows and underside.

Cloud.

He was closely followed by Milo Hertz, who staggered around the portal with one arm hanging loosely at his side and blood streaked across his face. Ribbon scrambled to her feet and inched back as Cloud stalked closer, baring his teeth.

"Yes, Fuzzball!" Ren cheered, punching the air.

Arthur tried to run forward but pain shot through his ankle and he fell against Cecily. She stabilized him and squeezed his hand, watching what was going on in front of them.

"It's over," Milo told Ribbon sternly. "Give me the time-key."

Edging away, Ribbon dipped a hand into her satchel and brought out the time-key. "Sorry to disappoint, but Deadlock doesn't give away anything for free." She dangled the time-key over the lava. "You and I are going to do a little negotiating."

Arthur drew his breath but Milo seemed unfazed. "That's where you're wrong," he replied, nodding at Cloud. "Your days of deal-making are done."

What followed happened so quickly Arthur could have blinked and missed it. With a dull *pfft*, Cloud transformed first into a haze of nano-particles, and then into a small monkey with a pale-pink face and beady black eyes.

Before anyone else had moved, Cloud leaped through the air, swinging his long tail for balance and landed on Ribbon's shoulder. He snatched the time-key right out of her hand and bounded back to the floor.

"Get off me!" she shrieked, waving her arms madly.

Arthur didn't understand how Cloud had transformed on his own. He'd never been able to before...

Howling with triumph, Cloud scampered towards Milo on his monkey hands and feet, with the time-key gripped safely in his tail. As Milo collected the device and slipped it into his top pocket, Arthur's chest caved. Finally, it was back in their possession.

Windows of light began opening all around the chamber as the UGP finally arrived. They were all wearing energy-batons similar to Griffon's strapped across their backs and battle-ready helmets with dark visors. As they stormed towards the raiders, they shouted warnings and drew their batons from over their shoulders. Ribbon stared at them, her expression a mixture of shock and defeat. There were so many officers, they easily overwhelmed the fleeing raiders, who yelled angrily as they were restrained. Arthur noticed Chief Inspector Doveton steaming straight towards Ribbon with her nostrils flared.

Ren dashed back and threw her arms around Arthur and Cecily. "It's over!" she cried. "We're going home."

29

Arthur wasn't sure if his eyes were watering from the pain in his ankle, or the intense heat in the lava cavern, or the relief that they had the time-key back. Probably a mixture of all three.

"I know it hurts, but try not to move it," said the UGP officer who was kneeling beside him. He was a slim man with long, delicate fingers. Very carefully, he rolled down Arthur's sock in order to examine his injury.

Arthur grimaced. His ankle looked like a pudgy ball of dough, the colour of cooked ham. "Is it broken?"

"Possibly." The officer fetched a cell-regenerator from his satchel. "But I'll have you up and walking again in a minute. Don't worry."

There were only seven minutes and forty seconds remaining on the timer on Arthur's watch. He surveyed his surroundings, looking for the others.

The cavern was bustling with activity. Ribbon and her band of raiders had already been escorted off the premises and taken directly into UGP custody. Milo was talking urgently with Chief Inspector Doveton, while Ren and Cecily were having their burns and scratches healed by another pair of officers.

Back in dog form, Cloud was sat at Arthur's side, peering up at him with his big dark eyes. Arthur reached over and patted him on the head. "You're a good boy," he said, moving his hand to scratch Cloud under the chin. "A very good boy."

Cloud gave a joyful bark, making Arthur smile.

"Now, hold still," the UGP officer said. He aimed the cell-regenerator at Arthur's ankle, and several pinpricks of blue light appeared on Arthur's skin. A wave of soothing cold spread throughout the area, as if Arthur's veins had been filled with ice water. The tenderness numbed.

After a few seconds, the cell-regenerator bleeped and the blue dots on Arthur's skin disappeared. "All right, now you can move it," the officer said, tucking the cell-regenerator back in his satchel. "How does it feel?"

Arthur made a few circles with his foot. There wasn't even a twinge of pain. His ankle felt strong and sturdy again, ready to put weight on. He tried to hide his surprise. "Yeah, it's better. Thanks."

"Take it easy for the next hour or so," the officer advised. "And no more I-RAGs for a few days, eh?"

"I think I can manage that," Arthur said, pushing himself up.

Ren and Cecily had already finished their treatments and were rushing over.

"How long do we have?" Ren asked, holding a hairband between her teeth as she smoothed her hair back into a ponytail.

"Seven minutes," Arthur answered. "Let's get Milo."

Cecily lifted Cloud into her arms and the four of them weaved past various UGP officers, to where Milo was still locked in conversation with the chief inspector. As he clocked sight of them, his eyebrows jumped. "Will you excuse me?" he told the inspector. "I haven't had a chance to check in with my team."

The inspector nodded. "There's a storeroom in the corridor outside where you can talk. It'll be cooler, and nobody will know you're there. Lazarus and his crew are already sniffing around outside and I don't know how much longer I can keep them away."

"Great," Milo said, smiling in thanks. He lowered his voice as he joined Arthur and the others. "Did you hear that? Let's get out of here."

They took a right turn out of the lava cavern and hastened along the tunnel until they reached an open door. The front of it was made to look like ashlar stone blocks, but on the inside, it was steel. Had it been closed, Arthur wasn't sure he would have even noticed it was there.

He stepped through the doorway ahead of the others, and felt goosebumps tingle all over his body. The room had *air conditioning*. Cecily normally disapproved of it because it was bad for the environment, but right now Arthur couldn't think of anything more heavenly. He heaved in a lungful of clean air, cooling his throat and nostrils as the others bundled in beside him. The room was small, but brightly lit. Stainless-steel shelves lined the walls, crammed with all sorts of props from Paititi, including the golden sun statues, Inca torch sconces and empty grain sacks. Milo shut the door, and everything fell quiet.

"We don't have a lot of time, so I'll quickly explain what happened," he said, removing the time-key from his top pocket. "The raiders overpowered me at the cavern entrance, but when I saw Ribbon holding Cloud, I remembered I'd added the option to activate him remotely using this." He tapped the ruby pendant around his neck. "At the same time, I initiated an experimental mode in Cloud's programming that allows him to transform of his own free will. He escaped and managed to save my life, but by that point Ribbon had already reached you."

Holding Cloud, Cecily rubbed him between the ears, gazing at him proudly. Arthur was losing count of the number of times Cloud had saved their lives now. Of all the incredible technology they'd encountered in the future, he was by far the most remarkable.

Scrutinizing the time-key, Milo rotated its dial in several different directions. "Earlier, when Ribbon mentioned there was a connection between Cloud and the time-key, I realized why that might be: I had used one of the mechanisms from Cloud's design in the time-key as well. I won't bore you with the details, but through a lesser-known astrophysical phenomenon, they were, therefore, linked." He shook his head, like he was annoyed at himself for not identifying it sooner. "But that's fixed now. I've set the time-key to deliver you back to Ren's garden at the exact moment that you left. To everyone else, it will be as if no time has passed at all."

Nerves fluttered in Arthur's insides. He was going home – back to his dad, his life, his future.

"Once you've safely departed, I'll use the time-key to make one last trip back in time a few hours," Milo said. "I need to access the recording equipment in that temple so I can alter some of the conversation between you and Ribbon that gets broadcast. That way, I can mask any mention of *time travel*." He signalled to the rock blaster, tucked into his belt. "After that, I'll destroy the time-key and no one will ever be able to use it again."

The sense of relief in Milo's voice was palpable. Arthur hoped he'd finally be able to move forward with his life now, free from the weight of his mistakes.

"What if Ribbon tells someone about the time-key?" Ren asked. "Do you think they'll believe her?"

Milo chuffed. "I doubt it. Ribbon has lied to a lot of people. Without proof, no one will be sure whether she's telling the truth or not. Time travel will be what it always should have been: a legend." He twisted the dial on the time-key one more time and a jet of mist spurted out of the hole in the centre. Very carefully, he placed the device in the middle of the floor.

Everyone took a step back as the mist swirled into a spinning vortex. Wind swept around the room, rattling the props on the shelves.

"Will you thank Griffon and Archimedes for us?" Cecily asked, lifting her voice above the din.

"I'll take care of everything," Milo answered. "Don't worry. I'm already planning to tell Lazarus Sloane that, just like your parents, you've gone into hiding to avoid the attention." He took a heavy sigh. "There is one more thing, though. I'm sorry, but Cloud needs to stay with me. It's too dangerous for everyone if he returns to the twenty-first century."

"What?" Cecily pulled Cloud closer to her chest. "No. I don't understand."

Cloud whimpered and lowered his tail. Arthur felt empty. Cloud had been with them through everything, first in the Wonderscape, and now in Legendarium. They couldn't never see him again.

Milo's eyes shone. "I know this is hard for you, but I can't risk anything like this happening again. I gave you Cloud because I thought he would help you cope with everything that happened in the Wonderscape."

"He did help us," Ren said quietly. "The Fuzzball's our best friend."

"But you don't need him any more," Milo said gently. "You three are already a great team. Do you know why? Because you're always reaching for the best in yourselves *and* the best in each other."

Arthur smiled half-heartedly. He supposed that was true, but it didn't lessen the pain of losing Cloud.

"Time's running out," Milo urged. "You have to say goodbye."

Cecily snivelled and kissed Cloud on the nose. "I'll never forget you, boy," she sobbed. "Be good."

"Fuzzball –" Ren's voice broke as she stretched out her hand and scratched Cloud under the chin – "thanks for everything, all right?"

A lump swelled at the back of Arthur's throat as he peered into Cloud's big bright eyes. "I'll miss you, buddy..." was all he managed to mumble before his bottom lip started wobbling.

The mist was swirling faster. Shaking, Cecily passed Cloud over to Milo. Arthur grabbed her hand, sensing she was about to burst into tears.

"Cloud and I will look for you in the history books to see what you did with your lives," Milo promised. "Don't let us down!"

"We won't," Arthur said, as he and the others lined up in front of the vortex. Ren took Cecily's other hand and, with a deep breath, they all stepped into the mist.

Brain freeze stabbed at Arthur's head. The ground

swayed under his feet. He squeezed Cecily's hand tighter…

And then the mist faded.

He was stood next to the pond at the bottom of Ren's garden, right where they'd vanished three days earlier. He could feel sunshine on his face and fresh air in his lungs. Birds were singing and, in the distance, he heard the drone of a neighbour's lawnmower.

Ren rubbed her eyes. "We're really home!"

All the tension in Arthur's muscles seemed to evaporate. The threat of Slimeageddon was no more.

"We'll have to tell our parents that Cloud ran away," Cecily said, sniffing and wiping her eyes on her jacket sleeve. "Come on, let's go inside. I want to see my mum and dad."

They set off up the garden, towards the house. With a breeze blowing in his face, Arthur felt lighter than air. Everything was going to be OK.

"We've still got the rest of the summer holidays!" Ren declared, swinging her arms. "I'm going to try that work experience my mum wants me to do. It might be cool. What about you two?"

Cecily smiled through her tears. "Nigeria. Definitely. My family is important and I can work hard to offset the carbon from the two flights. Arthur, you'd better go easy on the other students during that video games workshop."

He lifted his hands. "I know, I know. I'm gonna sign up for it tomorrow."

"*Tomorrow* is such a good word, don't you think?" Ren said.

"Absolutely," Arthur agreed. "It's like a promise. All sorts of things could happen tomorrow."

Acknowledgements

This sequel would not have been written without the generous support of booksellers up and down the country who encouraged readers to pick up *Wonderscape* – thank you. I'm exceptionally grateful to everyone at Walker Books, especially my editors Denise Johnstone-Burt and Megan Middleton, designer Ben Norland, illustrator Paddy Donnelly, typesetter Rebecca J Hall, publicist Kirsten Cozens and copyeditor Clare Baalham. Thank you also to my agent Polly Nolan, my dear friend Sarah Bryars, my boyfriend Peter and my sister Beth, who let me use her workshop to write in when there was no quiet space at home. Tara, thanks for being such a great listener and for always reading every draft. Lastly, a huge thank you to my mum, for everything and more.

Londoner **JENNIFER BELL** worked as a children's bookseller at a world-famous bookshop before becoming an author. Her debut novel, *The Uncommoners: The Crooked Sixpence*, was an international bestseller. She is also the author of Agents of the Wild, an adventure series for younger readers, and *Wonderscape*, which was selected as a Waterstones Children's Book of the Month and is inspired by some of her favourite heroes from history (there were too many to fit in the story) and her love of gaming. *Legendarium* celebrates incredible legends from across the world. Find out more about Jennifer at jennifer-bell-author.com.

"An expertly crafted, breakneck
speed adventure." *BookTrust*

When Arthur, Ren and Cecily investigate a mysterious
explosion, they find themselves trapped in the year 2473.
Lost in the Wonderscape, an epic in-reality adventure
game, they must call on the help of some unlikely historical
heroes to play their way home before time runs out.

"A whirlwind of fun and mystery
across space and time."
Thomas Taylor, author of *Malamander*

We hope you enjoyed

LEGENDARIM

We'd love to hear your thoughts.

#Legendarium

@WalkerBooksUK
@jenrosebell

@WalkerBooksUK
@jenbellauthor